PUBLIC
ANCHOVY #1

T0015050

PUBLIC ANCHOVY #1

MINDY QUIGLEY

St. Martin's Paperbacks

To the family of the late, great Isabel McPhee Berney.
May her memory be a blessing.

This is a work of fiction. All of the characters, organizations, and events portrayed in this novel are either products of the author's imagination or are used fictitiously.

First published in the United States by St. Martin's Paperbacks, an imprint of St. Martin's Publishing Group.

PUBLIC ANCHOVY #1

Copyright © 2024 by Mindy Quigley.

For information, address St. Martin's Publishing Group, 120 Broadway, New York, NY 10271.

www.stmartins.com

ISBN: 978-1-250-79247-1

Our books may be purchased in bulk for promotional, educational, or business use. Please contact your local bookseller or the Macmillan Corporate and Premium Sales Department at 1-800-221-7945, ext. 5442, or by email at MacmillanSpecialMarkets@macmillan.com.

Printed in the United States of America

St. Martin's Paperbacks edition / January 2024

10 9 8 7 6 5 4 3 2 1

ACKNOWLEDGMENTS

Some people have ghost writers. In Tanya Boughtflower, I have a ghost editor. She steers me right on dialogue and plot, corrects my grammar, tells me when my characters have the wrong names, and drops everything to meet me in Spain for tapas. I couldn't ask for a better friend.

Jaime Gagamov, Danna Agmon, and Jessica Taylor are wonderful humans and great beta readers, while Charlie Katz, Elisabeth Chaves, H. Scott Butler, Tom McGohey, Piper Durrell, and Caitlin Bean provided helpful insights along the way. Thanks to Matt Doherty, who has editorial eagle eyes. He can spot a weak section from fifty yards off and suggest five different great solutions. Special thanks to Tracee de Hahn—a veritable fountain of good ideas. Cat on the stairs! High fives!

Thank you to the indulgent Rev. Pamela Philips for allowing, nay, *encouraging* me to exercise full artistic license with her literally revered name. Elise Chandon also kindly lent her fancy French last name. Merci!

Thanks to my recipe researcher, Lori Hohenstein, aka Mom, for faithfully scouring the internet and tweaking recipes to help me make the Friends of the Library party's imagined menu a reality. If you like the tiramisu cookies, you have her to thank. Thanks also to Nancy Pontier and David Heyer for testing recipes and documenting the results, Aliya Razvi Chapman, Pam Malabad, and Denise Cranley for advice on gluten-free baking, and to Kristen Chang for the timely provision of xanthan gum.

James Whittle, Ginger Ashton, and Joe Hoyt—thank you for catering advice. James, I can't wait to use "body bags" in a future book!

I'm indebted to David Heyer and Kristi Giemza, who set aside their "do no harm" oaths to help me figure out how to realistically slip someone a Mickey. Jennifer Davis was another accomplice, turning her pharmacology Ph.D. to evil purposes and suggesting possible candidates for said Mickey.

Thanks to Anthony Wilson, retired chief of the Blacksburg, VA, police department, for his insights into small-town policing and willingness to play along with my "you find yourself trapped in a mansion with a killer . . ." scenarios. Thanks, also, to Jesse Bowman for answering questions about military reservist training and concealed carry.

Mike Zimmerman of All Seasons Marine Service answered many boat-related questions for me and also let me hang out with his cool dogs. *A mi informante Boricua*, Brian Huddleston, you finally get to be in the book! Gratitude to John Baute—if you need to know anything about anything, John's your man.

If you think something in the book is wrong or unrealistic, it's not the fault of any of the above people. They're all highly competent. Blame my characters, who occasionally go a little off-piste to bend the plot in the right direction.

Thanks to the booksellers (especially Barnes & Noble's Valley View, Electric Road, and Christiansburg locations; Blacksburg Books; Dust Bunny Books; and Book No Further) who've embraced the story of a type A pizza chef and her mischievous cat and helped get it into readers' hands. And thanks to you, readers, for reading! Because of you, I get to do this thing!

As ever, I'm grateful to the Talbot-Fortune Agency and Macmillan-St. Martin's. John Talbot, John Simko, John Rounds—thanks to all the Johns! Sara Beth Haring and Sara LaCotti—thanks to all the Saras! Many thanks to Danielle Christopher and Mary Ann Lasher for covers that capture Butterball in all his glory. And eleventy billion ups to Hannah O'Grady, part editor, part kindly wizard of words, all awesome.

Lastly, thanks to Paul, Alice, Patrick and the rest of my family. They have given me the precious gift of time to pursue this crazy obsession/job.

CHAPTER 1

Sonya Dokter, my sous chef and best friend, perched in the passenger's seat of our rented catering van, trying unsuccessfully to tune the radio to the weather report. Static blared, followed by a series of high-pitched snippets of Mariachi music, followed by more static.

"Can you turn it down?" I yelled.

She twisted the knobs, then jiggled them, but the noise continued to blast at full volume. "It's not working," she shouted.

Without taking my right foot off the gas pedal, I slipped off my left clog and used it to give the console a series of firm whacks. The radio let out one last shriek, then nothing but dead air.

As the van creaked out of the parking lot of Delilah & Son, my upscale pizzeria, the vehicle emitted a series of groans that made it seem bound for the scrapyard rather than its actual destination—Bluff Point, one of Geneva Bay, Wisconsin's most opulent private residences.

"So much for our grand entrance," Sonya muttered, idly tracing the cracks in the passenger's side window with her perfectly manicured index finger. "Heater's busted, too."

"I know," I said. "I wish we could afford our own van

instead of having to take the rental company's sloppy seconds. I'll be mortified pulling through the gates of Bluff Point in this."

Sonya lowered the visor, appraised her reflection in the dirty mirror, and sighed. She patted the sleek waves of her jet-black bob into place. "At least *I* look the part, even if this jalopy doesn't."

As I contorted myself to slip my shoe back on, I glanced over at Sonya's beaded flapper dress, which glittered even in the weak sunlight streaming through the grimy windshield. Her signature glammed-up fifties-style makeup had been swapped for toffee-colored lipstick and penciled-in high, arched brows—a look lifted straight out of a Mae West movie. She pulled an iridescent wrap around her shoulders to guard her bare arms against the October chill seeping into the van.

All day, the sun had been fighting a losing battle against a thickening wall of steel-gray clouds. The previous weeks had served up a string of sunshiny days, with postcard-worthy vistas of red and gold trees crowning Geneva Bay's glittering sapphire lake. Today, though, despite a daytime high poking into the sixties, the forecast predicted a plunge in temperatures, high winds, and a "wintry mix" kicking off around midnight. The storm would no doubt mark the start of our annual six months of hard weather. Typical Wisconsin winter, coming in like a planet-killing asteroid.

"You do look great," I told Sonya. "But I still don't get how you're planning to cook in that getup." I gave her outfit a skeptical once-over.

She flicked her wrist. "*Pshh*, catering is mostly just re-heating. I once catered a wedding in a full-on Victorian steampunk cosplay dress with a bustle and lace-up boots. This"—she gestured to her Roaring Twenties costume—

"is practically loungewear." She eyed my standard-issue white chef's jacket and black pants. A neat chignon corralled my long, chestnut hair at the nape of my neck, and the only adornment on my face was a hint of cherry-tinted ChapStick. "Isabel made a point of saying that when dinner service is over, we should stick around and enjoy ourselves. I can't believe you're not dressing up."

"I'm dressed as a chef," I deadpanned. "It's a timeless look."

"You might as well wear a nun's habit for all the fun you let yourself have," Sonya said, with a disapproving eye roll.

I wished I were the kind of person who could pivot from catering a fancy party to letting loose at one, but my focus remained firmly on the success of the restaurant. If I wanted to keep the business afloat, I couldn't take my eye off the ball.

"We've been *hired* to cater the party," I said. "The only reason we're allowed to stay and mingle is that Isabel is too nice to tell us to get lost the second the last canapé is served."

Isabel Berney, the head librarian at Geneva Bay's iconic library, had indeed encouraged me and my staff to join in the festivities at the Friends of the Library fundraising gala. The theme, Speakeasy Soirée, would see the town's upper crust turn out in their best gangster and moll getups for a dinner to aid in the preservation of the historic Frank Lloyd Wright–inspired lakefront library.

We'd provide a menu of Chicago-themed foods, like our signature deep-dish pizzas, along with Prohibition-era cocktails, to help turn back the clock to the days when Geneva Bay served as a hideout for the Windy City's mobsters and a popular stop on the booze-smuggling route between Canada and the Lower Forty-Eight. In addition to the pizzas, which would be served during the sit-down banquet portion of the evening's festivities, I'd crafted some portable snack options for the cocktail hour, including savory Italian beef crostini and my house-made version of the classic caramelly, nutty Chicago treat— Cracker Jack.

Tonight, I'd have a chance to show the who's who of Geneva Bay what my team and I could do, and to position us for the slew of party catering I was counting on to get us through until next summer. Geneva Bay depended on the tourist trade, and with the exodus of fair-weather residents well underway, I was already seeing our weekly revenue trend sharply downward. A shift to private party catering would be essential to undergirding our bottom line as winter set in.

My phone vibrated. Since the van predated Bluetooth by at least twenty years, Sonya reached into my pocket to answer it. As she pressed the speaker button, I saw the screen light up with Isabel Berney's name.

"Delilah, dear, I'm so glad I caught you. You haven't left for Bluff Point yet, have you?" Isabel chirped. She was tasked with coordinating logistics on behalf of the gala's wealthy sponsor. In the background, I heard the clink of glassware and other sounds of pre-party bustle.

"We have," I replied. "Son and I are on our way to pick up Jarka and then we'll head over. What's up?"

"I know what a miracle worker you are, so I have every confidence you'll figure out how to save the day," she began. My muscles tightened, and I girded myself for whatever was coming next. "You see, we've had a request from one of our very special guests for a 'free-from' pizza."

In my mind, I translated "very special" into "filthy rich."

"You mentioned that the other day. I've got three gluten-free pizzas set aside for the guests who can't eat gluten," I said.

"I'm afraid this is an additional request that I only just became aware of," Isabel explained. "The guest doesn't eat wheat, but she also doesn't eat meat."

"No prob," I said, glad I anticipated the possibility of someone needing a vegetarian *and* gluten-free option. "One of the gluten-free pies is topped with roasted tomatoes, Greek olives, and a mozzarella and feta blend. No meat. We should be good."

I heard paper crumpling as Isabel seemed to shift to reading from a list. "Let's see," she mumbled. "No gluten. Oh, she doesn't eat any dairy, either, or any animal-derived products whatsoever. And she avoids all nightshades, including tomatoes."

Sonya let out a whistle. "That's certainly 'free from,'" she said. "It's like an episode of *Chopped*, only the surprise ingredient basket's completely empty."

No question it would be a challenge, but I saw no reason to panic, certain I'd be able to figure out something from our planned menu that would meet this diner's request. This wasn't my first picky-eater rodeo.

"What about a warm root vegetable salad?" I said, in the direction of the phone's speaker. "I can use some of the roasted butternut squash from the pizza toppings, drizzle in some black truffle oil, and toss it with wilted greens. That's hearty enough for a main course."

"I'm afraid she has her heart set on a 'free-from' version of pizza," Isabel replied.

I glanced over to see Sonya's arched eyebrows shoot almost all the way to her hairline.

"Let me make sure I understand." I trained my eyes on the road but leaned closer to the phone. "No cheese, no wheat, no tomatoes. But she still wants to be served a pizza."

"That's right. She's very well-connected, so I hope you can pull a rabbit out of your chef's hat," Isabel replied brightly. "Well, not an *actual* rabbit, of course. She doesn't eat meat."

"This woman *does* know what a pizza is, doesn't she?" I muttered, unable to keep the sharp edge out of my voice. "Pretty much by definition, it's crust with tomato sauce and cheese on top."

"Of course, Delilah, and I can't thank you enough for being so accommodating."

I could almost picture Isabel's encouraging smile. Just north of seventy years old, she still worked full-time at the library. With her high-cut bangs, blunt bob, and inquisitive blue eyes, she bore a disarming resemblance to the iconic little Dutch boy. She was a dynamo, and her ability to bend people to her will was legendary. Much of the library's success over the decades rested on her shoulders.

"Pam already said that you can use anything you need from her kitchen," she continued.

Pam Philips, the party's sponsor and hostess, made her fortune by patenting a small feat of technical wizardry that allowed e-reader devices to wirelessly sync with phone apps and websites. She parlayed her innovation into a manufacturing company that supplied crucial internal components of almost every e-reader on the market. Unapologetically nerdy, Pam bore little likeness to the titans of industry and old-money families who comprised the bulk of Geneva Bay's lakeshore-dwelling elite. She bought Bluff Point the previous year, sinking a chunk of her e-reader fortune into purchasing, renovating, and furnishing the behemoth mansion. Since Pam moved into the house a few months earlier, Isabel had roped her into joining the Friends of the Library board, and she'd recently been elected as the incoming board chair.

"Thank her for me, but that doesn't really help," I explained. "All the food is premade so we can heat and serve when we arrive. Even if I were in my own kitchen, I couldn't create an entire recipe from scratch with this little notice. Recipe testing takes dozens of iterations sometimes. Plus, I don't have the ingredients I'd need. To make another gluten-free crust, I'd have to go back home or to the store to get more gluten-free flour. I used the last of the restaurant's stockpile, and we don't get another delivery until tomorrow."

I heard muted mumbling and then Isabel came back on the line. "We can send Pam's boat to pick you up at your house. That should save at least forty minutes. It's a straight shot over the water versus driving all the way around the lake." Bluff Point, in addition to being one of the grandest properties on the lake, was also one of the most secluded. Only a single, narrow road accessed the house, and the last few miles of it twisted through thick forest. "Your place has a dock, right? If the boat leaves now, it would be waiting for you there."

Time to shut this down once and for all. "Isabel, I can't," I said. "I want to make this work, believe me. I need to make a good impression on this crowd, and I appreciate you hiring me. But I can't."

Sonya gave me an appreciative nod, apparently impressed I'd been able to withstand the onslaught of Isabel's inveigling.

Little did we know that was only Isabel's opening salvo.

"Oh, I'm so sorry to hear that, but I understand," she said. "You've already been so accommodating. I wouldn't even have asked if this weren't so important. You know the town budget is under pressure, and without donated funds for the library, it's impossible to keep up with the preservation of such an architectural gem, much less undertake the needed renovations. Since the building was handcrafted, everything is custom—every door, every soffit, every toilet seat, for heaven's sake. How many libraries have stained-glass reading nooks overlooking a lake, like ours does? It's a true temple of the mind."

Isabel let out a heavy sigh before continuing. "I've written grants until my fingertips blistered and of course the town contributes what it can. But without a significant bump in private donations, I'm afraid of what will happen. There's been pressure to increase revenue, charging community groups more in rental fees and patrons more in fines. There's even been talk of selling the building and moving the library lock, stock, and carrel out near the Walmart." She paused and then added in a wistful voice, "No matter what happens, I can't think of anything I would have rather devoted my life to. To be able to offer unlimited knowledge, in a place of such exquisite beauty, for free, to anyone who loves reading . . . But, of course, I understand your decision not to make this *one* pizza."

A few beats of silence followed, as I felt my resolve crumbling. Damn Isabel Berney. She could convince the Great Wall of China to scooch ten feet to the right.

"Fine," I muttered. "So long as this lady knows that what she's getting is going to be 'free-from' actual pizza."

CHAPTER 2

Isabel and I finished working out the details and hung up just as I pulled in front of a two-story apartment building. Jarka Gagamova, our thirtysomething Bulgarian server, was waiting for us out front. She approached the van sporting a black three-piece suit, her shirt buttoned up to her long neck. Two small paintbrushes peeked out of her vest pocket, and she'd tucked her crayon-red hair into a bowler hat.

Sonya scooted to the middle of the bench seat to make way and contemplated the outfit. "Loving it." Her forehead creased. "Not totally *getting* it, though. Charlie Chaplin?"

Jarka straightened her spine indignantly. "I am Jules Pascin, most famous Bulgarian painter from my hometown. Everyone should know such great artist who creates so sensitive, so erotic, of pictures." When we continued to meet her with blank looks, she added, "He suffers very much for his art. In 1930, Pascin dies of alcoholism, leaving romantic suicide note to his French mistress written with his own blood."

Sonya's eyes widened. "So *not* Charlie Chaplin."

Jarka huffed loudly, pulled the seat belt across her thin torso, and snapped it into place.

"Change of plan," I explained, heaving the van into gear. "You and I are going to my house to collect ingredients that I'll somehow miracle into an acceptable free-from-pizza pizza, and Son will take the van to Bluff Point to meet the others. We'll head over separately on Pam Philips's yacht."

"The others" were Melody, our hostess; Daniel, our bartender; and Rabbit, our dishwasher/busser/jack-of-all-trades, all of whom had gone ahead to Bluff Point to begin setting up.

"Okay," Jarka said, imbuing her reply with the same level of enthusiasm she'd express if I'd asked her to put together a stack of cutlery roll-ups.

Her tune changed, though, when we pulled into the long, curving driveway of my Queen Anne mansion a few moments later. She inhaled sharply as the house's elaborate carved wood details, impressive wraparound porch, and cupcake-shaped turrets came into view.

"This is your house?" she asked.

I felt myself blush. I'd forgotten that Jarka, who'd only been working for me for a few months, had never seen where I lived, and didn't know the backstory of how I—a struggling small-business owner from a working-class family—came to reside in a glorious lakefront mansion with Melody and my great-aunt Biz.

"It's not Delilah's house," Sonya explained. "It's Butterball's. The rest of them just live there."

"Delilah's *cat* has this house?" Jarka asked.

I launched into the boiled-down recap of the very long story of how my curvaceous, ginger tabby cat was, in fact, the legal owner of a multi-million-dollar property. "My ex and I have joint custody of Butterball. When we broke up and he left for California, I moved into his house so Butterball could stay put. But Butterball's name is on the deed, or rather a trust set up in his name. I'm just here as his caretaker. And then my aunt and Melody needed a place to live, and there's enough room here . . ."

I trailed off. It wasn't that I was ashamed of the house. I'd been the one to oversee the renovations when my ex and I were still engaged, and I'd taken great pains perfecting every detail. However, the twin mantras of "no handouts" and "earn your own way in life" were deeply engrained in my psyche, and I couldn't bring myself to believe that me taking care of my much-adored cat justified free rent in a mansion. Plus, while this house represented my dream, my aunt was only here because the sweet lakefront cottage where she'd lived for over fifty years had fallen into foreclosure. And you better believe she didn't let me forget that living here wasn't her choice. The living arrangement was a gift horse, and Biz was determined to inspect its every last tooth. Thank goodness for Melody, who officially filled the role of Biz's live-in helper and unofficially kept the two of us from strangling each other.

As Jarka and I climbed out of the van and Sonya tooted a goodbye on the horn, my gaze was drawn down the gently sloping lawn toward the lake. Given the ominous sky and tanking air temperature, the lake was empty, save for the yacht gliding up to dock at my house's private pier. The boat, with its flawless white finish and double-decker height, called to mind an elegant wedding cake.

"That must be the boat Pam Philips sent," I said, observing the craft's impressive proportions. "Either that or a Russian oligarch is stopping in for a friendly chat."

Jarka and I hurried across the front lawn, bracing ourselves against the increasing force of the wind.

The boat's imposing presence reminded me of how

much was at stake. I never failed to be struck by the odd economics of these high-end philanthropic events—rich people lavishing vast sums of money on other rich people in the hopes that, what? A plate of buttery salmon *en croûte* and a chilled glass of Chenin Blanc would pry their wallets open a little wider? I supposed this was merely the fancy-pants version of the pancake breakfasts my parish held once a month when I was growing up.

Whatever my feelings about Geneva Bay's peculiar sort of noblesse oblige, I knew I needed to capitalize on this opportunity to showcase every arrow in my culinary quiver. I'd held my first kitchen job at sixteen, but even with twenty years as a professional cook under my belt, tonight's gig had my nerves winding themselves into knots.

I pushed my stress aside and opened the front door to my house. No sooner were Jarka and I inside than Butterball padded down the curving entryway staircase and sidled up to press his face into my shins.

"Hey, B-man," I said, running my hands along his wide, soft body. He purred his return greeting.

I let his calm presence wash over me like a sedative. *I can do this. I can cater an amazing event. I can see my staff safely through the winter months. I can create an enchanted friggin' unicorn of a pizza that contains no real ingredients and is somehow still mind-blowingly delicious.* I gave my cat's head another rub. What a shame that it was against health regulations to bring an emotional-support cat to work.

Jarka squatted down to get her share of Butterball's attention. "*Khubavo kote*," she crooned. Then, switching to English, she repeated, "Pretty kitty."

An appetizing, earthy aroma wafted down the hallway,

beckoning us toward the kitchen. I plopped Butterball onto the floor, and the three of us headed into the kitchen. I'd designed the inviting space, arranging everything to my exact specifications—restaurant-quality appliances, expansive countertops, and plenty of windows. Today, they granted a starkly beautiful view of waving branches, a lake the color of molten lead, and Pam Philips's big-ass boat, docked and waiting to whisk us across the lake.

My great-aunt, Elizabeth "Biz" O'Leary, stood in front of an open oven door, silicone mitts covering both her hands. She leaned down, extracting a tray of roasted baby beets. She gave the tray a gentle shake, which sent the amethyst-colored orbs colliding around the pan like miniature billiard balls.

Biz wore her usual stiff-collared blouse and slacks, and the white curls of her hair were arrayed in rows as orderly as the furrows in a freshly plowed field. She'd been petite all her life, and age had distilled her down to her bare essence. As with Isabel Berney, my aunt's small stature and advanced age belied her impressive energy. She removed the oversized oven mitts from her tiny hands, like a kid coming inside after playing in the snow.

"Aren't you supposed to be at Bluff Point by now? You'll be late," she chided. "And whose ridiculous aircraft carrier of a boat is that?"

I took in a calming breath. I'd moved from Chicago to Geneva Bay in part to be closer to Biz. She'd never married or had children, so my sister and I were her only living relatives. However, I hadn't envisioned living quite *this* close to her. Even in a house with plenty of square footage, we still found a way to step on each other's toes.

"We had to take a detour to gather ingredients. There were some special dietary requests," I explained.

"Hello, Miss O'Leary," Jarka said. She regarded the beets with motherly tenderness. "These beets are very beautiful. Like jewels from the earth."

Jarka wasn't as much of an obsessive foodie as the rest of the D&S crew. She disdained the fussiness of most restaurant dishes and gave short shrift to what she saw as the American excesses of our menus—too much seasoning, too much cheese, extravagant portions. However, she had a special appreciation for quality produce.

"Thank you, Jarka. They're very good, but they're nowhere near as good as the ones I used to grow in my garden," Biz replied. She shifted one of the beets onto a cutting board and sliced it for us to try.

I bit into the toothsome, perfectly cooked wedge. Biz had roasted it in a no-frills dressing, allowing the beet's sweetness and earthy tang to take center stage. Comparing these little balls of vegetable perfection unfavorably to her garden beets was like saying a Rembrandt was prettier than a Michelangelo.

"All those years enriching the soil in that garden," Biz said, as she swallowed her portion, "and the whole thing gets snatched out from under me by that tin-pot tycoon and his *weather girl*."

I pressed my eyes closed. I was in no mood to relitigate the circumstances of Biz losing her cottage a few months earlier in a foreclosure auction. She'd been going on about it practically every day since she'd moved in, poring over the terms of the sale and obsessing over the new owners' plans for the site. Even now, I could see a stack of records she'd copied from the town assessor's office sitting on the kitchen table. The long and the short of it was that she hadn't been able to come up with the money to pay the gargantuan property tax bill when it came due, and she had firmly rejected all offers of financial help. So off went her lakefront cottage to the highest bidders—her former next-door neighbors, Brian Lee "B.L." Huddleston and Kennedy Criss, a onetime TV meteorologist who'd recently become his third wife.

It wasn't that I expected Biz to fall down on her knees in gratitude simply because I'd offered her the opportunity to pass her golden years in a well-appointed lakefront mansion. Losing your beloved home of fifty years was hard. But I could do without the melodrama.

"Auntie Biz . . ." I began.

She held up her hand. "I know what you're going to say. I need to yank on my big-girl panties and be thankful I'm still on the right side of the dirt and didn't end up living in an old folks' home." She made her hand open and close like she was holding a sock puppet. *"Blah, blah, blah."*

"I wasn't going to say that," I began. Well, I *was*, but not in those exact words. To avoid further confrontation, I pivoted. "These beets are delicious."

She nodded. "They'll do. Roasted very simply with olive oil, salt, and thyme."

A lightbulb dinged in my brain.

"Can you spare some of them?" I asked. "I need something to make a pizza sauce without any nightshade vegetables. No tomatoes, eggplants, or peppers."

Biz tilted her head appreciatively. I was speaking our common language—the language of recipes—and suddenly all antagonism melted away. "Beets should be a good base, but where are you going to get the acid? Beets won't have the tang of a tomato."

I began to root through the cupboards and popped up with the bottle of red wine vinegar.

Biz nodded. "That and some spice ought to do it. You'll have to watch what you use, though. No red pepper flakes or chili powders if you're steering clear of nightshades."

"Good point," I said. "I'll stick to black pepper."

I stood for a moment, formulating the rest of my attack plan. From my previous forays into gluten-free crust making, I knew that almond flour would work to add bulk and sweetness to the crust, and in the absence of sticky gluten, xanthan gum could improve the texture and elasticity of the dough. But what could add the salty umami flavor of cheese, sans the dairy?

I rifled through my mental recipe cards, summoning up a recollection that vegan Parmesan could be fashioned from ground cashew nuts and "nooch," i.e., nutritional yeast.

"Jarka, can you scour the pantry? I think I've still got some nutritional yeast and almond flour that Sam used to use for his energy bars. There should be a couple boxes of his stuff on the bottom shelves."

Fortunately, my ex had been a devotee of various dietary trends and fitness fads. Plus, he'd shopped in bulk, meaning that I'd been left with a pantry full of the exact kind of whimsical hipster foodstuffs this situation required.

As Biz and I decanted the roasted beets into an oversized Tupperware container, Jarka emerged from the pantry carrying a large box. "Almond flour and nutritional yeast, yes?"

I peered inside. "Perfect."

"Are you making dinner or wallpaper paste?" Biz muttered.

I ignored her. "Jarka, can you box up the Breville, too? I'll need it to blitz the nuts for the vegan cheese." I surveyed the kitchen, tapping my fingers against my lips.

"And I want that stand mixer. Gluten-free dough is too sticky to knead by hand. There should be an empty box on the sunporch you can put it in." I hadn't planned to do much actual cooking at Bluff Point, so I hadn't sent over many appliances, pots, or pans. Given our tight timeline, I couldn't risk missing any necessary equipment. "Once you've got all that together, let's start bringing things down to the boat. Oh, and watch that Butterball doesn't slip out. He's under house arrest for catfighting."

Jarka addressed Biz as the two of them moved between the kitchen and the pantry, stacking boxes of ingredients and equipment. "Why you are not coming to the party?"

It was a fair question. Biz was an excellent amateur cook, and her extra pair of skilled hands often came in handy at the restaurant. But Biz had insisted on steering clear.

"A costume party with a bunch of preening Richie Riches? You couldn't drag me with a tow truck winch," Biz said. "The only thing I'll be sorry to miss is Lola Capone's performance. I used to have an LP of her back in the Eighties. That woman has a voice, I'll tell you that."

Jarka gave a nonchalant nod and headed out the back door. I, on the other hand, was squeezing the bag of carrots I was holding so tightly I was surprised the pressure didn't form it into a diamond. "Did you say Lola Capone is performing?"

"Didn't Isabel mention it?" Biz asked. "When I saw her at bridge club the other week, she was over the moon to book her. Lola Capone will be perfect for the Jazz Age theme."

I swallowed hard, trying to contain the swarm of butterflies that materialized in my stomach at the mention of the Capone name.

Biz peered at my face. "What's gotten into you? Do you still have the hots for that son of hers?"

"If you mean Detective Calvin Capone, I haven't seen him in months," I huffed. "Why should I care if his mother is singing at the party? I'm there to work. That's it."

In truth, I cared very much, as evidenced by the flocking tummy butterflies. Twice now, I'd fooled myself into thinking that Capone and I had the makings of a couple. But each time we got close, he pulled a disappearing act. I wasn't falling for that again.

I turned back to the fridge, catching a glimpse of myself in the mirror-like finish of its outer door. So Capone's mom would be there. So what? I doubted I'd even see her, and if I did, she'd probably have no idea who I was. Still, I couldn't help wishing I'd dressed for the occasion, or at least put on a little mascara.

I tamped down the butterflies and firmed up my jaw. Now wasn't the time to dwell on regrets, romantic entanglements, or lost opportunities. I had work to do.

CHAPTER 3

By the time I finished gathering every ingredient I could possibly need and headed down to the dock, Jarka was already halfway up the gangway, lugging the last of the supplies. The wind had sharpened to a knifepoint, cutting through my clothes and portending the fast-approaching evening. I prayed that my team would have everything in hand at Bluff Point when we arrived.

A uniformed crew member with heavy black braids and a bouncy stride hurried down to meet me as I climbed aboard the ship. "May I?" she asked, unburdening me of the canvas tote bags I was hauling.

She stowed the bags, unhitched the boat from its moorings, and then escorted Jarka and me up a set of stairs toward the enclosed helm. As we mounted the steps, the full power of the wind rose to meet us, causing me to grasp the handrails for balance. I was suddenly grateful for the boat's enormity. Even as the waves kicked up, it barely swayed.

"It was nice of Ms. Philips to send her boat to pick us up," I told the crew member, shouting to be heard over the gusts.

"Happy to," the woman, who'd introduced herself as Ciera, said, in a sunny Australian accent. "We'll have you across this puddle in two shakes. Have a squiz and you can just about make out Bluff Point." She pointed to a small dark speck on the far shore, set, as the name implied, on a bluff above the tree line.

I took a seat next to Ciera in the helm as Jarka explored the sizable interior of the boat. The room we occupied was roughly divided into steering, seating, cooking, and dining areas, all outfitted with high-end finishes. It had a leathery, pleasant scent, which I supposed was the boat equivalent of new car smell. Boat ownership was commonplace in Geneva Bay, but even the largest and nicest boats on the lake couldn't hold a candle to Pam Philips's yacht. It was Moby Dick in a school of minnows. Every time I thought I'd gotten used to the opulence of life in Geneva Bay—the thirty-bedroom mansions, the helicopter landing pads, the full-sized indoor basketball courts—the one-upsmanship found a new gear.

As the shoreline receded behind us, a knot of worry tightened in my chest. *Had we brought everything we'd need?* Once we were at Bluff Point, we'd be a good thirty minutes' drive one-way from the nearest grocery store. Catering was always stressful that way—unfamiliar space, unfamiliar layout, unfamiliar equipment—but this gig was especially so due to the location's remoteness. Something niggled. *What had we missed?* I tried again to still the whisper of worry that haunted the edge of my mind. *You're prepared.* The feeling was probably just a reaction to running late and to the unexpected, last-minute frenzy of the free-from pizza request. *No, there's something . . .*

Through the boat's large front window, Bluff Point loomed ever closer. One of the most recognizable of the lake's historic mansions, Bluff Point had been built as a summer getaway by a turn-of-the-century Chicago beer baron and had changed very little in the intervening hundred-plus years. A lighthouse-like turret, encircled by a 360-degree widow's walk, jutted from the front of the house like a ship's prow. The home was exquisite, a sumptuous jewel case of stained glass and carved wood. My own house hailed from the same genre of nineteenth-century architecture, and had its fair share of porches, balconies, and overhangs, but Bluff Point looked like a carpenter's fever dream.

"Just hang tight a minute while we dock," Ciera called out cheerily as we drew alongside the dock. She hadn't been kidding about getting across the lake in two shakes. I reckoned we'd made it in one and a half shakes, if that.

Once we'd disembarked, Jarka and I stood on the dock for a moment, looking up toward the house. The main approach from the lakeside appeared to be a dizzying arrangement of interconnected decks and stairways straight out of an M. C. Escher drawing. Late afternoon shadows crept over the property. A damp, chilly wind swept through, wrenching crisp leaves from the trees. Panicked squirrels darted around, crazed in their last-minute preparations for winter. If the structure seemed imposing from out on the water, from this angle it looked as impregnable as a medieval fortress.

Ciera joined us, toting a box of the supplies we'd brought. "We can zip up the hill in the ATV," she explained, gesturing to a small all-terrain vehicle parked beside the dock. "But," she continued, "if we're going to fit all this stuff in, I'm afraid there's only room for one person. If one of you wants to wait here, I can run the other up to the house and then circle back. Or we can leave your gear on the dock, take you both up, and I'll come back for it. Or one of you can take the stairs."

"I competed ultramarathon six times," Jarka said. "I will go by stairs. No problems."

Much as my pride goaded me to reject Jarka's offer, I knew I needed to save my energy for more important pursuits, like knocking this catering gig out of the park. With each minute that ticked by, my antsiness grew. Never one to leave things to chance, I'd started the day with a hefty time buffer, planning to arrive at Bluff Point at least two and a half hours before the six p.m. doors-open time. But little by little, those extra minutes melted away. It was four thirty-five, and I still had a brand-new pizza recipe to concoct from scratch.

Once all the gear was loaded, Jarka set off, taking the stairs two at a time. Ciera and I cruised around to the side of the house, where she pulled alongside a sturdy-looking oak door and cut the ATV's engine.

"This is the old tradesmen's entrance," she explained.

"I remember from the pre-party tour. This will take us in just below the kitchen, right?" I asked.

The previous week, I'd been part of the advance team that scoped out the venue, along with Isabel Berney and the members of the library board.

Ciera nodded, and we headed for the house, opening the door to reveal a hallway with a series of utilitarian rooms leading off of it. The door to a laundry room stood open on our right. To our left was a storage room with rows of shelves for extra linens and cleaning supplies. The space smelled of furniture polish and floor wax.

"Unfortunately, there isn't an entrance you can drive up to that's on the same level as the kitchen. Clearly not designed for people with disabilities," she said.

"Or for the convenience of the hired help." I added.

She flashed a smile. "I'm afraid historical authenticity won out over accessibility. Luckily, we can avoid carry-ing everything up those"—she gestured to a steep stair-case at the end of the hall—"by using this bad boy." She opened the door of what appeared to be a built-in cupboard, revealing a large dumbwaiter. She pulled a lever and the box set off, drawn upward into its vertical shaft by a pulley system. "Goes up to the kitchen and then from there up to the second floor, where the bedrooms are. They used to use it to send the tea trays up for breakfast."

"Not anymore?"

"No, Ms. Philips comes down and makes her own oatmeal in the kitchen like a normal person. It's not Downton Abbey." She laughed. "It hardly gets used, except to unload groceries."

"Does Ms. Philips live here all alone?" I asked.

"In the spring and summer, there's a full-time gardener who has a little cottage on the property. I'm Ms. Philips's assistant. I come every day to do all the girl Friday errands, captain the boat during the season, and generally try to keep the place from feeling too haunted. Other than that, just two housekeepers who come a few times a week to clean."

"Funny that she'd buy such a big house just for herself," I observed. "I'd get lonely out here."

"She wasn't initially interested in this property," Ciera explained. "Then she heard there was another offer on it, someone who was going to gut it and modernize it. She couldn't stand by and watch that happen, so she outbid them and got it. Once she owned it, she went all in on its restoration."

"It's beautiful," I said, admiring the craftsmanship that was evident even in this "back of house" area. "Are you coming to the party?"

She shook her head. "Not my scene. Anyhow, I've got work to do. I'm heading to the marina as soon as you're settled in to get the boat hauled out and help them start winterizing it. Just about everyone else is off the water already, but Ms. Philips loves the fall colors, so she wanted to wring out every last drop of the season. The weather's been so nice up until today."

Ciera offered to help carry my supplies up to the kitchen, but, not wanting to take further advantage of her kindness, I assured her that I could take over. After she helped me unload everything from the ATV, she said goodbye.

I hurried up the servants' staircase and rounded the corner toward the kitchen so quickly that I nearly collided with a trim, elderly man.

"Ah, Ms. O'Leary. A pleasure." Edgar Clemmons leaned heavily on a gilt-topped cane and gave a courtly bow.

Clemmons, the outgoing Friends of the Library board chair, straightened the striped tie of his dark wool suit. He had a precise, genteel voice and faultless manners, but his unexpected presence sent a little tremor of unease up the back of my neck. Sonya, who loved nothing more than playing mother hen to an odd duck, had struck up a friendship of sorts with Clemmons, based on their shared love of film noir. To me, though, his manner had always been unsettling. I'd seen a lot of him over the preceding months, since I'd convinced Isabel to move the Friends of the Library board's regular monthly meetings to my restaurant by offering them a free bottle of wine at each meeting.

From my limited vantage point in the restaurant kitchen, the meeting during which the library board voted to replace Clemmons with Pam Philips seemed to follow the usual unremarkable bureaucratic orderliness of a small-town institution. However, when I'd popped out to say hello to the group, the mood was tense, and I sensed a barely repressed rage radiating off Clemmons. Since then, every time I saw him, I felt that he sat just a little too straight and measured his words just a little too carefully.

I surveyed his formal suit. Initially, I felt unsure he was in costume, given that his day-to-day attire tended toward the overly prim. Upon closer inspection, however, I noticed that he seemed to be dressed as a specific person, like Jarka was, rather than in a generic Prohibition-era outfit.

"Pretty Boy Floyd?" I ventured, basing my guess on his dapper attire and neat grooming.

"Hardly," Clemmons bristled. "I'm J. Edgar Hoover. He was my namesake, and I've always felt an affinity toward him."

What kind of whack-a-doodle parents named their kid after J. Edgar Hoover?

The only pictures I could ever remember seeing of the famous mob-busting federal agent were of a man with a paunchy, snub-nosed boxer's face wearing a perpetually irritated scowl. Clemmons's features were more refined, but I could make out a resemblance between him and the FBI director. That broad, intelligent forehead. That uncomfortable, penetrating gaze.

"A lawman. You're expecting a rowdy crowd, then?" I said with a smile.

Instead of matching my light tone, Clemmons grew serious, and the creases around his mouth deepened. "It felt necessary tonight." He paused and turned away, his face falling into shadow. "Certain matters need to be set to rights."

"Have you come early to help with the party setup?" I asked. Maybe his melodramatic phrasing was merely his way of saying that he was going to double-check seating assignments or fluff up some centerpiece flowers.

"No," he said. "I'm sure *Isabel* has planned everything perfectly."

"Well, enjoy the party," I said. I was anxious to get to the kitchen, and even more anxious to avoid hearing whatever was behind the bitter emphasis he placed on the town librarian's name. I took a step to pass him. I knew from experience that Clemmons was a know-it-all who could make ordering an appetizer into a ten-minute monologue.

"I've been uneasy for some time," he said, not taking the hint. "And finally the pieces clicked into place as I prepared for the event tonight. It was in fact Sonya who connected the dots for me. She and I share a love for old movies, you see." There was something about Clemmons's tone that crept under my skin like a slow-motion shiver. His voice dropped almost to a whisper. "There are things in this house that concern me deeply. Things are amiss."

"Amiss?" I asked. Yeesh, this felt more like a mind game than a conversation.

"Yes. I saw some things in Pam's book collection that are of particular interest to me, to Pam herself, and to many others, I suspect. I have suspicions." He lifted his chin haughtily. "That woman. As if it weren't enough for her to degrade the written word with her technological *innovations*"—he scrunched his nose as he spoke the word—"she hoodwinked Isabel into letting her take over the library board, I'm sure of it. Isabel will get her comeuppance soon enough, once Pam starts replacing all the books with computer screens and trading human librarians for robots."

"Riiight . . ." I said. "Should I tell Pam you're looking for her? Or you could call her and tell her you're here? I'm sure she's around somewhere."

"I don't use a mobile phone. Opiate of the masses, designed to keep us from thinking. If you see Pam, tell her to meet me in the appointed place." He paused, casting a dramatic gaze around the long hallway. With his prim suit and slicked-back hair, he looked so much like a B-movie actor that I began to wonder if he was intentionally jerking me around. I battened down my natural curiosity, refusing to take the bait, waiting for him to continue on his own. And waiting.

"Well, I've got to get to the kitchen," I said at last. I was done playing twenty questions with this weirdo.

"It's up to me to set matters to rights. The guilty must be held accountable," he said.

"The guilty?" I asked. *Dang it.* He'd gotten me.

Now that he'd piqued my interest, though, he didn't launch into one of his legendary monologues. Instead, he was already advancing toward the same staircase I'd just ascended, but upward toward the second floor. He leaned heavily on his cane with each step he took.

"Are you okay on those stairs?" I asked, watching him teeter slightly on the landing. "I think the staircase in the drawing room is less steep."

"I can manage," he said, waving me off.

"Great. Well, whatever is 'amiss' with 'the guilty,' I hope you get it figured out," I called.

He turned and took a few steps back toward me, training his probing gaze on me once more. "Until I know for certain, I'd appreciate your discretion." There was a note of reproach in his voice.

"I don't really have a choice, since I have no idea what you're talking about," I said. I'm a cut-to-the-chase kind of gal, and I found Clemmons's slow drip of innuendo irritating. Plus, the guy gave me the heebie-jeebies.

With a swift, formal nod, he headed off, leaving me just as in the dark as I'd been at the outset of the conversation.

CHAPTER 4

Bluff Point's kitchen was one of the few areas of the house where convenience had taken precedence over historical authenticity. While the original wall of storage cabinets and plate rails had been preserved, the rest of the space was modernized with stunning black-and-copper-finish appliances and plenty of well-lit workspace. As I approached, I heard the familiar bass thump of our Chop and Bop prep playlist. I was relieved to smell the tantalizing aroma of roasted garlic and oregano, underlaid with a comforting waft of slow-cooked beef. Judging by the smell, our Italian beef crostini hors d'oeuvres were underway.

I found Sonya at the long center island, stacking bite-sized tamale apps into steamer baskets to warm through. Her hair and makeup still looked flawless, which at least signaled that the apocalypse wasn't imminent. However, the fact that she wore an expression of grim concentration, rather than her usual carefree smile, hinted that the pressure was on. She prepped another round of tamales with the focus of a submariner loading a cache of torpedoes into their firing chutes.

"Where are we up to?" I asked, tying on an apron.

"Apps are on, but we're way behind on thawing the pies," she said, not looking up.

I took a deep breath and blew it out slowly. "Okay, entrees don't need to go out until seven. As long as the apps go on time, we can catch up on the entrees. Have you seen Melody or Jarka? We're going to need their help."

"No sign of Jarka," Sonya said. "I thought she was with you?"

I shook my head. "She came up from the dock a different way."

"Well, Melody went to change into her costume, and she didn't come back," Sonya said.

Where was everybody? I checked my watch. I couldn't remember ever showing up at a catering gig with this little time to spare, and I still had an entire pizza recipe to invent. The extra servers we'd hired to supplement my staff would be arriving shortly, and we'd have to brief them on the menu. By now, Melody should've finished setting the tables and transforming a Chicago-style hot dog cart we'd rented into Delilah & Son's very own "Haute Dog Cart," offering the traditional fixings— mustard, chopped onion, relish, dill pickle and tomato wedges, pickled peppers, and celery salt—with our signature careful attention to high-quality, freshly prepared ingredients. Daniel, I prayed, would have his Prohibition-themed cocktails ready to go. And where was Jarka? At the pace she set off up the stairs, I'd expected her to beat me to the kitchen.

"Did you make sure the ovens are up to temp?" I asked. "They'll need to be at three seventy-five by quarter to six."

"Yeah, and for my next trick, I'm going to spin twenty plates while I juggle these tamales with my boobs," Sonya snapped, as she shifted another batch of tamales into the steamer.

"Is that a no?" I asked.

"I've only been here a few minutes! Go look at the ovens yourself!" she shouted. Then under her breath she added, "I'm a sous chef, not a freaking magician."

Whoops. It seemed as if I'd stepped across the fine line between micromanaging and signing my own death warrant.

By way of apology to Sonya, I hustled over and started cranking the dials on our battalion of rented ovens. When it comes to deep dish, moisture is kryptonite. Every step of the process is designed to cut your chances of ending up with the dreaded soggy bottom crust. Fat repels moisture, so we rely on low-moisture, high-fat cheeses, like Wisconsin mozzarella, to create a protective layer, and we also add fat to the crust itself in the form of both melted butter and olive or corn oil. Fresh toppings like spinach and mushrooms are precooked and wrung out or laid out to dry on racks before being added.

At the restaurant, high-temp cooking and immediate service did the trick to ensure a crispy, flaky finish to the crust. When filling a large catering order, though, there was no easy way to transport pizzas en masse without the moisture from the ingredients seeping into the crust. And obviously it would be impractical to assemble dozens of pizzas from scratch on-site and serve them all at once.

After some trial and error, I'd hit upon another method. We baked the pizzas in advance at Delilah & Son, then flash-froze them on rolling racks in our walk-in so we could load the racks straight into the catering van. When we got to the venue, we re-baked them on-site to bring them to serving temperature. Not the most elegant solution, but large-scale catering is rarely elegant. Hopefully we'd figure out a way to make our quick-bake method extra quick today.

Just then, Robert "Rabbit" Blakemore hurried across the kitchen carrying tubs of greens and quart-sized containers of sliced Granny Smith apples, dried cranberries, and crunchy pepitas for the dinner salads. He nodded toward me as he set them down.

"Hey, Chef," he said. "We were startin' to get worried that the boat had taken you and Jarka on one of them *Gilligan's Island* three-hour tours."

Rabbit wasn't known for his sartorial style, usually showing up to work in black jeans and a backward-facing Milwaukee Brewers cap. Today, however, his wiry frame looked positively debonair in a starched white shirt with suspenders and a bow tie.

"Nice outfit," I commented.

A smile creased his careworn features, causing the wrinkles next to his green eyes to fan out toward the prematurely gray hair at his temples. He removed the tweed newsboy hat from his head and ran a hand self-consciously over his closely cropped hair.

Rabbit had only a few years on me in age, but he wore them heavily. He'd spent the better part of a decade, on and off, behind bars, and had wrestled with a drinking problem in his younger days as well. Determined to make a better life for himself and his young daughter, he'd finally cleaned up his act and put his admirable work ethic to productive use. I suspected that among the many gangsters and molls who'd be in attendance at the party, Rabbit would be one of the few who'd actually lived a life of crime.

"Thanks, Chef. The hat and suspenders were my grandpa's. Probably from the forties instead of the twenties or thirties"—he stretched the suspenders and let them snap back against his chest—"but it looks the part good enough."

"Well, serving deep dish at a Prohibition party isn't totally authentic, either. It wasn't invented until the early forties," I said. "And I doubt Bugsy Siegel ever saw a mini tamale in his life. Hey, I don't suppose you've seen Jarka?" I scanned the room again, as if she might leap out of a cupboard. "I hope she didn't fall down the stairs or something."

Rabbit's eyes trailed past me, through the glass patio doors that opened onto the lawn. "Jarka's right there."

Sure enough, about twenty feet beyond the glass, Jarka stood close to a man, beneath a pergola covered in dead vines. Her companion was tall and trim, with an athletic build and elegant carriage. He wore an exquisitely tailored suit, with a fedora low over his face.

The weather outside had grown even more ominous since my arrival. My slightly elevated vantage point afforded a far-reaching view over the rear garden and down the steep hill to the lake. Mirroring my unsettled mood, the wind gusted again and the trees frantically waved their browning leaves. The lake water swished back and forth, reflecting back the dishwater color of the sky.

"She's been out there for a while with that guy," Rabbit said. "They seem to know each other, but I don't like the look of it."

I could sense why Rabbit, with his built-in jailbird antennae finely tuned to lurking threats, had been keeping his eyes on the pair. Although much of the man's face was veiled in shadow, I could make out a tight jaw and a sneer on his lips. Jarka wasn't much for sharing personal information, but last I'd heard, she was in a serious relationship with the director of Geneva Bay's Chamber of

Commerce—a sweet, awkward man who was the total opposite of this dude. So who was he to her?

It was clear this wasn't a casual chat. Jarka stood firm, her chin angled up, her gaze boring straight into the man as he carried on what appeared to be an impassioned, and unwelcome, soliloquy.

"Do you recognize him?" I asked.

"No," Rabbit said, "but he looks like trouble."

Confirming his assessment, the man lunged at Jarka, pulling her toward him by one arm. Before my brain could even piece together what I was seeing, my body was halfway out the door.

CHAPTER 5

A blast of wind hit me as I rushed out the door, followed closely by Rabbit. As I approached Jarka and the mystery man, I heard rapid-fire words in a language I couldn't understand. Bulgarian, I supposed. Bounding past me, Rabbit was on the man in ten steps, taking hold of him by the scruff of his collar and pulling him away from the pergola and Jarka.

"Let me go!" The man wheeled around. The hat flew off his head as he confronted Rabbit. He aimed a punch at Rabbit's midsection, which Rabbit barely dodged.

The two men circled each other. The stranger assumed a formal boxing stance; Rabbit held his arms wide apart as if he were trying to corral a wild horse.

By the time I reached the group, Jarka had jumped between Rabbit and the man, her face reddened from a combination of windburn and strong emotion. She hissed something at the man in a foreign language. Then she turned to Rabbit. "Thank you, but there is no need."

"You sure?" Rabbit asked, not lowering his guard. He eyed the man suspiciously.

"Whoever you are, this is no business of yours," the man snapped, moving toward Jarka.

I stepped in front of him. "When I see someone grab one of my employees, it literally is my business."

The man's fists were still balled and ready for action. My muscles tightened, preparing for whatever might come next. I stood almost five-ten, and my curvaceous build had helped me out more than once when it came to physical confrontations. I might not have Rabbit's quickness or scrappy prison yard experience, but my forceful personality and fend-for-yourself, South-Side-of-Chicago upbringing had afforded me no shortage of sparring practice.

"I am fine," Jarka said, coming alongside me and tucking the blowing strands of her vivid red hair back under her bowler hat. "This person is Victor. He is leaving now." She shot Victor a glare that would've made Attila the Hun consider taking a desk job.

Victor dropped his hands to his side. Without his hat on, I finally got a clear glimpse of the man's face. He was handsome, but in a highly unconventional, Benedict Cumberbatchian way. The skin on his face was so taut, I feared it might snap if he opened his mouth too wide. His eyebrows arched broad and black across his forehead, like a child's drawing of bird wings. Cheekbones, nose, jawline—every angle was sharp. Overall, he looked like a bust whose sculptor hadn't had time to go back and chisel away the overly severe edges.

Victor regarded Jarka with pleading eyes. By degrees, her expression softened, and an ineffable look passed between them. I glanced at Rabbit, whose face bore the same puzzled expression mine must have, and whose mind I suspected held the same question. *Had that been an embrace or an assault?*

"I am the artist Count Leka Simeon Victor Hohenstaufen-Chandon. I apologize for the disturbance," the man said. He spoke in an unidentifiable European accent, tinged with posh British inflections. "I shall take my leave of you." He gave a curt bow and stalked into the house.

Jarka's thin lips compressed into a tiny dot. Her expression was unreadable. Most people would've felt the need to offer some explanation for the scene. Not Jarka. She trooped past us toward the house, and Rabbit and I followed. Behind her back, I shot him a "What the hell?" look, which he met with a baffled shrug.

"Who did he say he was dressed as?" Rabbit called to Jarka. "The artist formerly known as Count Dracula? Did he think this was an early Halloween party?"

"Is not costume," Jarka replied, slowing her stride. "He *is* Count Leka Simeon Victor Hohenstaufen-Chandon. That is his given name. His ancestor was Margrave of Bohemia."

"Mangrove of what?" Rabbit said.

"*Margrave*. Nobility. Victor is a painter." She cast a disgusted look back outside to the spot where they'd been standing. "Let us speak no more of this. There is much work to be done, and we are late."

By the time we got inside, our four rent-a-servers had arrived and were milling around, awaiting their marching orders. Over my long career as a chef, I'd catered hundreds of events of all sizes, and had a firmly established routine. Arrive at the venue two and a half hours early. Unload the food and gear. Organize the team. Organize the courses. Organize the stations. Get the food warming. About forty-five minutes before go time, the hired event staff arrived. Next came the stand-up—the quick briefing before the madness of service began, to explain the menu, answer questions, and assign tasks. Then I'd return to the kitchen to buzz through the last-minute prep and troubleshoot any issues that had arisen. Everything proceeded according to a predetermined, methodical rhythm.

Catering is the same as any complex task, like flying a plane. Can you just hit the throttle and zoom off into the clear blue sky? Sure. But the chances of a successful take-off and landing greatly increase if you take the time to do your preflight checks. Today, though, I'd run out of time for my usual routines. I was going to have to rely on my crew and fly by the seat of my pants.

I turned to Jarka. Even if she hadn't just experienced an emotional shock, she wouldn't have been my go-to person when it came to soft skills. She was whip-smart and incredibly efficient, but her English could be dubious at times, and her approach to personal interactions was matter-of-fact. The same way a cattle prod is matter-of-fact.

However, I had no choice but to trust her. "Are you okay to lead the stand-up alone?"

"Of course, Chef," she replied, her face as expressive as a manila envelope. If she'd been rattled by the encounter with Victor, she wasn't showing it.

"Great. Make sure the servers understand the timings of the courses. Dirty plates should be cleared immediately and wine- and water glasses should never be empty."

"I will demand this of them," Jarka said.

I grimaced, hoping "demand this of them" was just a poor translation of "cheerfully motivate them."

I hastily explained the dumbwaiter system to Rabbit and asked him to collect the pizza-making supplies, which were still languishing downstairs. Meanwhile, I began to make the rounds of the kitchen, getting the most urgent things underway, and taking stock of what still needed to be done.

"Everything okay with Jarka?" Sonya asked.

"I think so?" I said, with an uncertain glance back toward the dining room. "Apparently, she has some kind of . . . *thing* with a count."

Sonya furrowed her brow. "That guy was an accountant?"

"No, a *count*."

She set down the jar of house-made *giardiniera* she was holding. "As in the *Count of Monte Cristo*? Like, royalty?"

I shrugged, moving across the kitchen to begin unpacking the gear Rabbit had sent up in the dumbwaiter. "I guess. The only count I know is that little purple vampire from *Sesame Street*, and I'm ninety-nine percent sure that wasn't him."

She shook her head and picked the jar back up. "Man, Jarka is a dark horse."

"You can say that again," I agreed. I leaned down to lift the stand mixer box and gasped. It was weightless.

"What's wrong?" Sonya asked.

I flipped open the lid. "The stand mixer isn't in here. We somehow brought an empty box." I pressed my finger to my temples. My premonition on the boat—that we were missing something important—apparently wasn't just a product of my overactive control-freak brain. "The gluten-free crust is next to impossible to mix by hand. It's like spackle." I swore under my breath. "I don't get how Jarka didn't realize the box was empty, but never mind. I should've double-checked." I looked around. "Look in the cabinets. Maybe Pam has one we can borrow."

We flew around the room, opening door after door. Just as I'd given up hope, Sonya shouted a triumphant, "Found it!" She hefted a gleaming KitchenAid model onto the counter. "Crisis averted."

"Hopefully that was the last heart attack I'll have today," I said, putting a hand to my chest. "Before I start on the gluten-free dough, I'm going to check in with Daniel and Melody. We need all hands on deck when service starts. I don't want any more blips."

"Okay, but don't abandon me again. This is turning into one of those 'don't go into the barn' slasher movies. Even *I'm* stressing out," she said.

I beelined it through the dining room, where dinner would be served. Although there was no sign of Melody, I took some comfort in the fact that she appeared to have finished laying the rented tables with crisp, white linens and white-gold cutlery (also rented) for the sixty guests who were expected to attend. Tall, thin vases stood at the center of each of the round tables, brimming with sprays of cream roses and white ostrich plumes. Melody had been chipping away at a degree in graphic design, and she had a real eye for all things visual. She'd created a historically accurate monochromatic effect with enough texture and variation to feel fresh and modern. Even to my exacting eye, it was perfect. *Phew.* The dining space would be ready, at least, even if the food wasn't.

As I hustled down a short hallway that separated the dining room from the drawing room, I heard a sound like the air being let out of a tire.

I paused and listened. *Pssst.* There it was again.

Two wide blue eyes peeked out of a partially open door. As I approached, a hand reached out to pull me inside a pale pink powder room.

"Melody, what in the world . . . ?"

My young housemate looked distraught. Her complexion was splotchy, her face puffy and streaked with tears. She was clad in an oversized Geneva Bay Badgers sweatshirt and torn jeans.

"What's wrong? Are you feeling okay?"

Checking to make sure the door was closed, she tugged the sweatshirt over her head, and then pulled off her jeans. Underneath, a silver fringed minidress was practically suctioned to her petite curves. The deep V in the neckline nearly met the high slit in the microscopic skirt. The top was encrusted with diamanté sparkles. There seemed to be more material in her elbow-length satin gloves than there was in the rest of the outfit combined. The getup left little to the imagination, or maybe sent the imagination into overdrive, depending on the imaginer's inclinations. Shy farm-girl Melody rarely showed skin, but her natural assets were undeniable.

"I look like a slutty disco ball," she sniveled. "I borrowed this from my cousin without trying it on. She wore it a few Halloweens ago, and she said it would cover a lot more on me because I'm five inches shorter than she is. I bet she lied to me on purpose. She's always teasing me about being a prude. There's some kind of built-in corset in here that just . . ."—she gestured to the perky, round tops of her breasts—"exhibits things."

I grabbed a hand towel, ran it under a stream of cold water, and pressed it to her tear-swollen cheeks. "It's a cute dress. You look lovely," I said.

"How am I going to serve people?" She pushed the towel away and put her face in her hands. "Oh, for Pete's sake, I should've made sure it fit before I left."

I pulled her hands away from her face. How I wished Sonya had been the one to discover this predicament. Sonya had a gift for all the touchy-feely, you-go-girl, pep-talky mumbo jumbo that I absolutely sucked at.

"You'll be fine, Mel. It's just a dress."

She bit her lip and crossed her arms over her chest.

"I know you're counting on me, Chef. Sonya's probably stressing."

"All that's true. But I know how you feel." I gestured to my chef's clothes. "If you're not comfortable in the dress, put an apron over it or wear your jeans and sweatshirt instead."

"Then I'll look unprofessional," she countered.

"I don't know what to tell you. It's a long way to the mall, and we don't have any spare clothes," I said. I'd tried empathy, but maybe laying out the bald facts and appealing to reason was the way to go. "I've barely set foot in the kitchen. We're way behind. Sonya will implode if I don't get back in there to help, and the guests will be arriving any minute."

"I know. But this"—she waved her hands over her bosom—"isn't me."

My blood pressure crept toward the red zone. I adored Melody—it was impossible not to. At her best, she was eager to please, buoyantly energetic, and a natural peacemaker. However, she hated to be the center of attention, hated to be caught unprepared, and she'd been known to dig in her heels when it came to things she considered matters of principle. It didn't take Sonya's gift for interpersonal intuition to see how the "slutty disco ball" dress dilemma could trigger a Melody Meltdown. Managing a situation like this required time, patience, and finesse, three things I did not possess.

"Everyone will be looking at my *everything*." She cast her eyes downward and contemplated her "everything" with a dismayed frown.

I heard footsteps in the hallway coming from the direction of the kitchen, and flung the door open, praying that it would be Sonya. She would know how to fix this. Instead, I found Daniel Castillo, Delilah & Son's bartender, cradling an armload of ripe honeydews. He sported a gray suit with thick white pinstripes, the impeccable tailoring of which set off his toned physique. His usual spiky faux-hawk hairdo was slicked back, framing his chiseled jawline, bronze complexion, and ebony eyes.

"*Jefa,* I realized I'd forgotten . . ." His gaze drifted past me to where a wide-eyed Melody was leaning backward against the sink, clutching its edge like she might float off the floor if she let go. "Melons," Daniel sputtered. Then, blinking, he cleared his throat and clarified, "I need to puree the honeydew for the melon Bellinis."

Melody had been enamored of Daniel since the moment she'd laid eyes on him, and tended to follow him around like a smitten puppy. This was the first time, though, I'd seen him regard her with anything other than brotherly affection.

Noting her distress, his voice softened. "What's the matter, *mija*?"

"Nothing, I . . . I just . . . I just . . ." she said.

"You're not trying to steal my tips, are you? Looking even more beautiful than me?" Daniel had regained his composure, and the usual mischievous sparkle returned to his eye.

Another set of footsteps echoed in the hallway, and Pam Philips appeared in the doorway.

"Getting the party started early?" she asked. Pam was attired in a standard-issue flapper outfit, a knee-length purple fringed dress and a feather boa so gigantic it could've passed for a feather anaconda. A beaded headband fought a losing battle to contain the nest of frizzy salt-and-pepper hair atop her head.

"We're dealing with a little wardrobe malfunction," I explained. "R-rated dress on a PG gal."

Melody looked from me to Daniel to Pam with wide eyes, as if she might die on the spot from sheer mortification.

Pam took note of Melody's chagrin and removed her boa. She reached into a drawer of the vanity behind Melody and extracted a pair of cuticle scissors. "May I?" she asked, holding them aloft. Melody nodded, seeming unsure what she was agreeing to.

Pam used the scissors to snip her boa in half. She put one segment back around her own throat, and wrapped the other around Melody, taking a moment to strategically arrange the feathers. "There, now, all the crucial bits of lady meat are covered."

Melody looked down at her concealing plumage and broke into a relieved smile.

"You good?" I asked.

She nodded.

"Honestly," Pam said, "I didn't expect people to get so into the costume thing. I ordered my dress on Amazon and got this"—she twirled the ends of the enormous boa—"at Goodwill."

That seemed pretty on-brand, from what I knew of Pam Philips. While her fishnet stockings and low-cut bodice might not be age-appropriate, from what I'd been able to observe of her at library board dinners, I'd come to believe she was one of the rare women who truly couldn't have cared less what others thought of her. She wouldn't hesitate to spend a princely fortune on a yacht if she wanted one, but she didn't splash cash needlessly on things she didn't care about.

Pam started her company, Invisible Inc., when she was still a graduate student at UW-Madison. Some naysayers scoffed at her obsession with a dedicated device for e-reading—why purchase another screen when a computer, tablet, or smartphone could do the same job? And why purchase an e-reader at all when tried-and-true ink-and-paper books had shown their staying power over the centuries? As she expanded her technology business and went looking for investors, bankers shunned her. She was plump and dark-skinned, with a determined chin and a loud, easy laugh. She grew up in Sherman Park, a working-class Black neighborhood in Milwaukee, and made her way through school on scholarships and part-time jobs. Not exactly the type to win over the Wharton-educated suits who controlled the money spigots. But she succeeded despite them all, or maybe because of them.

Pam patted Melody's cheek. "You've gotta be you, right? Being you is the most comfortable outfit you can wear." She adjusted her own "lady meat" using the back-sides of her hands and took hold of one of the melons Daniel was carrying. "Now, let's party."

CHAPTER 6

I must've done something good in a past life, because by some divine grace, the first round of apps went out right on time. Daniel seemed to be keeping the cocktail hour lubricated, while Jarka's "demands" ensured that the servers were in the right places at the right times. Melody fluttered back and forth, her usual good cheer restored, leaving a trail of purple feathers in her wake. In the kitchen, Rabbit, Sonya, and I made a frantic team effort, working at a sprint pace, a blur of suspenders, sauces, and flying fringe.

I barely registered the clamor as I rushed to put the finishing touches on the free-from pizza. I tasted the dairy-free Parm. Nutty and savory, it zinged across my tongue. Satisfied that it was the closest you could get to real cheese without squeezing an udder, I sprinkled it over the top of the nightshade-free "no-mato" sauce I'd whipped up from Auntie Biz's roast beets.

"Well, it looks the part," I muttered to myself, placing my concoction into the oven. "In about thirty minutes, we'll know if it tastes like a pizza."

Just then, Pam entered the kitchen. "The appetizers are delicious," she said. "I've heard nothing but praise. Everything is going great. Well, except for Gloria."

"Who's Gloria?" Sonya asked, spooning softened butter into the metal stand mixer bowl.

"My cat. Apparently, she's taking swipes at anyone who tries to go upstairs," Pam explained, her forehead creasing in concern. "She didn't come in here, did she?"

I shook my head. "Haven't seen her."

"She's never done anything remotely like this before," Pam said, "but a number of people mentioned a cat lying in wait in one of the alcoves on the stairs trying to take a chunk out of them. I guess you never know with pets. This is the first time this many people have been in the house at once. Maybe she's feeling territorial, poor baby. I'd lock her in my bedroom, but I can't find her," Pam said. "That's one downside of this house. You could spend all day walking up and down stairs and in and out of rooms and never find the person, or in this case, cat, you're looking for. It's like a real-life game of Clue."

"Speaking of which, did Edgar Clemmons find you?" I asked. "I ran into him earlier in the back hallway."

She shook her head.

"Really?" I said. Even in a house of this size, I was surprised they hadn't crossed paths, given the seeming urgency of Clemmons's mysterious mission. "He said he was meeting you in 'the appointed place.'"

"Yeah, the library. That's where he said to meet him." She plucked a loose feather from her boa. "I went, but I didn't see him."

"Any idea what he wanted? It seemed important," I said.

"He called this morning to say he *had* to talk to me," she explained. "I tried to get him to tell me whatever it was over the phone, but he said he'd have to show me in person. Then he told me he was coming early. I said it wasn't convenient, but he insisted. What kind of person tries to buttonhole the hostess right before a big party? Isabel and I were running around, and I had to get dressed, so I was running late. I guess I missed him." She shrugged. "Did he tell you what it was about?"

"No. He swore me to secrecy, but I'm not sure why, because all he did was spew out a bunch of meaningless innuendo," I explained.

Pam rolled her eyes. "Edgar can be such a drama queen." She turned to Sonya. "I'm sorry, I know he's your friend, but he's working my last nerve. I'll be so relieved when the torch is officially passed tonight and he's off the board."

Sonya frowned, dropping a handful of chopped parsley into the bowl along with the butter. "That does sound melodramatic, even for Edgar."

"Come to think of it," I said to her. "The only specific thing he mentioned was that *you* had helped him connect the dots to figure out whatever mysterious thing he thought he'd discovered in this house."

Sonya did a double take. "*Me?* I don't remember connecting any dots."

"Something to do with old movies?"

She shook her head. "No clue."

I shrugged. "That's what he said."

"Well, whatever it's all about, it'll have to wait," Pam said. "I'm here because Zaria Singhal asked to meet you. She wants to thank you for accommodating her request for the free-from pizza."

"Who's Zaria Singhal?" I asked.

"A collector and dealer of rare books and antiquities from Chicago," Pam explained. "She's got connections to every wealthy book lover in Geneva Bay and is quite wealthy in her own right, so Isabel wants to keep her happy."

I wanted to protest that we were in the middle of service, that I didn't even know if the magical wonder-pizza was going to turn out okay. Instead, I sighed. Easier to get it over with than spend time fighting what would no doubt be a losing battle with Isabel or her proxies. I dutifully tramped out to the drawing room.

Outside the windows, the sky had blackened, and the promised storm had finally kicked off in the form of an icy-cold rain. Inside, though, the atmosphere glowed, warm and inviting. The room brimmed with flapper-era opulence and gaiety. Behind the bar, an elegant wrought-iron staircase curved up to the second floor. At the other end of the room stood a baby grand piano and a microphone, ready, presumably, for Lola Capone's performance.

What if Capone's mom hates your food? What if the food all comes out late because you're not in the kitchen to oversee things and she thinks you're a train wreck? Why do you even care what Lola Capone thinks of you? You still have a thing for him, don't you? Thanks, brain. That's all I needed. A brand-new set of things to stress out about.

"Now where did Zaria go?" Pam asked aloud, scanning the room.

We worked our way toward the bar, where we found Isabel Berney, draped in an ill-fitting, floor-length black coat that swamped her petite frame. She'd replaced her usual half-moon readers with small, round wire-frame glasses, which perched on the end of her button nose. A black lace veil framed her intelligent face like a wimple, and a papier-mâché-and-foil replica of an axe was tucked into a leather belt at her waist.

Noting my quizzical expression, she asked, "Do you like it?" She straightened up to her full height—all four feet, nine inches of it—lifted her axe, and intoned, "'God commands me to rid this nation of the demon drink!'"

I frowned and shook my head, still in the dark. "That old priest from *The Exorcist*?"

"I told her it was too obscure," Pam said to me. "But you know Isabel. She insisted."

"I certainly did," Isabel agreed.

"You're going to have to spend all night explaining who you are, so you might as well practice on Delilah," Pam said to Isabel.

Isabel smiled obligingly. "Happy to." She turned to me. "I'm Carrie Nation, the temperance activist. Without Nation and the Woman's Christian Temperance Union there would have been no Eighteenth Amendment, and therefore no Prohibition," she explained. "Of course, if I wanted to be really authentic, I'd use my hatchet to smash up this bar and threaten this destroyer of men's souls." She waggled her papier-mâché axe cheerfully toward Daniel and his wares.

Behind the bar, Daniel had shed his jacket and rolled up his sleeves. His workspace looked like a cross between a chemistry lab and an herbalist's shop, with a wide assortment of syrups, specialty liqueurs, and garnishes that were particular to his signature cocktails.

"Well, lucky for Daniel, Carrie's cause failed in the end," Pam said.

"I'll drink to that," Isabel replied. She re-holstered her axe and slammed her hand on the bar. "What's on the menu, barkeep?"

"Two Prohibition-era specials tonight," Daniel replied. "The South Side Fizz and"—he poured jiggers of gin and sweet vermouth into a cocktail shaker along with a dash of bitters; then he gave the concoction a seductive jiggle, showing off his muscular forearms—"the Hanky

Panky." He strained the contents into three ice-filled glasses and garnished the drinks with twists of orange.

Pam reached out for one of the proffered glasses and Daniel threw a wink her way. I swear the man could seduce a floor lamp.

"You're not trying to line me up as a sugar mama, are you?" Pam asked, letting out her signature high-decibel laugh.

Daniel leaned against the bar and made a clicking noise inside of his cheek as he pointed a finger gun at her. "Maybe you can support me in the style I'd like to become accustomed to?"

"Oh, I've had my fill of fortune hunters over the years," she said.

Daniel put his hands over his heart. "You wound me. But I'm a patient man. I can make you as many cocktails as it takes to change your mind."

He handed the other Hanky Panky cocktails around, and we clinked our glasses. I wanted to down the drink like a tequila shot and rush back to the kitchen, where Sonya was no doubt drowning in appetizers and cursing my name. Instead, I forced myself to inhale the herbal fragrance of the claret liquid and take a slow sip. If I'd learned one thing in my two decades in the hospitality business, it was that no matter what was going on in the kitchen, the front of house should betray no hint of chaos.

I allowed the intense cascade of flavors to hit my tongue—spicy, sweet, and bitter, with the faintest note of citrus from the fruit peel.

Daniel smiled, watching me take in the flavor profile. "Bold, no? Many Prohibition cocktails use gin because it could be made in people's houses," he explained. "They called it bathtub gin for a reason. A lot of the popular drinks from that time had strong flavorings to hide harshness in case the bathtub turned out a bad batch."

"Clearly you've done your research," Isabel said. "Warms my librarian's heart."

Pam downed her drink. "Any idea what became of Zaria?"

"She was right here," Isabel said, standing on her tip-toes to peer into the crowd.

"I'll see if I can find her," Pam said, disappearing into the scrum of partygoers.

My eyes stopped dead on a pair of faces moving straight toward the bar—Kennedy Criss and B.L. Huddleston, the couple who'd purchased my aunt's cottage. *Ugh.* I'd almost forgotten that Kennedy had recently joined the Friends of the Library board. When our gazes met, the smile on Kennedy's heavily made-up face became as immobilized as her stiffly coiffed blond bob. Her husband's dark mustache twitched, as if his nose had picked up an unpleasant odor. Unfortunately, we were too close to pretend we hadn't seen each other.

"Delilah," Kennedy crooned. "What are you doing here?" Her eyes trailed down to my chef's coat. "I guess you've been hired to work?" She spoke with the chipper, sunny-day cadence that had spewed forth from TV screens in the greater Milwaukee area for the better part of a decade, but her tone conveyed the sheer impossibility that I could be there as an invited guest.

Isabel, too, seemed to register the slight. "Yes, Delilah orchestrated tonight's phenomenal menu. Aren't the appetizers incredible?" she said. She gestured toward the window. "What do you make of this weather, anyway? Does it make you want to get back in front of a green screen?" Her tone did an impressive tightrope walk between being a gracious hostess and putting the woman in her place.

"I don't do forecasts anymore," Kennedy said, flashing a saccharine smile. "Brian didn't like me working." She turned back to me. "How's your aunt?"

"Same as ever," I replied acidly.

It wasn't their fault, I reminded myself. *They were in a position to benefit from Biz's misfortune. That's all.* Still, they'd made it clear that they always considered my aunt's slightly ramshackle property an eyesore, and they'd tried many times to pressure her into selling. Kennedy was barely able to contain her glee when the tax sale finally allowed her to take control of it.

In my prior interactions with the couple, B.L. Huddleston had always seemed the nicer of the pair, although, in my opinion, his ingratiating air veered into smarminess. He possessed a distinguished virility reminiscent of commercials for erectile dysfunction medications and luxury SUVs. "Give her our regards," he said, displaying his large, white teeth. An impressive swoop of black hair, delicately feathered with salt-and-pepper, crowned his ruggedly handsome face. "I hope she understands about the sale."

I pressed my lips together.

"Well, we'll finally have space to expand. Our new pool is going to look great in the spot where her garden was," Kennedy added. "Plenty of sunlight."

Okay, that was it. There was no way Kennedy didn't know how much Biz's garden had meant to her. After months spent trying to talk my aunt out of holding a grudge, I was ready to go full O'Leary on this chick.

CHAPTER 7

Kennedy had pushed me over the edge with her cheap shot about my aunt's prized garden. Before I could let fly the string of highly descriptive profanity I was concocting, Isabel shouted, "Zaria! There you are!" and dragged me toward an especially glamorous knot of party guests. "Good thing my axe is a fake," she mumbled, looking back toward Kennedy and B.L.

A striking woman disentangled herself from the group and stepped toward us. "So pleased to meet you. I'm Zaria Singhal." She was tall and impossibly thin, with an aquiline nose and a complexion that glowed like polished gold. Her dress was similarly gilded, fashioned out of metallic lamé fabric. An emerald-colored turban perched atop her head, adorned with a peacock feather. Around her neck, a gumball-sized rock of jade dangled from a thick chain, setting off clavicle bones so sharp they looked like they should be registered as dangerous weapons.

Before Isabel and I could return Zaria's greeting, Kennedy Criss stepped in front of us.

"Are you enjoying yourself?" Kennedy crossed her arms over her chest as she addressed the other woman.

Zaria's smile tightened and she threw her hands up.

"Always!" Given her shiny dress and slender frame, the gesture caused her to bear a remarkable resemblance to a candelabra. "Can I do something for you, Kennedy?"

"You can stop selling behind my back. You know I was going to buy those books for Brian's birthday," Kennedy continued.

Zaria tilted her chin down, but her black eyes remained defiant, almost mischievous. "Darling, you know I'd love to do you a favor, but I run a business, not a charity. If someone is consistently willing to pay more for my wares than you are, then I *have* to sell to them. Standard practice. All very aboveboard." Her creamy tone had a thick syrup of condescension drizzled into it.

"Kennedy, maybe you could take this up another time . . ." Isabel began.

Kennedy wheeled around to face the smaller woman. "Butt out, Berney. You and your little library are even deeper in Pam Philips's pocket than *she* is." She thrust a thumb toward Zaria.

"It's *our* little library now, though, right?" Isabel answered. "You're on the board, part of the leadership team. I'm sure we'll have a productive exchange, considering your views on public libraries. Edgar's already told us about some of the . . . *fresh* ideas you'll be bringing. Why don't we get a drink at the bar and you can tell me more about your plans?" She put her hand on Kennedy's back and guided her away. Looking back over her shoulder, she mouthed, "You're welcome."

"Wow," I said, turning to Zaria. "That was a *lot*."

Zaria rolled her eyes. "Kennedy wanted a couple of first editions as a gift for her husband. But there were multiple interested buyers and the volumes went to auction. Her maximum bid was less than another bidder's, so she lost. She apparently thinks we're all in some kind of conspiracy against her."

"What did she mean about everyone being in Pam Philips's pocket?" I asked.

"Guess who the winning bidder was?" Zaria looked at me expectantly but didn't wait for an answer before continuing. "Kennedy has tried a number of times to buy rare books for her husband. Almost every time she does, Pam outbids her or buys the volume before Kennedy can get to it. I know it's hard to believe, but B.L. Huddleston is a real bibliophile."

"That *is* a surprise. I guess you can't judge a book by its cover," I said.

She laughed. "First thing you learn in my business. Anyway, I think it's become a bit of a game for Pam, but Kennedy doesn't see it that way, as you witnessed for yourself."

I let the irony of Kennedy's stance sink in. She and B.L. bought my aunt's property at auction, a sale I'm sure she'd consider fair. But when the shoe was on the other foot, she didn't seem too happy about it. Still, if it was true that Pam only bought the books Kennedy wanted out of spite, I couldn't help feeling the whole thing was a little petty. After all, Pam was a powerful businesswoman, well educated, and wealthy in her own right. Kennedy, on the other hand, was a weather-girl-cum-trophy-wife trying to please her husband with a thoughtful present.

"I guess you make out well from their feud, if it drives up sales prices," I noted.

"My income is mostly from commissions, so I'm not complaining," Zaria said, with a laugh. "But I didn't ask you out here to talk shop. I wanted to thank you for accommodating my request for the special pizza. I'm sorry it was so last-minute. My fiancé and I were supposed to go back to the city tonight, but the weather forecast changed our plans. I'm glad, though. I adore the library. Books have always been an obsession of mine. We didn't have a lot of money growing up, and in the summer, I would go to the public library every day."

"My sister and I did that, too," I replied.

"What do you like to read?" she asked.

I cringed. "Actually, we hung out there for the air conditioning," I said. "I'm obsessed with cookbooks, but other than that, I'm not much of a reader."

"Well, I'm the lucky beneficiary of your cookbook obsession, I suppose. I know the particular combination of intolerances and allergies I have can be a challenge, but I have to be extremely strict about my diet." She looked over my shoulder, waggling her fingers toward someone behind me. "While I have you, I want you to meet my fiancé."

I turned to find myself face to face with the man who'd been talking to Jarka before the party, Count Victor von Creepazoid Whatshisname Jingleheimer Schmidt. *Fiancé, eh?* I wondered what Zaria would make of the scene that transpired between him and Jarka. He glowered at me, looking none too pleased to have to speak to me again. Strangely, the radiating sphere of his animosity appeared to encompass Zaria, who stiffened as he took his place alongside her.

He leaned his head toward her ear. "I must speak with you. *Now.*"

She kept smiling, but under the painful weight of his gaze, her expression sank. "Victor, I was just telling Ms. O'Leary how grateful I am about the pizza."

He and I both opened our mouths—to say what, I don't know—when the tinkling notes of a piano sounded, casting a hush over the room, and blessedly derailing our conversation. I recognized the opening notes of "Mack the Knife." The crowd gradually shifted, forming a half ring around the piano, and I gained a clear view of Lola Capone.

I'd seen her perform years earlier at the Green Mill, an iconic jazz club in Chicago. At least a decade had passed since then, but she didn't seem to have aged a day. Cocoa skin, a black pixie cut, and round, expressive features. A trim figure and hands that seemed to cast a spell, amplifying the emotion of her words. And that voice. It vibrated on a special frequency that could be heard deep inside the soul.

Although I needed to get back to the kitchen, I watched for a moment, mesmerized. Like many working-class workaholics, I'm essentially an uncultured philistine. I went to culinary school instead of college, and the last time I'd been to a museum was on a high school field trip. I spent fourteen hours a day cooking for work, and to relax, I cooked. While I was as ignorant about musical styles as I was about most other types of fine art, I still had the capacity to be transported by a beautiful song. And Lola Capone's voice was a magic carpet.

Not more than ten bars in, though, I had the neck-tickling feeling of eyes resting on me. I turned to find Edgar Clemmons standing next to me, seeming to have materialized from thin air.

"I must beg a favor." He spoke in a low voice right into my ear. His hot breath on my neck gave me a cold shiver.

"I've got to get back to the kitchen . . ." I began.

He pressed an object against my arm. "It's urgent." I looked down and saw two small books, which Clemmons kept partially concealed in a fold of his jacket. "Please give these to Sonya, along with this message, and I ask that you convey it as precisely as possible." He tapped the cover of the first book, which, judging by the cover, looked like a thriller. "Here's a title that I know all too well." He ran his finger along the cover of the second book. "And the plot of *The Maltese Falcon* is more realistic than you might imagine. These books are a small part of a much larger collection." He hastily pressed both books into my hands.

"You could give them to her yourself," I pointed out. "She's in the kitchen."

"I have a rendezvous. This room is awash with guilt, and it's time I called the guilty parties to account. I hope I'm mistaken, but I feel I must take precautions. When we did our walk-through of the venue last week, I noticed that something was amiss, but the implications were slow to dawn on me. Now I believe I have proof, and it's in your hands." He scanned the room again and I noticed that he had a reddish welt rising on his left cheek.

"What happened to your face?" I asked.

He didn't answer. I followed his gaze, which was firmly planted on Lola Capone. Isabel, Pam, B.L., Kennedy, and all the other guests seemed transfixed by the performance as well, but Clemmons's eyes regarded her differently. Instead of widening in wonder, his eyelids narrowed. "Please remember the message for Sonya. Exactly those words. I hope I'm wrong, but if I'm not, it may become important."

I tucked the books into one of the large pockets on the front of my apron and turned toward the kitchen. "Right-o. Speaking of Sonya, I'd best be getting back," I said.

Before I could even take a step, Clemmons took hold

of my arm. "Lola Capone has a rare talent—one I hope she won't squander."

I shook my arm free. "Meaning?" Even as I asked the question, I cursed myself for once again falling victim to Clemmons's verbal snares. I resolved that I'd mothball my curiosity, no matter how enigmatic his reply was.

His lips curved into a bitter smile. "Ms. Capone really must start making better choices in her associates if she knows what's good for her. You know she had a child with Al Capone's grandson, don't you? You'd think she would've learned her lesson. Ironic that her son would become a police officer, given that notorious bloodline and his mother's questionable character." He paused. "He's an excellent pianist, though, I'll grant him that."

As I watched Clemmons walk away, his words zapped me like an electric shock. Captivated as I was by Lola Capone's singing, I hadn't bothered to look at the pianist, only vaguely registering a tuxedo and moving hands behind the instrument's open lid. But from this angle, there was no mistaking the chiseled contours, amber eyes, and honey-toast complexion of Calvin Capone's face. The *whoosh-whoosh* of my heartbeat drowned out all other noise, and my internal thermostat spiked.

Capone looked up at that moment and our eyes locked. His lips flashed a hint of a smile, but his gaze felt like it was x-raying my soul.

I had no idea he could play the piano. Damn him, he could probably perform open heart surgery while catching the winning pass at the Super Bowl. No doubt Capone occasionally got something stuck in his teeth or forgot his coworker's name. But I couldn't imagine it.

A few months previously, I'd literally thrown myself into his arms. We'd shared a moment; I was sure of it. And then months passed, and nothing. Not a call, not a text. I supposed he'd decided he could do better than a type-A chef whose main talents were knife skills and being able to identify dozens of obscure varieties of cheese by smell alone. His loss, if he couldn't see that I was also loyal, passionate, and fun. Capone had had his chance, and he missed it. I'd moved on. Well, maybe not *on* on, but I had my restaurant, my friends, Butterball, and, well, maybe not *a ton* else, but I had enough self-respect to keep myself from being a Waity Katie—for Capone or any other man.

Lola Capone crooned the next lyric from "Mack the Knife," and Capone's eyes flew back to the piano. As I turned to leave, I became aware of low, angry voices speaking nearby.

Zaria and the Count, who'd been standing close to me, were arguing in hushed tones. He noticed me watching them, and took Zaria brusquely by the arm, leading her past me to the very back of the room. She shot me a look as they passed, a mixture of embarrassment and wretchedness I recognized from the faces of maltreated women I'd known over the years. The two of them moved farther from the crowd, and ducked behind a black lacquer Japanese folding screen in the adjacent hallway.

I followed them, cracking my knuckles. If Victor was going to get aggressive with Zaria, he was going to learn the same lesson Marco Jablonsky did our junior year of high school when I saw him smack Sharon Probst in the Dairy Queen parking lot.

I edged closer, wondering if I should intervene now or wait to see how this played out. After all, I still wasn't sure if what Rabbit and I witnessed between the Count and Jarka had been violence. I was acutely aware that I needed to get back into the kitchen ASAP, but I decided that, in this case, sticking around to eavesdrop wasn't nosiness so much as a moral imperative. Sonya would forgive me for abandoning her in the middle of service once I filled her in on why.

I could see the tops of their heads clearly above the folding screen—Victor's sleek, dark hair and high forehead, Zaria's jewel-green turban, with its single delicately fluttering feather. I leaned against the corner of the wall, where I could watch them in my peripheral vision. If they came out abruptly, I was only a few short steps from disappearing into the crowd or hustling down the hallway to the kitchen. If I heard anything violent, I was only a few short steps from kicking Victor's royal ass.

"She's here, isn't she?" Zaria asked.

"You're behaving like a ridiculous child, as if I engineered this situation somehow," Victor replied testily.

"Didn't you?" she asked. "How else do you explain the coincidence?"

"Geneva Bay is a small town," he growled.

The feather on her turban dipped, as if acknowledging the truth of his words. Then, he switched into a language I vaguely recognized—Bulgarian, I thought, based on the times I'd heard Jarka speak her native tongue—and continued his diatribe. She responded with a tremulous mm-hmm and then fell silent as he carried on. His tone gradually softened, and I heard Zaria sniffling. I stole a glance and saw that they'd moved into an embrace, and heard him murmuring gently.

The smoochy sounds of their reconciliation were drowned out by the sound of thunderous applause as Lola Capone belted the final notes of "Mack the Knife."

"Lola Capone, everyone!" Isabel Berney called out as she lowered the microphone stand. She gestured to the singer, who made a graceful bow as she melted into the crowd. Capone remained seated at the piano, his hands folded neatly in his lap. "Lola's going to take a very brief break while I say a few quick thank-yous. First off, I want to thank you all for being here. Public libraries are of the people, by the people, and for the people, and only with your continued commitment can Geneva Bay's treasured institution flourish. Please continue to give generously."

I turned to leave as Isabel began to reel off the obligatory expressions of gratitude. Clearly, Zaria and the Count had made their peace and she wasn't in need of my protection. I reckoned they were one of those couples with a toxic dynamic, and nothing I or anybody else could do would change that.

"I'd also like to thank incoming chair Pamela Philips for hosting this magnificent party," Isabel continued. "Pam? I know she's here somewhere. She must've stepped out, but thank her when you see her. And of course we owe an enormous debt of gratitude to Edgar Clemmons for his many years of faithful service as board chair." She searched the room once again. "Edgar?" She gasped and then screamed. "Edgar!"

In an instant, her intonation changed from humdrum to horrified, and even before I turned around, I knew something had happened. Something terrible.

CHAPTER 8

Isabel Berney's shriek rose in volume, like the siren of an approaching ambulance. The next sounds were a series of thuds. Isabel put one hand over her mouth and swept the other toward the staircase that curved up the back wall of the drawing room. My eyes, along with those of the assembled guests, turned. I glimpsed a blur of motion, a figure tumbling. A nauseating crack could be heard as Isabel's scream trailed off and the body hit the floor. The whole thing was over in a matter of seconds.

Since I'd already separated myself from the crowd to spy on Zaria and Victor, I was the first to the base of the staircase, where the broken body of Edgar Clemmons lay in a ruined heap. His hips jutted unnaturally sideways, and his bloodied head lay at an almost ninety-degree angle to his neck. The limbs were a jumble; he looked like a marionette whose strings had been abruptly cut. Those probing eyes, so unsettling in life, were even more so in death. While he was alive, I felt they could look through me. Now, he could see through everyone and everything, to whatever lay beyond.

Daniel arrived next. He'd spent several years as an Army reservist, and with his military-honed reactions, he was around the bar and on the floor next to me almost instantly. He went through the motions of checking for signs of life. "His neck is broken. These injuries . . ." He shook his head.

I murmured an Our Father. Even though I lacked medical training, I had no doubt Clemmons was beyond hope.

Now that the initial shock was over, I gradually became aware of sights and sounds. Gasps and murmurs arose from the small knot of people who edged closer. An attractive older woman who'd been standing nearby caught sight of Clemmons's body and turned to retch delicately into a large potted palm.

I felt a hand on the small of my back and the familiar, warm scent of vanilla and sandalwood washed over me. "Did you touch him? Did you move anything?" Capone's silky baritone asked. I turned my face toward his. Despite the horror in front of us, a surge of attraction cascaded through my body. Capone looked impossibly handsome in his tuxedo, and I had to physically resist the invisible magnets that tried to pull me into his embrace.

"No, and Daniel said CPR isn't going to help . . ." I trailed off.

"I'll call it in," Capone said. "You and Daniel, keep people away from him."

He stepped aside and spoke quietly into his cell phone. By now, more people had worked their way to the front. I registered their faces as if I were looking at them through a kaleidoscope, fragmented images displayed before me in hypercolor. First, Jarka appeared out of the scrum. She had practiced as a physician in Bulgaria before moving to America, and she instinctively crouched alongside Daniel, assessing Clemmons with her experienced eye. She looked from Daniel to me in a wordless acknowledgment that her patient was past help and gently eased his eyes closed.

Pam emerged from the crowd in mute shock, still clutching her cocktail glass. Melody came next, wide-eyed. When she saw Clemmons, her small body began shaking head to toe. Daniel, seeing her distress, rose and led her gently toward the bar, where he draped his jacket around her shoulders. Zaria and Victor rushed over next. Zaria caught sight of Clemmons's body and stopped in her tracks. She buried her face against her fiancé's chest, her face flushed, her shoulders heaving. Victor held her to him, their earlier discord forgotten. Even the pathologically talkative Kennedy Criss seemed at a loss for words, standing alone, her mouth hanging open as if her jawbone had dissolved into gelatin.

"What should we do?" Isabel asked aloud, eyeing the expectant crowd. She pressed her knuckles to her mouth. "Oh, this is terrible." For the first time since I'd known her, she didn't have an action plan.

Finally, I snapped to my senses. "We should keep everyone away," I said, at last heeding Capone's instructions. Probably less than a minute had passed since Clemmons fell, but it felt like I'd traveled to the moon and back. "Please, everyone. Let's give the man some dignity." I held out my arms to push back the massing crowd.

Pam and Isabel fell in alongside me, and the three of us formed a sort of human wall.

"The party's over. That's for sure," I heard Pam mumble flatly, to no one in particular.

Capone rejoined us and addressed the crowd. "I'm Detective Capone of the Geneva Bay Police. EMS is on the way, but given our location and the storm, it'll be a while before they arrive. If you witnessed anything that might help us understand what happened, please stay behind so I can take your statement. The rest of you are free to leave, although we might get in touch with some follow-up questions. Please be careful on your way home. The roads may be slick."

Most of the crowd took the hint and shuffled away, but about a dozen people remained frozen in place by either shock, morbid fascination, or both. By now, Lola Capone had appeared.

B.L. Huddleston, too, joined his wife near the front of the remaining onlookers. Both Kennedy and B.L.'s clothes were damp, speckled with raindrops, and I wondered briefly why they'd gone outside in the howling gale.

"So that's all you're going to do?" Kennedy said. She looked around as if to say, *Can you believe this guy?*

"What else did you have in mind?" Capone asked mildly.

"Question the witnesses. Secure the scene," she said.

"Oh, for heaven's sake, Kennedy," Isabel snapped. "It's an invitation-only party. Everyone knows everyone. Must you always make it sound like there's something nefarious going on?"

"What about the hired help? They're probably not on any list," Zaria said, her eyes stopping on Jarka. "And they seem to have been on the scene before anyone else."

"What are you implying?" the Count said irritably. "This isn't an Agatha Christie novel. An old man fell down the stairs. These things happen."

"That's right. It was clearly an accident," Pam agreed, her voice taking on a higher pitch than usual. "We all saw him fall."

Even the preternaturally calm Calvin Capone seemed to be reaching his limit with the comments from the peanut gallery. "Unless one of you has something useful to add, please clear the room." He turned to Pam. "Do you have anything we can use to shield the body from view?"

"There's a folding screen," I interjected, pointing to the place were Zaria and Victor had secreted themselves earlier. "And we can cover him with one of the extra tablecloths."

Capone nodded to me and I rushed to put my plan into action. I grabbed a clean, white tablecloth from our spare stash behind the bar and tucked it under my arm. The screen, though, wasn't planning to come along so easily. It was far heavier than it looked. Even with my adrenaline still surging, I nearly knocked over a tall coatrack that stood in the hallway as I wrestled with it. Noticing my struggle, Pam hurried over to help me.

As she lifted her end, she dropped her voice to a panicky whisper. "You don't think Edgar could've tripped over Gloria, do you? With his mobility problems, he might've lost his balance if she took a swipe at him."

The thought hadn't occurred to me, but as a fellow cat owner, I understood the worry in Pam's eyes. How to conceive that your beloved fur-baby could cause a man's death? Could the police arrest you for that kind of thing, the way they might if you'd let a dangerous dog loose? No wonder she seemed anxious to write off the death as an accident.

As Pam and I arranged the screen in front of Edgar's body, I tried to imbue my voice with maximum conviction. "I'm sure he just tripped. He wasn't steady on his feet."

Capone herded the others from the room. Pam and I, meanwhile, spread the tablecloth over Clemmons's body and maneuvered the screen into place, trying not to let our eyes wander toward the floor. Instead, I looked outside, where sleet had replaced the driving rain. Illuminated by the exterior lights, fat, angry drops plummeted through the black night. The room, which only minutes before had been abuzz with the sounds of celebration, was silent, as if an entire party's worth of people had been raptured into the sky. Half-drunk cocktails and half-eaten canapés littered the tables, and even the floor.

What would we do with all the uneaten food? Did poor Sonya, toiling away in the kitchen, even know what happened? Probably best that she didn't. Sonya and I had been at culinary school together, and she'd faked a bout of mono to avoid the butchery component of our course. The sight of blood—hers or anyone else's—could make her swoon like a Victorian gentlewoman. When it came to meat, she'd mostly overcome her tendency to pass out through repeated exposure, but if she didn't brace herself, the sight of someone cutting into an overly rare steak could still make her turn the color of pistachio ice cream.

Suddenly, the lid of the piano slammed down with a dissonant clang, and Lola Capone let out a cry, lower in volume than the one Isabel emitted when Clemmons fell, but no less alarming. Pam, Capone, and I hurried over to the spot where she stood, pressing her hands to her chest.

"Mom, are you okay?" Capone rushed to her side, concern flooding his handsome face.

She held out her hand for his. "Just got a fright, honey."

Capone put his arm around her and pressed his lips to the top of her head. "I know. That was terrible to see."

"Not that," she said, glancing toward the stairs. "Well, *yes*, that. But I'm talking about the piano. I was going to close the lid and put the cover on, but I saw . . ." She shook her head. "There's some sort of animal inside it." She pointed at the instrument with a shaky finger.

"Could a bird have flown in?" I glanced around the large room.

"No, no, it was furry," Capone's mother explained.

Pam and I exchanged glances. "Could it have been a cat?" she asked. "My Gloria has been known to climb into some strange places."

"I only caught a glimpse, but it looked too big to be a cat," Lola replied.

To emphasize the fact, we heard a series of angry thumps and the dull, tuneless sounds of piano wires being struck. Whatever was trapped in there wasn't happy about it.

"I had a raccoon in the basement a few months ago," Pam said. "With old houses, you never know."

Another thump emanated from the piano. "We can't leave it in there," Lola said. "It'll destroy the instrument."

Capone nodded grimly. "It's a Steinway B. Probably costs a hundred grand."

I picked up the piano cover from where Lola dropped it. "You open the lid," I said to Capone. "I'll catch it." I hoped the thick material of the cover would be enough to keep me from getting my face scratched off by whatever demon-possessed creature sprang out.

Capone nodded and we moved into position. He swept his arms backward to indicate that Pam and his mother should move behind him. "It's probably scared, so watch yourself," he cautioned. "On the count of three. One . . . two . . . three!"

The lid flew open and an almighty screech emanated from a ferocious mass of flailing fur. I launched myself at the creature, ensnaring it in the piano cover as Capone bolted over to help me complete the capture. We lowered the roiling mass of fur and fabric to the floor as the animal continued to struggle. When it finally grew still,

Capone and I sat face-to-face, breathing hard, with the piano cover and its contents between us. Pam and Lola inched closer.

"Did you see what it was?" Capone asked. "A fox, maybe?"

"I didn't get a good look," I said, swiping a strand of sweaty hair behind my ear. "But . . ." I shook my head. *It couldn't be.*

"What is it?" He peered into my face.

"It looked like . . ." I carefully scrunched the material of the piano cover until it formed a sort of loose sack around the wriggling animal. I lifted it off the floor, testing the heft of it, confirming my suspicions. Baffled, I shifted the familiar weight of the makeshift sack's contents from hand to hand.

"Be careful," Pam cautioned. "It could be rabid."

My throat constricted as I struggled to form coherent words. "The cat. Swiping people on the stairs. Clemmons. Oh my god. I think . . . Oh god." I pressed my eyes shut and swallowed. I was in serious danger of hyperventilating as I lowered the animal to the floor and gently unwrapped it.

Lola gasped. "What are you doing?"

My ragged breathing almost ceased altogether as the cloth fell away, revealing a tubby, strawberry-blond tabby.

Butterball confronted us, back arched, teeth bared.

"It's okay, B-man," I crooned, trying to keep from crying. "Were you scared?" *Sweet baby, did you accidentally kill somebody?* "You're okay now." *And I am very much not.*

As he heard my voice, the tension in the cat's spine gradually slackened and his face relaxed into its usual placid expression. He sidled over first to me, and then to Capone, nuzzling his face into our ankles, his ordeal in the piano already ancient history. Looking around at the assembly of horrified humans, he settled back on to his haunches and began to lick his paws, exuding an air of injured dignity.

After a moment, he turned his round-eyed gaze up to me. *Me-ow*, he declared. His nom-noms voice. He trotted over to a low bench, where a plate of appetizers had been abandoned. No one stopped him when he tucked into an Italian beef crostino, gulping down the meat before making a satisfied *Purr-up* trill of approval. From Butterball's point of view, he was fed and all was right with the world.

CHAPTER 9

Uneaten food was stacked on every available surface of Pam Philips's kitchen. We'd sent home as much as we could with the departing guests, but it barely made a dent. Isabel, who stayed behind to help in the aftermath, offered to take some pizzas to the hospital and fire station, the only places likely to be open late on a night like this. Jarka was boxing those up, while the rest of my team busied themselves packing and cleaning. Meanwhile, I slumped on a stool at the massive center island, Butterball cradled in my lap. I petted him robotically, as he munched with greedy abandon on a dish of anchovies I'd placed on the countertop for him.

Sonya and Daniel eyed me with concern. "Do you think she needs liquor or coffee?" Sonya asked him.

Daniel took my chin in his hand and tilted my head from side to side, taking stock of my dead-eyed expression. "Both," he said firmly. "Definitely both. You brew some coffee and I'll get what I need from the bar."

After he left, Jarka spoke. "Chef, again I apologize for accident how I pack Butterball into a box," she said. She regarded me and my cat with pity. "Now, because of my mistake, he has become a murderer."

"It wasn't murder," Melody said. "We don't know that Butterball killed Mr. Clemmons. And even if he did, it was a random accident, not murder."

"It wasn't your fault anyway," I said to Jarka. "Butterball loves hiding in boxes. And he weighs the same as a stand mixer. He probably went catatonic when you picked up the box from the porch, and even if he was meowing or something, you wouldn't have heard him over the sound of the wind. Once he got stowed in the ship's hold with all the other stuff stacked on top of him, there's no chance any of us would've realized. And it's no wonder he took off and found a place to hide once we got here. He hates storms."

We'd spent the time while we were waiting for the emergency responders to arrive trying to reconstruct the sequence of events that led Butterball to end up at Bluff Point, and managed to piece together the most likely scenario. When I racked my brain, I recalled a detail that seemed unimportant at the time: the box for my stand mixer had traveled across the lake, but when we wanted it, the mixer itself was nowhere in evidence. And indeed, when we looked closely at the box, it contained telltale claw marks and tufts of lemony-orange fur.

I shoved what remained of a Red Hot Mama pizza into my mouth. I'd stress-eaten half a pizza. Even in my misery, I had to admit that I'd outdone myself. Crisp, buttery crust, fiery tomato sauce, and the satisfying chew of spicy Italian sausage.

Sonya checked the wall clock. "Shouldn't the emergency responders have arrived? It's been over half an hour since Capone called." She looked toward the windows, but the night was so black the only view they offered was a reflected tableau of misery—the dregs of the aborted party, the pervasive horror of Clemmons's death, and the heavy weight of my guilt. "I don't like the idea of having a dead body two rooms over. Poor Edgar."

Melody hugged herself. "It's awful, 'n so?" she said, using the Wisconsinese contraction of "isn't it so?" "I need to pee," she continued, "but I'm afraid to even go into the hall in case I see it again. I've seen dead animals on the farm a bunch of times, but that was real different."

Sonya held her hands up to ward off further description. "Don't tell me any details."

Butterball shifted on my lap and I felt something solid dig into my thigh. "Oh, Son, I completely forgot that Clemmons gave me some books for you. Right before he died." I removed them from my apron pocket and handed them to her. "He had a message, too." I frowned. "I was supposed to give it to you in his exact words, but with everything that happened since then, I'm not sure I remember it." I closed my eyes for a moment and then opened them with a snap of my fingers. "Oh, wait, I've got it. First he said, 'Here's a book that I know all too well.'" I shook my head. "No, he said 'title.' 'Here's a *title* that I know all too well.' Then he said that 'the plot of *The Maltese Falcon* is more realistic than you'd think.'"

"Was that the whole thing?" she said, frowning in confusion.

"There was one more bit," I explained, doing my best to convey the message verbatim. "He said that these books are a small part of a larger collection. What's it mean?"

Sonya took the books and turned them over in her hands. "Huh. I'm not sure. He's lent me books before. We were talking about *The Maltese Falcon* recently, but I don't know why he gave this to me. He knows I have my own copy, and I've seen the movie a dozen times, too."

She regarded the other book and read the title aloud. "*The Man Who Knew Too Much* by G. K. Chesterton."

"That's a movie, too, right?" Rabbit said. "My mom likes to watch Turner Classics."

"Yeah, Hitchcock," Sonya said, paging through the volume. "He actually made two movies with that title. One in the 1930s and another in the fifties, with Jimmy Stewart and Doris Day. I've seen them both, but I've never read the book. The movie plots are different from each other, and from what I understand, neither one has anything in common with this book, other than they all have the same title." She turned back to me. "That's all he said? Just to give these to me? No note or anything?"

"It seemed important," I said. "He made it seem like you would know what he meant. And earlier he said that thing about you unlocking a mystery for him." I leaned on the counter. "No guesses?"

"Nope," she replied.

"Weird. The way he looked around, it seemed like he thought he was being watched. He said he had to take precautions," I said. "Any chance that he was right about that?"

She shrugged. "If he said it, it was probably true. He's an eccentric guy, but I don't think he'd make something like that up. But who knows?"

By now, Daniel had returned. He mixed the hot coffee that Sonya brewed with Kahlúa, brandy, sugar, and Grand Marnier, then expertly sliced a fine curl of peel from an orange. He lit the gas burner, singed the edge of the peel, and plunged it into a glass mug. "To bring out the oils," he explained. He topped the drink with whipped cream and handed it to me. "Sip slowly. I call this Port in a Storm."

I took a long swig of the coffee cocktail and hoped the boozy warmth would anesthetize my brain. It was divine, like a creamy, slightly bitter chocolate orange. If I hadn't been so miserable, I would've savored it. Instead, I drained it in four gulps, burped, and wiped the whipped cream from my lips with the back of my hand.

"So much for slow sips," Sonya said.

"What am I going to tell Sam?" I groaned. "He leaves Butterball in my custody for less than three months and this happens."

"I doubt they can indict a cat for manslaughter," Daniel said.

"Of course not," I replied, clutching Butterball closer. Then, turning to Sonya I asked, "They can't, can they? I've heard of cases where dangerous dogs were put down."

"Butterball's not dangerous," she said. "This was a freak thing."

I buried my face in Butterball's fur. "And I thought it was bad when you brought home dead birds."

I looked up at the sound of someone clearing his throat. Capone stood in the doorway. "Delilah, are you ready to talk? Someone can stop by the restaurant in the morning if you're not up to it."

I sighed. "Might as well get it over with." I off-loaded Butterball into Sonya's waiting arms and followed Capone.

"I set up an impromptu command center upstairs in the library. I've already spoken with Isabel and Pam and obviously my mother," Capone said, leading the way up the servants' staircase.

"Command center? Is this a full-blown investigation?" I asked, as we made our way up the narrow staircase.

"Not yet. Let's not rush into anything," Capone answered.

"Yeah, I know you like to take things slow," I muttered, thinking of our months-long, near-miss, quasi courtship.

If he registered the snide comment, he ignored it. We padded down the hallway and he continued. "At minimum, I want to get the facts straight to help with the ME's report. It'll also make it easier when we break the news to Clemmons's next of kin, and with any insurance claims that might be filed."

"Oh god, I hadn't even considered that I might get sued," I said.

Capone placed a reassuring hand on my back. "It's going to be okay, Delilah. There is no indication that you were negligent in any way. Pam has a cat, and she understands completely. It could easily have been her cat. In fact, she said she originally thought it was."

"Maybe it was. How do we know that Butterball was the culprit? Just because he was near the scene doesn't mean he's guilty, right?" I asked hopefully. "Did anyone actually see the cat that was swiping at people on the stairs?"

"Several people," Capone said. "Sorry, I know this is hard. They described a large, orange tabby. Gloria Philips is a long-haired, small, white Ragdoll breed."

I grimaced. "Even if no one sues me and Butterball doesn't end up in cat jail, I don't know how I'm going to live with myself. I know it was an accident, but I want to hide under a rock and never come out."

Capone gave me a sympathetic smile, but there wasn't much else he could offer. He, too, had a cat, and no doubt could imagine the boa constrictor of guilt squeezing the air from my lungs. I'd always found Butterball's antics—the catfights, the travel-related freak-outs, the bursts of kitty rage—amusing. My ex wanted to call in a feline behaviorist, but I thought he was blowing things out of proportion. "Our cat doesn't need a shrink," I'd told him. Never in a million years did I think my sweet kitty was capable of causing a man's death.

Capone and I continued on to the library. Compared to the vast, crowd-ready expanses of the downstairs rooms, the upstairs had been designed on a more domestic scale. The library was richly appointed—wingback leather chairs, a granite reading table, and a grand inlaid maple desk—but still cozy. Someone had lit a fire in the hearth and Lola Capone stood in front of it, warming herself.

"There you are, sugar," she said to her son, relief flooding her voice. "It's eerie up here alone." Walking toward to me, she offered her hand. "Ms. O'Leary, we haven't been properly introduced. Although I feel like I've known you for ten years already after all that's happened. And, of course, Calvin has told me about you."

I turned to Capone with raised eyebrows.

"He keeps promising to take me to your restaurant for a mother-son dinner," she explained, "but his work always seems to get in the way." She shot him a reproachful look. "Why have dinner with your mother when you can spend all your time with robbers and drug dealers?" Her voice was deep and musical. I knew from Capone that she spent her early childhood in Cuba, but her voice held only the merest sprinkle of an island accent.

"Well, you convinced me to be here tonight, so don't say we never spend quality time together," Capone replied.

I got the sense that this was a well-worn conversational path for them.

Lola smiled at her son's dark humor but then shivered, setting off a cascade of sparkles as the beads in her gown caught the firelight. The wind kicked up again and rattled the panes of leaded glass in the windows. "What a strange night," she said, rubbing her gloved hands against her bare arms. Her eyes were far off, entranced by some distant thought or memory. "That poor man."

"Did you know him?" I asked.

"Never saw him before tonight," she said.

"He spoke about you, just before he died."

Her eyes widened. "About me?"

"Yes, a few minutes before he fell."

Lola swayed, as if the wind outside managed to pierce the walls and buffet her slim body. I reached out to steady her, fearing she would fall.

Capone's forehead wrinkled into a worried frown. "Come back where it's warm, Mom." He settled her into a chair by the fire and covered her with a plaid blanket that had been draped over the opposite chair.

Lola flashed a tight smile. "Thank you."

Capone peered into his mother's face, and I thought I sensed him shifting into detective mode. "Did you know him, Mom?"

She pulled the blanket more tightly around her and stared into the fire. "I just told you. I never laid eyes on Edgar Clemmons before tonight." She shivered again. Then turning to her son, she asked, "Will we be much longer? Should I call an Uber?"

Capone shook his head and looked at his watch. "Sorry, I thought the EMS would be here by now. Delilah is the last person I want to talk to, and then I'll take you home. I can't imagine an Uber would come out here in this weather anyway. It's getting worse by the minute."

"Has everyone else left?" she asked me.

"Yes, other than my crew, Isabel, and Pam. The last of the stragglers drove off about ten minutes ago," I said.

"I should leave you two to speak in private," Lola

said, pulling the blanket over her shoulders like a shawl and rising from the chair.

"There's no need," I replied. "You saw all the same things that I did."

She nodded sadly. "If you really don't mind, I do think I'll stay. The rest of the house is so drafty, and I don't want to go back downstairs until they take the body away."

"It's okay if she stays, right?" I asked Capone. "You said this isn't an interrogation."

"It's fine with me if you're okay with it."

The three of us settled in front of the fire and I recounted the day's events as best as I could—the abrupt change of plans with the free-from pizza, the unexpected boat ride, my two melodramatic encounters with Clemmons. Capone, for once, didn't have his briefcase and laptop, so he took notes on a large, yellow legal pad. Lola, like her son, listened intently, with an open expression that made it easy—too easy—to unburden yourself of information.

Capone tapped the eraser side of his pencil on the notepad. "So Clemmons gave you two books? What were they?"

"Mysteries, I guess," I replied. "*The Man Who Knew Too Much* and *The Maltese Falcon*. He said they were for Sonya, but she didn't know why he'd given them to her. She put them away with her stuff, I think, if you want to take a look."

"And earlier, before the party, you ran into Clemmons in the back hallway?" he clarified.

"That's right," I said. "I remember being worried about the steepness of those stairs because of his mobility problems. I actually suggested he take the main staircase, the one he fell down, because I thought it would be safer. And we know how that panned out," I added ruefully.

"Pam Philips mentioned he had trouble walking," Capone said. "Could help explain why he fell."

"I don't suppose Isabel mentioned seeing his cane get caught on the rug or something? Those wooden panels shield the top of the stairs from view, but maybe she had a better angle than the rest of us." I sighed. "I guess I'm still hoping we'll discover that it was a pure accident. Nothing to do with Butterball."

Capone gripped the arms of his chair as he waited for me to finish speaking. "Did you say 'cane'?"

"Yes, Clemmons used a cane," I replied.

"Always? It wasn't part of his costume or something?"

"No," I said. "He needs it. He parks in the ADA space when he comes to the restaurant. I think Sonya said it was some problem with his spine."

Capone's face grew grave. "Where's the cane, then?"

CHAPTER 10

Lola fixed her eyes on her son's face. "Now, Calvin. I don't like that look." She turned to me. "I've seen that face on him too many times. When he gets like that, I know he's got the bit between his teeth."

A log on the fire cracked, sending up a small shower of sparks and making us all jump.

We sat quietly for a moment, and I thought back over my encounter with Clemmons. "Maybe the cane fell underneath him somehow. Could you have missed it? After all, you didn't even know you were looking for it."

"No," Capone replied. "It wasn't with the body. And I checked around the top of the stairs to see if Clemmons could've tripped on something other than Butterball. There was nothing there. No cane. Nothing."

Lola clicked her tongue. "Baby, you always think the worst. What are you suggesting? That somebody pushed the man down the stairs and then stole his cane? Or grabbed his cane to make him fall? Why would anyone do that? Isn't the most likely situation that this poor man set down his cane someplace out of the way so he didn't have it with him when he fell? Maybe in the restroom or somewhere like that? From what Delilah is saying, without his cane, he'd have been even more likely to lose his balance and fall down."

I frowned. I didn't like the implications, either, but Capone wasn't the only one with a suspicious mind. I'd seen Clemmons walk, and I couldn't imagine him forgetting or misplacing his mobility aid. "I don't think he would've left his cane somewhere. He relied on it," I said. "There's something else, too," I added.

Capone's eyebrow lifted, his signal that I should continue.

"Clemmons had a mark on his face when I saw him just before he fell. Like he'd been hit."

"That's interesting. And he didn't have it when you saw him before the party?"

I shook my head.

Capone ran his eyes down his notes and leaned closer to me. "You're sure you don't have any idea what he meant about things being 'amiss' in this house or why he gave Sonya those books?"

"None at all," I said. "He was annoyingly vague. He said some stuff about old movies and then he gave me those books for Sonya with the weird message. I mentioned the conversation to Sonya, since he said she helped him figure out whatever he thought he'd figured out, but she had no clue what he meant. He clearly thought it was important, and it seemed like he'd chosen the J. Edgar Hoover costume because he believed he'd uncovered something shady and wanted to expose it. Like it was *his* job to hold 'the guilty parties' to account."

Capone flipped back to another page on his notepad. "I asked both Isabel and Pam about the changing of the guard on the library board. It seems that Edgar wasn't happy about it."

"What did they say?" I asked.

"That the change was a long time coming," he explained. "That Edgar tends to rub people the wrong way, and the board was concerned that he wasn't the best person to lead the fundraising effort. Sounds like he was a man who made some enemies."

I leaned forward in my chair and looked intently at Capone's face. His amber eyes were unsettled, reflecting the flickering dance of the firelight. "I thought he was just being over-the-top with his cloak-and-dagger routine, but maybe he was right. What if someone went after him to avoid some secret being exposed?"

Lola threw up her hands. "Not you, too. Now I understand why C.J. thinks you two would make a good couple."

Capone's mouth dropped open and his skin turned from bronze to cherry pink. He reeled backward into his seat. "Mom," he sputtered.

I, meanwhile, had an uncomfortable flashback to sixth grade, like I'd just been accused of sitting in a tree, k-i-s-s-i-n-g Calvin Capone. I'd met Capone's adult son, C.J., the previous summer, and Lola's statement confirmed that I hadn't been wrong to sense C.J. was nudging his father toward making a move with me. But it also reminded me of my own misgivings about getting involved with Capone. His family tree was almost biblically complicated. As if being a direct descendant of Al Capone wasn't enough, Capone continued the excitement by becoming a teenage father. His son, C.J., now a medical student, himself became a widower at a young age and was the single father to a button-cute toddler—making Capone, at age forty-two, a grandfather. I was only thirty-five. Did I really want a relationship with somebody's grandpa?

Lola waved her hand, dismissing her son's embarrassment.

"Mom, we're talking about a dead body downstairs," Capone said, straining to regain his composure.

"Proves my point. Life's. Too. Short." She leaned forward and punctuated each word by poking her finger onto the table next to her.

"Well, some of us have responsibilities," Capone countered. "And we take those responsibilities seriously." His voice took on a hard edge.

"What's that supposed to mean?" Lola asked.

Capone stood up. "Look, forget it. I don't want to argue. We need to find this cane." He consulted his notes again. "Maybe it's in this room, since Pam said Clemmons told her to meet him in here."

I was only too glad for an excuse to move away from the topic of romance. Capone's family was pushing him to make a move. He talked about me to them. I felt like I'd made my interest about as clear as I could without hiring one of those skywriting planes. So what was stopping him? What were these "responsibilities" he mentioned? Was there something about me that he'd decided was a deal breaker? *His loss*, I reminded myself.

The three of us made a quick search of the room. Two walls were covered, floor to ceiling, with built-in bookshelves. Many of the books were beautiful, leather-bound, gilt-edged volumes—showpieces of the type wealthy people liked to display for aesthetic effect. However, there were whole shelves of paperbacks and other popular novels that had clearly been well thumbed. While the rest of the house adhered to the period motif, here, it seemed, Pam Philips's love of reading had overcome her devotion to historical accuracy. It was surprising to see such an abundance of paper in the possession of a woman who'd done more to usher in the digital book age than almost anyone.

Coming up empty on our search for the cane, we proceeded along the hallway to the upper landing, from where Clemmons had fallen. A richly hued Turkish carpet ran along the length of the hall, stopping at the top of the stairs. Gilt-framed portraits hung on the walls. Capone was right: there were no obvious tripping hazards, and nowhere the cane could have been overlooked. Nothing appeared out of place. On the stairs themselves, as I'd recalled, carved wooden panels shielded the view of the top of the stairs from anyone down in the drawing room. A tall alcove, set into one of the panels, stood next to the top step. Inside it was a large potted plant.

"That's where Butterball was, according to the guests he swiped at," Capone said. "Behind the plant." He took out his phone and shined the flashlight into the recess. "Orange fur," he said, playing the flashlight's beam across a telltale tuft.

My heart sank. Unfortunately, it didn't take much imagination to picture Butterball ensconced in that space, hissing and swiping at passersby. With "his" people, he was a love muffin—friendly, affectionate, and very people focused. But he defended his turf fiercely and had strong, and decidedly negative, opinions on being taken out of his element. Plus, he *hated* storms, and the one raging outside was a doozy.

I swallowed hard. Maybe my concern about the missing cane was as much wishful thinking as true suspicion of foul play. What was wrong with me? I actually preferred to believe Clemmons was *murdered* over thinking that my sweet Butterball could've caused the accident that led to his death.

Before we could continue our search, the sound of voices rose from downstairs.

"That must be the EMS people," Lola said, putting her hands on her hips. "Finally."

I took a few steps down, but Capone put his hand on my shoulder. "Probably better if we take the other staircase. I'm used to stepping over dead bodies, but not everybody is."

When we reached the front hall a few moments later, I was surprised to see—instead of the bevy of police officers and paramedics I'd expected—Zaria Singhal and Count Victor. A moment later, B.L. Huddleston and Kennedy Criss came in the front door, complaining loudly and brushing raindrops from their hair.

"What on earth . . . ?" Lola began.

Pam and Isabel emerged from the lower-level staircase.

"We had to turn back," Victor said testily. "The path is blocked just before you get to the main road."

"The wind is terrible," Zaria agreed. "Fallen trees everywhere."

"Our car almost ran into a ditch trying to dodge one," B.L. added.

Kennedy removed her fur coat and pushed it toward me. "Hang this up, would you?"

"Excuse me?" I asked. Outrage exuded from my pores.

Noting the expression on my face, Capone shot me a look that suggested I should think twice about committing assault and battery in front of a police detective. "I'll take it," he said, hanging the coat over the back of a nearby chair to dry out.

My glare remained locked on Kennedy, as I wondered why her husband put up with her. From what I'd seen, she went out of her way to be nice to him, but surely he could see what a monster she was? Or did youth and a pretty face cancel out a radioactive personality? Having never shopped for a trophy wife myself, I didn't know the ins and outs of the market.

Capone's phone rang and he stepped aside to answer it.

"I'm so sorry to impose on you," Zaria said, "but we don't have anywhere else to go. Can we wait here until they clear the way?"

"Of course," Pam said.

Just then, Daniel rounded the corner into the hallway. "*Jefa*, there you are. We were wondering what to do with the . . ." Then, when he noticed the assembled crowd, his forehead creased. "What's going on?"

"The road's blocked," Isabel explained.

Capone returned to the group, his expression grim. "That was one of my colleagues. They can't get through, either, and the equipment they'd need to clear the road is in use out on Highway 12. Since there's no urgent need for medical care, our situation has been 'de-prioritized.' The dispatcher thought it could be early tomorrow morning before they can send someone out."

"Tomorrow?" Lola said, her dark eyes widening in dismay.

"But there's a dead body in the other room!" Kennedy clutched her throat in alarm. "Does this mean we have to leave him there all night?"

"I'm afraid so," Capone replied.

"I'm not spending an entire night in a house with Edgar Clemmons's corpse. I can't," Zaria said, scanning the room frantically. "Don't you have a boat, Pam? I know the lake will be rough, but all we'd have to do is dock it a few houses over and we'd be able to get to a road that's open."

"The boat's at the marina, being winterized," Pam replied. "Ciera, my assistant, took it this afternoon. I wouldn't want anyone to risk the lake in this weather anyway."

"We could walk, couldn't we?" B.L. said. "Can't be that far to one of the neighbors' houses."

"If we go along the shoreline, it's about a mile to the Chadwicks', a little less on the forest path," Pam said. "But their house is closed for the season."

"What about Doug and Cookie Blankenship's place?" Kennedy suggested. "It's probably a little further, but the forest isn't so thick in that direction. They've cleared a lot of their land for their helipad."

"They're in Aspen for the winter. They mentioned it when they RSVPed 'no' for tonight," Isabel said.

Kennedy grabbed her husband's arm with both hands. "Brian, please do something."

"We must be able to get the trees cleared from the road," B.L. blustered. "Pam, do you have a chainsaw and some ropes? I'm sure the menfolk can handle this." He sized up Daniel and patted him on the back. "What do you say?"

Daniel raised an eyebrow. Despite his powerful physique and military background, Daniel was a lover, not a fighter. With his razor-sharp cheekbones, coal-dark eyes, and mobster suit, however, he gave off an aura of menace. Taking note of the bartender's expression, B.L. quickly moved his hand from Daniel's back into his own pocket and took a couple of steps backward.

"You seriously think you're going to convince anyone halfway sane to go out into a raging storm with trees falling all around them?" I asked.

"We'd pay anyone who volunteers," Kennedy said.

"Implying that my staff needs the money badly enough to risk their lives?" I snapped.

"No one's going out in these conditions," Capone said. He laid a restraining hand on my arm, interrupting me before I could give voice to a vivid description of what the Huddleston-Crisses could do with their money, their chainsaw, and their ropes. "The house is secure," he continued. "We have plenty of provisions. The best thing we can do is stay here until the storm subsides."

"So that's it, then." Zaria worried her hands together. I followed her eyes as she looked at the faces of the remaining guests, their expressions ranging from resignation to tension to downright fear. Quietly, in a near whisper, she gave voice to what each one of us had come to realize. "We're trapped here."

CHAPTER 11

We stood silently for a moment, taking stock of our situation. Trapped in the house with a dead body and a group of strangers for what could be a very long evening. The festive atmosphere of a few hours earlier had evaporated completely, leaving behind a residue of anxiety, rancor, and distrust.

"I don't like this at all," Zaria said, her voice trembling.

Victor shushed his fiancée. "Calm down, Zaria. You're becoming upset for no reason. The man is dead. What harm can he do? It's no different than having a side of beef in one's freezer."

Being a chef, I was more habituated to sides of beef than the average person. But even for me, hearing the comparison, said aloud with such crisp detachment, was jarring.

Pam addressed the group. "Well, then, that's decided. We'd better make ourselves comfortable, because you're all spending the night."

Her words settled over the group like a freezing fog.

"Everyone must be hungry," Isabel said, trying to calm the waters. "Delilah, is there any chance we could warm up some of the leftovers? I'm not sure anyone has eaten properly."

"My pleasure," I said, narrowing my eyes at the assembled guests. With all my years of fine dining training, I was fully capable of putting on a show of polite deference when it was called for, but never before had I been expected to sleep in the same house as my patrons.

"Wonderful," Pam said. "We can sit in the dining room, away from . . ." She paused, probably realizing that mentioning a dead body in the same sentence as dinner plans wasn't terribly appetizing.

Isabel counted on her fingers. "The Capones, Delilah, her staff, me, Pam, the Huddleston-Crisses, Zaria, and Victor. That's fourteen place settings."

"We're all going to eat together?" Zaria seemed caught off guard by the idea.

"I think the upstairs-downstairs distinction is moot at this point, don't you?" Isabel asked, with a tone of mild reproach.

"Oh, sorry, I didn't mean to sound snobbish. It's just hard to fathom that we really *are* all trapped here together." Her eyes darted nervously from face to face. "It's a bit claustrophobic, that's all."

Pam opened her arms wide, taking in the grand scale of the entryway. "*This* is claustrophobic?" I was glad to see that she seemed more amused than offended. There was already enough ill will floating around.

"I'll go and make some cocktails while the food is prepared," Daniel offered. "Who wants a South Side Fizz?"

Every hand except Capone's went up. I supposed he considered himself on duty now. Did that mean he was taking the possibility that Clemmons was murdered seriously? Or simply that he wanted to remain alert and prepared?

"Let's go get that drink," Isabel said.

Daniel took a few steps to follow her. I touched his shoulder. "What was it you came to ask me about?" I asked.

"Oh, we're having some issues with the dumbwaiter," he explained. "Rabbit and Melody were starting to load the supplies and leftover food into the van. But I guess it doesn't matter if we're all staying."

I made my way to the kitchen, where my crew was busily demobilizing our operation. Jarka stacked the dirty dishes into their crates, ready to ship back to the restaurant for later washing. The rest of my crew, though, were engaged in a slightly less conventional operation. The door of the dumbwaiter stood open, the box barely visible, its top peeking over the horizon of the doorframe. Rabbit was on his hands and knees on the floor next to the contraption, with a barefoot Melody standing on his back. Only her legs were in view. Her top half leaned into the miniature elevator shaft. Sonya stood next to them, one hand on Melody's lower back for support, the other shining her phone's flashlight up into the dark space. With everyone in their period attire, it looked like a slapstick scene from a small-town dinner theater production.

"What are you guys doing?" I asked.

"There's something wedged in the pulley up there," Sonya explained. "A load of tiramisu cookies is stuck partway down to the basement."

Melody's muffled voice echoed from within the shaft. "I've almost got it."

"Are you sure this is safe?" I asked dubiously.

"Melody said she's the go-to person for fixing stuff on the farm—the hay baler, the hay conveyer, the Cow O' Matic 5000," Sonya said.

"Cow O' Matic?" I asked.

"Yeah, I made that last one up, but I'm pretty sure the first two are real," Sonya replied. "She definitely said a number of things about hay and cows."

"Plus, she's the only one small enough to get up in there," Rabbit said from the floor.

"Well, don't spend too much more time on it. We need to serve dinner," I said.

"Serve dinner?" Jarka repeated.

"Yeah, for all the people staying over," I explained.

"What people staying over?" Rabbit asked.

I tied on my apron and went to the sink to wash my hands. "There are fallen trees blocking the road, and they probably can't be cleared until tomorrow morning. Several of the party guests didn't make it out in time and will have to stay the night."

"Us, too?" Melody popped out of the shaft like a jack-in-the-box, her blue eyes wide.

I nodded. "'Fraid so. And I told Pam we'd serve dinner for everyone, since none of us have eaten yet."

Jarka's perma-frown deepened. "Who are these people? The people trapped here with us?"

"Pam, of course, and Isabel. Then there's my aunt's former neighbors, Kennedy and B.L." I paused. "And also Zaria Singhal and Count Victor, her *fiancé*." I wasn't sure if Jarka knew of his betrothal, but it seemed better to put it out there now, rather than risk her coming across the pair unprepared during the course of the evening.

If I'd expected a big emotional reaction from Jarka at the news that the subject of her mysterious entanglement and his fiancée were trapped in a remote mansion with her overnight, I was, as usual, disappointed. Instead of a dramatic response, she simply picked up a clean C-fold towel, ran it under the tap, and continued to wipe down the counters. The Statue of Liberty could learn a thing or two from Jarka about keeping a straight face.

"We're almost done with this." Melody's voice was barely audible as she ducked back into the shaft. "One more tug should do it. It feels like some kind of rod got tangled in the pulley ropes. There!"

She handed the troublesome object to Sonya and began to climb down. Before I knew what was happening, the entire pyramid collapsed into a human sandwich. Sonya was the bottom layer, followed by Rabbit, and topped by Melody.

"Oh my god! Are you okay?" I called, hurrying around the counter.

Jarka beat me to the scene and had already pulled Melody and Rabbit up before I reached them.

"I don't understand what happened," Rabbit was saying. "Sonya just fell into me all of a sudden. Knocked my knees right out."

Sonya didn't try to explain. Instead, she lay limp on the floor, face down.

"Son?" I called, dropping to my knees. I rolled her onto her back. Her eyes were closed, her complexion ghostly pale.

Her eyes fluttered, and she groaned.

"Is she hurt?" Rabbit asked.

Jarka pressed her fingers to Sonya's neck to check her pulse and surveyed her for injuries. "I think no. She only is faint."

My body went numb. I'd only ever known Sonya to faint at the sight of blood.

Rabbit turned slightly toward the counter. On his back was a red smear. "Oh, geez, Rabbit, are you bleeding?" I asked.

He looked over his shoulder, trying to see the spot I was pointing to. "Where'd that come from? I ain't hurt." He turned to Melody. "You all right, Mel?"

She looked herself up and down, "Yeah, I'm fine."

Jarka began to fan Sonya with a kitchen towel. "Is not her blood. She has no wound."

That's when I saw it. On the gleaming parquet floor, a few feet from where Sonya fell, lay Edgar Clemmons's gilt-topped cane. Instead of the well-worn patina you'd expect on the handle, though, the top of the cane was encrusted with a substance that looked like sour cherry jam.

"Is that what I think it is?"

My question was rhetorical, but Jarka answered it. "Blood," she said.

I turned to Rabbit. "Get Capone in here. Because Butterball sure as hell didn't do *that*."

CHAPTER 12

By the time Capone arrived, my emotional cocktail was a heady blend of relief and horror, shaken *and* stirred. I cradled Butterball in my arms, whispering sweet nothings into his ear. *How could I have thought my beautiful baby would be capable of causing a man's death? Maybe I spoiled him a little, but I hadn't created a monster.* Given that the revelation of my cat's innocence was tied up with the discovery of a murder weapon, though, it was hard to find cause for celebration.

After confirming Sonya's vital signs for himself, Capone turned to address the rest of my staff. "Anyone want to fill in the blanks here? Did this cane fall from the sky or what?"

"I pulled it out of the chute," Melody said. Her voice sounded a bit thready, but she seemed to have recovered from the initial shock. With her farm upbringing, when it came to blood and guts, she was made of pretty stern stuff. "We'd sent a couple of loads down and the dumbwaiter box kept sticking on the way back up. I realized the problem was probably that something was getting wedged in the mechanism. I'm the smallest one here, so I kind of climbed in with Rabbit and Sonya holding me. I reached up, felt what I thought was a loose rod, gave it a good yank, and handed it to Sonya." She glanced down at Sonya, who was finally starting to come around. "I wouldn't have handed it to her if I'd realized what it was and what was on it. It was dark in there."

"It's not your fault," I soothed.

Sonya was lying on her back, eyes still closed, but she managed to say, "She's right, Mel. It's not your fault that I was born with a defective on-off switch."

"Oh, thank goodness you're okay," Melody gushed, joining Capone and Jarka on the floor next to Sonya. "We thought you were hurt."

"How are you feeling, Son?" I asked. I set Butterball down and crouched next to her, placing my hand on her cheek.

"I can't believe I touched it," Sonya said, suppressing a gag and then taking hold of my hand. "I didn't realize what was on it. Although, some part of me did, maybe? You know, like when milk's gone bad, and you *know* it, but you have to taste it just to be sure? I touched the"—she swallowed and lowered her voice—"blood, like with my *actual fingers*." She held out her other hand, which was indeed smeared with crimson. "The last thing I remember was looking at the handprint I made on Rabbit's back and thinking this is how Lady Macbeth must've felt."

"Is that Shakespeare?" I asked.

"'Out damned spot'?" Sonya prompted.

"Never read it," I said. "If we're talking books, I can pretty much guarantee I haven't read it unless it was assigned in high school. And even then, I probably did CliffsNotes."

Sonya said, "You're such a barbarian."

"*I'm* a barbarian? I'm not the one laying on the floor next to a murder weapon with blood all over my hand," I replied.

Sonya gagged. "Don't say the B-word." She squeezed her eyes tighter shut but then cracked one lid open just a smidgeon. "Is the cane still there?"

"Yes," I said.

"Thought so. I can sense it." She turned her head away.

"This *has* to be the murder weapon, right? There's no other explanation," I said to Capone.

"There's always another explanation," Capone replied. "But it does seem likely. If the assailant was known to Clemmons, they could have easily been walking alongside him, grabbed his cane, and assaulted him at the top of the stairs. It could've been done in the heat of the moment or planned in advance."

"Right," I said, continuing to play out the scenario. "Then the killer would be standing there, with the party in full flow downstairs, holding a cane covered in"—I looked at Sonya—"in *you know what*. They can't throw it down the stairs at this point, because Clemmons is already halfway down. And they can't plant it at the top of the stairs with *you know what* all over it because then it would be immediately obvious how he died. They probably can't take the time to try to clean it, either, not knowing if someone would rush upstairs at any moment. So they hid it in the dumbwaiter on the way back downstairs, maybe hoping to pick it up before they left, or least hoping to buy enough time to be long gone before it was found."

"But then we started using the dumbwaiter and the cane fell down into the pulley rope and got stuck, 'n all," Melody finished.

"It's plausible," Capone agreed.

"Did Clemmons have a head wound?" I asked Capone.

Capone shot me an "Are you serious?" look. "He fell down a flight of wooden stairs."

I glared back at him. "I wondered if you'd noticed

an *unusual* head wound. Not consistent with the fall, I mean," I said.

"He did have a wound on his forehead, but I couldn't say what caused it. That's the ME's job," he said.

"I don't think a medical examiner is going to make it out here tonight," I said, glancing out the sleet-speckled windows.

"*I* am here," Jarka said. "I am not trained to say what causes a death, but I have worked in emergency department and seen many such injuries of falling people."

"What's your take?" I asked.

"Many times when people fall down stairs, they slip with their feet and land here." She stopped fanning Sonya and pointed to her rump to indicate the area in question. "And hit head here." She touched the base of her own skull. "I see many times this kind of fall when I was doctor in hospital. Mr. Clemmons falls, I think, like this." She rotated her hands to demonstrate a head-over-heels fall, starting with the person's back to the stairs. "The breaks to the spine and neck are very bad. With normal slip onto butt end, injuries are different. If he trips over Butterball, he would fall forward, not back. Just I am guessing, but this is what I think."

I sometimes forgot how overqualified Jarka, aka Dr. Jarka Gagamova, was for a waitressing job. She planned to regain her medical license in the U.S. but had failed the language portion of the qualification on her first attempt and was saving up money while she studied to retake it.

"If he were facing his attacker, he'd fall backward like that, right?" I asked. "Say, if he were hit with his own cane on the upper landing of the stairs?"

"Is possible," she replied.

"Let's not jump to conclusions," Capone said. "The

ME will be able to tell us more, but what Jarka is describing is consistent with what Isabel saw. She said it looked like Clemmons came tumbling head over heels down the stairs. He fell with force."

Over the course of the few moments since the discovery of the cane, his demeanor had undergone a rapid shift. While he could never be said to be truly off duty—he was too practiced in the art of hypervigilance for that—he'd seemed relaxed at the party. Following Clemmons's accident, he'd moved into a lowish gear—his "professional witness" mode. He'd focused on getting organized, communicating, and keeping everyone calm. Now, though, I could see him walling himself in. Shutting out distractions. Sealing off emotions. Going through procedural checklists in his head. Things had gotten serious, and it was time to be Cop Capone. Observing the change was like watching someone put on body armor, piece by piece.

"That doesn't sound like a case of his feet going out from underneath him," I argued. "Surely the cane proves he was murdered?"

"Nothing is proven until a judge and jury say it is. Bear in mind that a forceful fall could also happen if he tripped," Capone said. "No fall down a steep wooden staircase is likely to end well, especially not for an elderly person."

"How can you ignore the bloody cane? It's practically throwing itself at you and you're acting like that means nothing!" I threw up my hands in frustration. Why couldn't Capone just grab hold of the sure thing in front of him, whether it be a perfect piece of evidence or a hot-to-trot pizza chef?

Capone sighed. "Look, Delilah, I'm not ignoring the obvious. But a defense attorney can bring down a case on what-ifs. It's my job to always keep that in mind."

"Maybe we should get this cane out of here so Sonya doesn't pass out again," Rabbit suggested.

"Oh, yeah. Sorry, Son," I said, taking her non-bloody hand again. I turned to Capone. "I know it's crime scene evidence, but I don't suppose we could move Edgar's cane? And clean Sonya up?"

"Sonya, I need to you hang tight for a minute," Capone said. He snapped a few dozen pictures of the cane with his phone. "I don't suppose you have any cotton gauze or a very clean kitchen towel I can cut up?" he asked.

"I saw a box of Q-tips in the bathroom," Melody replied.

He nodded. "Get them."

As she went to get the supplies, Capone looked around the vast expanse of countertop until he found a gigantic roll of plastic wrap and some catering gloves. He donned the gloves and laid out a sheet of plastic wrap on the floor next to the cane. Then, he carefully eased the object on top. When Melody returned, Capone swabbed samples from the cane and Sonya's hand, placing each Q-tip into a separate plastic bag and labeling them with one of the black Sharpies we used to label our foil-topped food containers. Finally, he wrapped the cane in the plastic wrap.

"Is not wrong to move and touch these things?" Jarka asked.

"The evidence has already been disturbed from its original position," Capone explained. "Melody grabbed the cane in multiple places, and Sonya also touched it. Best thing we can do now is preserve what's left the best we can, and with all the people staying overnight in the house, that means putting it somewhere out of the way."

"Is it safe for me to open my eyes yet?" Sonya asked.

"One more minute," Capone replied.

"Conceal the Cane is a fun party game. It's like a goyish version of hiding the afikomen at Passover, only you throw in a murder," Sonya deadpanned. "We should patent this. Or at least have the rest of the guests join in."

At the mention of the others, Melody clutched her boa-covered throat, her gaze trailing to the open doorway. "Maybe they already did join in. It could be one of *them* who put the cane there. What if the killer comes looking for it and finds out we moved it?"

"All the more reason to get it out of the way and keep this development to ourselves." Capone raised his index finger to his lips. "Understood? No one but the people in this room need to know what was found or who found it."

I looked around the kitchen and suddenly noticed something missing. A big, orange, furry something. "Has anyone seen Butterball?"

"He was just there a minute ago, eating a haute dog," Rabbit said, gesturing to an empty plate.

"Oh, geez, he could be anywhere," I groaned. "We've got to find him. God knows what he could get up to here. He's probably hiding in a crazy place because of the storm."

"Hope he'll be okay using Miss Philips's cat's litter box," Rabbit observed. "He's been here for quite a while."

"*Yuck.* I hadn't even thought about that," I groaned.

"Once I've got the evidence squared away, we can organize a search party," Capone said.

"Luckily, we're serving dinner, so he'll probably come to us," I said.

"I'll get the food started," Rabbit said. "The pizzas should still be okay. I'll get the ovens going again to warm them."

I said a silent prayer that the Pizza Gods would be forgiving of the *re*-reheating. Even though this had turned from a big, splashy affair into a big, messy murder scene, I still cared about the quality of what I served.

"I will set table," Jarka said.

"I'll help," Melody said.

"Great. We're serving family-style," I said.

"We're all gonna sit together?" Rabbit asked, his sparse eyebrows shooting up.

I nodded. Apparently, the hoity-toity folks weren't the only ones taken by surprise by the sudden shift to communal dining.

"I should call Biz and let her know we're not coming back tonight," I said. "Wait till she hears we're stuck here with her archenemies."

Inwardly, I breathed a sigh of relief that she hadn't come. She'd have had no qualms about framing B.L. and Kennedy for Clemmons's murder if she thought it would lead to her getting her cottage back.

"Any way you could prioritize moving the cane?" Sonya asked. "Or should I just plan to spend the night down here?"

"Sorry, Son," I said. Turning to Capone, I continued, "I think we can put it in the butler's pantry, where all the china and glassware is stored. It locks with an old-fashioned skeleton key. Pam gave it to me in case we needed anything out of there, and to use as a place for us to keep our personal belongings."

Capone gently took hold of the plastic-wrapped cane, aiming to jostle it as little as possible. With his other hand, he picked up the Ziploc bags.

"Let's go," he said to me.

As I led him in the direction of the pantry, I heard Sonya say, "Looks like Capone and Delilah win this round of Conceal the Cane. Game over, I guess."

But as we walked along the darkened hallway, I had a bad feeling that the game was only beginning.

CHAPTER 13

The narrow confines of the butler's pantry were lit by a single fixture, which cast shadows throughout the small space. I began to clear a shelf that held china soup tureens, while Capone kept his careful hold of the cane and bagged Q-tips. Despite the grim task before us, I couldn't help noticing his proximity to me and the warmth of his skin.

"Is your mother okay? She seemed a little shaken when we were talking in the library," I said.

"She's tough," he replied. "The entertainment business is hard, and it was even harder for her to get a break as a young single mom."

"Was your father supportive of her career?" I asked, hoping the question didn't seem like too much of a non sequitur. After Clemmons's insinuations about Lola Capone's private life, I was anxious to know more.

"They never got married, and he wasn't involved in our lives. I've never asked her, but I suspect she took the Capone name for the cachet of it, to help open doors. Which is ironic, because Al's own son had his name legally changed to Albert Brown in the sixties. The generation after that reversed course and started embracing the connection. I guess by then the advantages of being gangster royalty outweighed the disadvantages."

"I suppose." I hesitated. "Clemmons seemed to have a problem with it, though."

Up to that point, Capone had only been half engaged in the conversation, focused instead on arranging the evidence and cataloging it with his phone. Now, though, his attention was on me. "What do you mean?"

I hadn't planned on mentioning the details of my last conversation with Clemmons, but in light of the evidence of foul play, it seemed better to get everything out in the open. Still, I knew it wasn't going to be easy to tell Capone that the dead man's last words had disparaged his mother.

"He accused your mother of associating with the wrong kind of people." I paused again, grimacing. "And . . ."

"Out with it," Capone said, clearly in no mood for pussyfooting around.

Most likely for the best, since there was no way to put it delicately. "And he implied that her morals weren't up to scratch."

Capone's jaw clenched. "He said what, exactly?"

"That she was a great singer," I said, "but he thought she should make better choices about who she associates with. And that it was ironic that you'd become a cop, considering who your great-grandfather was, and . . ."

"And?" A single muscle twitched in his neck.

"And that your mother's character was questionable."

"Is that all?" His expression was neutral, but anger bubbled like magma beneath his words.

"Yes." I turned my eyes back to the shelf. "Clemmons was probably one of those old fuddy-duddies who think that everyone in the entertainment industry is immoral."

"Probably," he said, his lips so tight they barely moved.

While any son would naturally be fuming about a suggestion like the one Clemmons had made about Lola Capone, there was something in Capone's demeanor, some whirling tempest of suppressed emotion, that made me think the accusation struck a very specific nerve with him. Cop-Mode Capone was usually calm and clinical. When I'd seen him show emotion during an investigation, it was carefully calibrated to the situation—a gentle hand on the back of a reluctant witness, a menacing warning to a suspected lawbreaker. Now, though, he was clearly struggling to keep his feelings in check.

"You know what? Forget I said anything." I waved my hand. Given the look on Capone's face, it was probably just as well that Clemmons had already been killed. Time to change the subject. "Do you know anything about Count Victor?" I asked. "I saw him getting aggressive with Jarka earlier, and then again with Zaria Singhal."

Capone, although still clearly angry about Clemmons's questioning his mother's virtue, seemed intrigued. "Are you shopping him as a suspect already?"

"I'd like to, but sadly, I think he's off the list. If Clemmons was hit with his own cane and then immediately fell, I don't think the Count or Zaria could've done it. They were standing right next to me when he came down the stairs."

"We need to keep an open mind. Maybe he was killed at a different time and they *wanted* you to see them there so you could be their alibi."

I let out a dismissive snort. "If one of them magically suspended the body and then dropped it when they were safely away from him, I'll give you ten bucks. Besides, they didn't know I was standing there. I snuck up on them to eavesdrop."

He gave me the side-eye but didn't pass comment

on my nosiness. "You don't work in this business for twenty-plus years without seeing some weird things," he said. "We still don't even know for sure that he *was* murdered. There could be some other explanation for the cane. Once the physical evidence is analyzed and we can start a proper investigation, we'll know more."

By then, I'd made enough space on the shelf for Capone to carefully lay down each piece of evidence he'd been holding. We stood shoulder to shoulder as he finished arranging the cane and the blood samples in a neat row. With each movement, our bodies brushed against each other, and the subtle scent of his cologne left me flustered and struggling to maintain concentration.

As he laid the final bag on the shelf, Capone suddenly stopped and reached his arms toward me. His muscles were taut, and I felt his breath quicken. Mere inches separated us. After all of our near misses, *this* was the time he was going to pick to make his move? Sure, I was attracted to him, but didn't I deserve a little wooing? What did he think this was, five minutes in the closet with Delilah? I opened my mouth, ready to give him a thick, salty piece of my mind.

"Are those the books?" he asked, reaching past me.

I spun around, quickly enough, I hoped, to conceal the blush in my cheeks. *Quit imagining things. He's not into you.*

He pushed aside Sonya's purse and iridescent wrap and took hold of the two books Clemmons had given to me during the last few minutes of his life.

"Uh, yeah," I said. "Son must have put them there."

Capone picked up the slim volume of *The Maltese Falcon*. The cover was striking—a stark image of a black bird perched on a bright yellow background. The copy of *The Man Who Knew Too Much* was even more overtly eye-catching. An image of a cowering, grey-suited man dominated the dust jacket, and the book's title was printed in a garish red font.

He flipped slowly through the pages of each book, then held the volumes up to the light, examining them from various angles.

"No note," Capone said, with a disappointed sigh.

"Maybe he wrote a message in invisible ink, Hardy Boys–style. I wouldn't put it past him." I crossed my arms and huffed. "All this jabroni had to do was tell me in plain English who he thought was after him. Or, better yet, he could've called up the police and said, 'Gee, I think so-and-so is up to dinky-donk.' If he had, we wouldn't be in this situation. Instead, we're standing in a closet with two old books and a bloody cane."

"Maybe he didn't want to name names because he didn't want to spread rumors or make false accusations," Capone suggested.

"Could be," I granted, although that seemed to give Clemmons too much credit. To me, it was more likely the man wanted to mess with my head than it was that he wanted to protect an innocent person from being falsely accused. "But something must've changed in the meantime to confirm, or at least reinforce, his fears. When I saw him the second time, he felt threatened enough to want to make sure his message got passed along."

"So why *not* just tell you, as you so eloquently put it, 'so-and-so is up to dinky-donk'?" Capone asked. "Even if he *was* right that he was being watched?"

I tapped my fingernail against my lip. "Unless so-and-so was following him, standing within earshot, and he was trying not to tip them off."

"Do you remember who was near you?" Capone asked.

"Basically everyone. I was right near the bar. People

were coming and going. Dozens of people were crowded around, and I wasn't paying particular attention. Really anyone at the party could've been close by other than you, since you were at the piano."

He sighed and slipped the books into the inner pockets of his tuxedo jacket. "Well, these could shed some light on what happened. I'll get Sonya to take another look. Maybe jog something loose."

We locked the pantry door and made our way back to the kitchen, where we found my staff, minus Daniel, busily resurrecting a dinner from the remains of the abandoned earlier attempt. The kitchen was awash with the fragrance of baking pizza—the aromatic equivalent of a cozy blanket.

"You know, it's remarkable how you're the head chef and yet you've managed to cook for all of five minutes tonight," Sonya said, pulling a pizza from the oven. Despite her ordeal, her glistening helmet of marcelled waves remained intact, and she'd applied some fresh powder to her face.

"Glad to see you've recovered," I replied, hip-checking her as I walked past. "I've been dealing with a few small distractions, in case you hadn't noticed."

"Haven't we all," she replied.

"I know I left you hanging," I said, turning off the sarcasm. "You handled it like a pro, and I don't know what I'd do without you."

"You're forgiven, but it's time for you to bring some of that Delilah magic. Isabel has already been in once to check the status of dinner. I gather that a few of the guests are hangry. Plus, Daniel has been serving drinks. We don't want hanger to turn into dranger."

"Dranger?" Capone repeated.

"Drunk-anger," I explained. I walked to the sink to

wash my hands. "For catering gigs, you ideally don't want to let guests have more than one cocktail before you start bringing out food. If people go too long on empty stomachs, suddenly you've got a frat party on your hands and things can get a little wild."

"Even at high-society gigs?" Capone asked.

"*Especially* at high-society gigs," I replied.

Melody looked up from her spot at the kitchen island. "The more I think about it, the more I don't like being trapped here with strangers. What if one of *them* murdered Mr. Clemmons? It had to be someone from the party, right?"

"Someone could've come in from outside," I said, trying to reassure both myself and her.

Capone nodded. "Could've been. There are no security cameras on this property, though, so it's impossible to check."

"No cameras?" Sonya said. "That seems a little nuts considering all the valuable art and stuff in here."

"Apparently, Pam Philips is anti-technology," Capone replied.

"How can she be against technology?" I asked. "She made her money inventing some hi-tech doohickey to make e-books sync up on different devices."

Capone threw his hands up. "She said she likes to keep her home life as tech-free as possible to maintain separation between her work and her home. She still uses a computer and cell phone, but hasn't installed any smart technology in her house other than the very basics. Apparently, that's part of the reason she restored this house the way she did."

"Look, I'm a poster girl for vintage and retro things, and I can barely work my TV, but tonight I wish this house was plastered with security cameras," Sonya said.

"I'm talking real-time, wall-to-wall Big Brother record-ing devices."

"I'm with you," Capone agreed. "I'd very much like to know who was upstairs at the time Clemmons fell, and if any of those people are still in this house."

"Even if it was one of the guests, what are the odds of it being one of the people stuck here now?" Rabbit said. It was rare for him to speak voluntarily in Capone's pres-ence. For obvious reasons, the sight of a badge made him reflexively want to invoke his right to remain silent. But his curiosity and desire to calm Melody's shaky nerves seemed to have gotten the better of him. "Probably some creep from outside. A jilted ex of Ms. Philips or some-thing."

"Rabbit says what probability also says," Jarka agreed. "There were so many other people at the party, and only six are left besides of us. Why it should be any of those who are here and not one who left?"

I turned to Capone. "But in a way it's good news if it *is* someone from the party, right? Because Isabel has a list of everyone who attended. Once we get back to civiliza-tion, you can try to match fingerprints with people who were here, or swab the cane for DNA and then check it against everyone who came until you match it."

"The perpetrator's DNA and fingerprints may or may not be on the cane," Capone said.

Sonya let out a grim chuckle. "And even if there theo-retically is fingerprint or DNA evidence, I'd like to meet the judge who would grant a blanket warrant to do DNA swabs on dozens of Geneva Bay's most prominent citi-zens. It's not like their fingerprints are likely to be in the FBI database, either." She turned to Capone. "You're going to need to build an ironclad case if you have any hope of getting a warrant to collect that kind of evidence."

Despite the "Dokter" last name, Sonya hailed from a family of prominent lawyers, and she'd learned the basics of criminal law like other kids learn their multiplication tables.

Capone's phone rang, and he stepped out of the room to answer it.

"I know it's not nice to say so, but I don't like most of the ones we're stuck here with," Melody said in a low voice. "I like Ms. Philips and Ms. Berney, but not Count Victor. He's mean, and Ms. Singhal seems fake to me. Mr. Huddleston seems like a phony, too. And Kennedy Criss! She's so awful that I'm actually embarrassed for her. She seemed so much nicer on TV."

"That reminds me," I said. "I need to call Biz and let her know what's going on." I dialed her number and set the phone on the counter, pressing the speaker button.

She answered on the third ring. "Make it quick. I'm doing a Mornay sauce and I don't want my milk to boil over."

"Hi, Biz," Melody called from across the kitchen.

Biz's voice brightened. "Is that Melody's voice I hear?" As usual, her snappishness was reserved for blood relatives. The more DNA you shared with her, the less tolerant she became.

"Yep. We're all here," I replied. "You're on speaker." Everyone chimed in with hellos, and I gave her a quick rundown of our situation. Upon hearing that we'd be spending the evening with her nemeses, Biz grunted in disgust.

"Sounds like the wrong person was murdered," she said.

"I can't understand why Huddleston doesn't just show that wife of his the door," Rabbit said. "She's a real piece of work."

"Mr. Huddleston would not want to lose so much money if he leaves her," Jarka said.

Sonya nodded. "I bet their prenup agreement is rock-solid. People as rich as that don't mess around."

"Oh, for sure. Biz heard from a former student of hers who's a paralegal downtown that their prenup accounts for, like, everything and he won't see a penny," Melody added.

"What are you guys talking about?" I asked. "If he has a prenup with her, then shouldn't that protect his money?"

Sonya's delicately penciled eyebrow arched upward. "*His* money?" She shook her head. "*She's* the heiress."

Biz's tinny voice came through the speaker of the phone. "Everything is hers—the house, the boat, every dime of the money."

Seeing my confused look, Melody continued in a slow, deliberate tone—the kind you might use to explain something to someone who'd recently undergone a frontal lobotomy. "Her parents own Criss Communications. That's how she got that job doing the weather for one of their TV stations."

I looked at them blankly. "You're saying B.L. can't leave Kennedy because she has a prenup to protect her money?"

"That's right," Biz said. "He'd probably come away with nothing in a divorce."

"I thought Huddleston was some kind of bigwig." I shook my head. "I'm sure he said he was an investment manager."

"Kennedy gave him some of her money to play around

with, to keep him busy, but he doesn't have a bean of his own," Biz said.

"Maybe a little from his previous divorce settlements," Sonya said. "But Kennedy is the one with the dinero. B.L. is her trophy husband. Apparently, he's a charmer. Personally, I don't see the appeal, but then I'm not really much of a lady's man's lady, if you know what I mean." She winked playfully. "She's his third wife, and each time he marries up the ladder."

"This is what Biz has discovered," Jarka said.

Yeesh. Apparently, even Jarka knew more about the results of my aunt's months-long stalking efforts than I did. I had to admit that I'd been less than generous with my attention when it came to Biz's quest to reclaim her cottage. Every time she'd brought it up, I'd shut her down. I didn't want to admit it, even to myself, but on some level I resented that she wasn't grateful to me for uprooting my life to live near her. I was also hurt that she'd barely acknowledged how I went out of my way to make her comfortable in mine and Butterball's house. As the unkind thoughts bubbled to the surface, a pang of guilt tickled my solar plexus. She didn't ask for any of it. Those had been my choices. She'd lost her house in part because *I* hadn't been able to protect her. All she wanted was someone to empathize with her. To listen.

And I, feminist that I claimed to be, had been so sure that the picture before me—a suave older man with a younger, blond wife—was the typical sugar daddy scenario that I hadn't even considered that Kennedy could be the one calling the shots.

"Haven't you been listening to me for the past two months?" Biz demanded. "Why do you think I've been pulling all those property deeds and public records since they took my cottage?"

"Please, Auntie Biz. Stop saying they took it. They *bought* it out of foreclosure," I reminded her. "And you need to stop with the research. You have an unhealthy obsession with them."

"Well, I guess not everyone is lucky enough to have a fiancé ride in on his white Tesla to give them a big mansion to live in," Biz said.

"You live in that big mansion, too," I countered.

"Only because those people took my house. I have a right to know what they're doing to it."

"It's not your house anymore," I seethed, gritting my teeth. Biz's sauce wasn't the only thing in danger of boiling over. I took a deep, steadying breath. "You know what? We've got work to do. Make sure you have a flashlight and pellets for the woodstove in case the power goes out. We'll see you in the morning."

"I was riding out Wisconsin storms long before you were born, missy," Biz retorted. She hung up before I could.

Why did Auntie Biz have to be so hardheaded? Why did she have to goad me?

I looked around the kitchen, expecting to see my exasperation mirrored on the faces of my staff. Instead of agreement, though, I saw a gallery of reproachful expressions.

"You didn't know about any of that?" Sonya asked. "Biz talks about them all the time. I know more about their money situation than I do about my own."

"Why should I know about the financial and marital arrangements of my aunt's former neighbors? It's none of my business. Or yours. Or *hers*!" I barked toward the now-blank phone screen.

"You're right, Chef. Miss O'Leary seems to care a lot

about it, though," Rabbit said, not meeting my eyes. "I suppose I listened for her sake."

I grimaced. I'd tuned Biz out. Shut her down whenever she brought up the subject.

I shook my head, trying to deflect blame. "Oh, come on! You know how she can be. You said yourselves she talks about it all the time. She's been like a broken record for months. It's driving me nuts."

They all turned back to their work.

I sighed, conceding defeat. "Fine."

"You're going to apologize to her?" Melody looked up, surprised.

"No, she'd hate that." I sighed again, the weight of guilt heavy in my chest. "I'll bake her a fruit pie. That's the traditional act of contrition in our family."

Sonya gave her head a weary shake. "O'Leary women. Some shrink should write a book about you."

"I wouldn't read it, and neither would Biz. She's more of a crossword puzzle gal," I said with a sad smile.

Sonya laid a sympathetic hand on my back, which somehow made me feel worse.

I turned to her and lowered my head. A rush of words tumbled out, unbidden. "Why does Biz hate living with me so much? She's so desperate to find a loophole so she can get her old place back. I've tried to make the house nice for her, but she just wants to get away from me."

"Oh, Dee. Her beef with the Huddleston-Crisses isn't about you," Sonya said. "She misses her old life. She's frustrated with herself for getting in the financial position to lose her independence. But that doesn't mean she doesn't love you. She's a stubborn woman who has trouble accepting defeat or admitting mistakes." She tipped her chin toward me. "Not that you'd know anything about that."

My crew had stopped working, their eyes trained on me. As we were talking, I'd been julienning fresh basil to sprinkle over our finished pies. I looked down to find a pile of wet, green smithereens. I firmed up my quivering jaw and slapped the knife down. "Am I the only one who has a dinner to prep? Get to it."

"*Oui*, Chef," they said in unison.

They scurried back to their tasks while I scraped the ruined herbs into the garbage disposal and began again. *O'Leary women don't cry.* That, at least, Auntie Biz and I could agree on.

CHAPTER 14

Capone returned to the kitchen just as the Delilah and Biz soap opera was wrapping up. He cleared his throat, his face stern.

"Were you outside?" I asked, noticing that he was wet from the rain.

"Yeah, while I was on the phone with the station, I got my service weapon. It was locked in my car," he replied.

The air in the room got heavier. My team and I stopped working for a moment and looked at one another. *Did he say he went to get his gun?*

"Why do you get this weapon?" Jarka asked.

"For protection. Yours and everyone else's." Turning to address the whole group, he said, "You do realize that finding the cane changes things significantly?"

"You said you talked to the police station," Sonya said. "Does that mean they're sending someone to clear the road so we can get out of here?"

"They will, won't they? They can't just leave us," Melody said.

While Melody looked distressed, Rabbit looked solemn. He put a pan of garlic knots in the oven to warm. "They ain't gonna help us."

"I'm afraid Rabbit's right," Capone said. "There are

motor vehicle collisions all over the county and live power lines down. They're not going to pull crews off of those scenes to attend to a hypothetical danger. We just don't have the manpower."

"So we're stuck in the middle of a crime scene," I said. "Geez, this is crazy. If Melody hadn't found the cane, that could've led to someone getting away with murder."

"They still might get away with it if I don't do my job," Capone said. "Sloppy police work lets bad guys off the hook all the time. I can't be a one-man police force, though. I need you all to be my allies, extra sets of eyes and ears. When help arrives, I want to be able to hand over an organized, methodical report, and well-preserved physical evidence. If this was a murder, I want to make sure when we catch the person who killed Edgar Clemmons we haven't compromised the investigation by being careless or getting caught up in distractions. And more than anything, I want fourteen people and two cats safe at the end of this."

I dropped my eyes. He was right. I'd been caught up in my family drama with Biz and led my crew into a gossipfest about Kennedy and B.L.'s prenup. Meanwhile Edgar Clemmons lay dead, most likely murdered, two rooms away. There was no way on earth I'd ever make it as a detective. An Old West sheriff? That, you could sign me up for. But the job of a modern police officer required too much patience and restraint. I'd watched Capone work enough times to know that I wasn't cut out to gradually build a case or file a bunch of hoop-jumping paperwork just to be able to arrest someone, especially someone whose guilt was obvious.

"I appreciate that this is a strange situation," he continued. "Officer Rettberg's at the station trying to build up some background on Clemmons, figure out his connections to the other guests. Sonya, could you answer a few questions about him to help us fill in the blanks?" He looked at me. "I know you're in the middle of service."

"Well, considering I left Sonya fifty different times during prep, the least I can do is give her a break now. Besides, I think we're ready to serve," I said.

Capone took a seat on one of the stools at the center island. He picked up his pencil and note-filled legal pad from where he'd left them earlier.

Sonya wiped her hands on her apron and leaned on the counter opposite him.

"I'll go get everyone gathered at the table real quick," Melody said.

"And me and Jarka can start bringing the food in," Rabbit said, following in her wake.

I picked up a silicone mitt and used it to take hold of a hot pizza pan, intending to clear the kitchen so that Sonya and Capone could speak alone.

"Do you mind hanging back?" Capone asked. "Since you were the last one to talk to Clemmons, I might need you."

"Of course."

Once the three of us were alone, Capone turned to Sonya. He held out the two books. "I was hoping you could take another look at these. See if you can think why Clemmons would've given them to you. What message was he trying to send?"

Sonya paged through them slowly and wrinkled her forehead. "Dee, tell me again what he said."

I repeated it back to her. "'Here's a title that I know all too well. And the plot of *The Maltese Falcon* is more realistic than you might imagine.' And then, 'These books are a small part of a much larger collection.'"

"Edgar loved word puzzles and riddles," Sonya said.

"He was so precise in his language." She looked up to the ceiling, thinking. "*The Man Who Knew Too Much*," she said aloud. Her eyes narrowed. "He said it was a *title* he knew all too well?"

"Yep."

"Why would he say 'title' instead of 'book'? That's odd, right?" she said. She ran her finger over the words on the book's cover.

"'Title,'" I repeated, picking up on her line of reasoning. "You said that the book had nothing in common with the movies, other than the title, right?"

"Exactly. He knew that I'd know that, which must be why he emphasized that the message was for me in particular. The title of this book is the message, not the contents," she said. "I'd say Clemmons was trying to say *he* was a man who knew too much."

"You might be on to something," Capone said. "But what did he know too much about? Or who? What do you know about Clemmons? What's his background?"

"We mainly talked about old movies. I only met him a few months ago, and he wasn't very forthcoming about his private life," she said. "From the snippets I know, he worked in the rare manuscripts collection at the Newberry Library in Chicago for his whole career, and retired to Geneva Bay. He's been chairing the Friends of the Library board up until now. Pam Philips was supposed to take over as of tonight."

"How did he feel about that?" Capone asked.

"He wasn't happy about it, that's for sure. He referred to it as a coup," she said.

"A coup?" Capone's face remained impassive, but he scribbled furiously into his notebook.

"I got the impression that he was forced out. I tried to avoid the subject because he got so worked up when he talked about it," Sonya explained. "Isabel would know more about that backstory."

"He told Delilah you'd connected the dots for him about something. Any idea what he meant?"

She shook her head.

"Do you remember your last conversation with him?" Capone asked.

"Just the usual stuff. Humphrey Bogart. I said I thought *The Maltese Falcon* was better than *Key Largo*, which might be why he gave me that book. It was just a normal conversation." She paused, her forehead creasing. "Except . . ."

Capone tilted his head expectantly.

"He got up suddenly and said he had to make a call. When he came back, he seemed distracted and he left shortly after. That was a few days ago, the last time we talked."

Capone took down the details of the approximate date and time of the call. "I'll ask Rettberg to start working on a warrant for his phone records so we can find out who he might've called that day," he explained.

"He used my cell phone. He doesn't have his own."

"No phone?" he asked.

"Nope, he's kind of quirky that way," Sonya said. "Very anti-technology."

"Like Pam Philips," Capone noted. "Do you mind if I take a look at your call log?"

"Sure." Sonya reached into her cleavage and, with a little wiggling, extracted her phone from somewhere deep within her bra. Capone's mouth fell open as she held it out for him. "What?" She shrugged. "This dress doesn't have pockets."

"It's a chick thing," I assured him, taking the phone to hand it over to him. Glancing at the screen, though,

I noticed it hadn't lit up when I touched it. "Son, I think your battery's dead."

"Shoot. I need to get a new one. I was running the GPS on the way over and then playing music. Those apps always drain it."

"No problem," Capone said, looking a little relieved he didn't have to handle Sonya's boob phone. "I'll get Rettberg working on it. She should be able to get the logs from your provider." Looking over his notes, he asked, "What about friends? Who did he spend time with? Did he have a romantic partner?"

"Not that I know of," Sonya said. "He was a bit of a loner."

"What about enemies? Anyone who didn't like him?" Capone asked.

"Why would anyone not like him?" Sonya said.

I let out a dry laugh. "Really?"

"Well, *I* liked him."

"You like everyone." I turned to Capone. "I'm not sure she's a fair judge of who's normal. With some notable exceptions"—I said, laying my hand on my chest—"she gravitates toward weirdos."

Sonya crossed her arms over her chest. "I do not."

"What about when we were in culinary school and Weird Giana asked you to be her bridesmaid after you'd known her less than a month?" I asked.

"She wasn't weird," she countered. "She just had strong views on JFK's assassination."

"She had an emotional support snake," I reminded her. "And what about when Creepy Monica asked you to be her *actual bride* after you'd known each other less than a week?"

"Can we please return to the matter at hand?" Capone said.

Ignoring him, Sonya raised her palm in a "talk to the hand" gesture. "No, this needs to be settled once and for all. That was a misunderstanding. Monica's astrologer said she'd meet her soulmate that night and she assumed it was me because we were the only lesbians at that party and we both had tattoos of jukeboxes."

"Her tattoo was on her face."

"You're so judgmental sometimes," Sonya huffed.

"I love that you can make friends with anyone, Son. All I'm saying is that sometimes I wish you'd be more careful. Clemmons gave me some kind of coded message to pass along to you a few minutes before he died. If he was worried someone was after him, why did he tangle you up in this mess? That, plus the thing about you being the one to 'connect the dots' for him, like you held the key to why he was murdered. That's a lot of pressure to put on you."

"I'm sure I can figure it out if I just think about it long enough," Sonya said. "I don't want to let him down if giving me that message was the last thing he did."

"You shouldn't *have to* figure it out," I countered. "Think about it. Having access to information about his murderer puts a target on your back."

A crash sounded from the entrance to the kitchen. I turned to see Isabel, Zaria, Lola, and Pam standing there, slack-jawed. A large metal serving tray wobbled back and forth on the floor, before settling into stillness with a final clatter. Zaria bent down hastily to retrieve it, while Lola stood stiffer than a shop-window mannequin. Pam looked just plain confused.

Isabel's eyes were saucer-round. "Did you say '*murderer*'?"

CHAPTER 15

The kitchen fell silent. So much for keeping the circumstances of Clemmons's death under wraps. Capone closed his eyes and leaned his forehead against his knuckles. I pressed my lips tightly together, but it was too late. The cat was out of the bag—for the second time that night.

"Did you just say Edgar Clemmons was murdered?" Isabel asked.

"What are you all doing in here?" I stammered.

"We came to help bring out the food so you could come join us," Pam explained. "Now what was this about a murder?"

"I was speculating," I said.

"That didn't sound like speculation," Isabel countered, undeterred. "What were you saying about a coded message? Did something happen?"

"An accident is bad enough, but murder?" Zaria shook her head. "It doesn't even bear thinking about."

"I'm talking nonsense," I said. "I'm just worried about my cat. He probably feels guilty about what happened, and I can't find him." None of them seemed to be even remotely enticed by the red herring I was trying to offer them.

Capone's gaze caught on his mother. Of the four women,

she was the only one who'd remained motionless after the initial shock. "Are you okay, Mom?"

She attempted a half-hearted smile, but it morphed into a grimace. "Sure, baby, sure."

I'd almost forgotten about the storm outside, but it chose that moment to reassert itself. A white streak of lightning blazed across the sky, illuminating the kitchen. All of us, even Capone, jumped. The lights flickered and the air tingled with the electricity of the near-miss strike.

"It was a dark and stormy night," Sonya muttered.

Lola put her hand to her heart and turned to her son. "Could you go get my purse? It's with my coat in the front hall. I need to take a pill." Capone left the room, and returned a moment later with his mother's beaded clutch. She removed a prescription bottle, shook out a pill, and downed it without water. "For my nerves," she explained.

Isabel put a gentle hand on her back. "It's been a night, hasn't it?"

Pam removed her boa and placed it on the back of a chair. "I can't understand why someone would want Edgar dead."

"Can't you?" Isabel's eyebrows shot over the top of her round glasses.

"Do you know something? Was someone out to get him?" Capone asked.

"All of us, according to Edgar," Pam said.

"Don't joke, Pam," Isabel said. Turning to Capone, she explained. "Edgar was very bitter about being removed as the chair of the library board." She sighed. "Don't get me wrong. I got along fine with Edgar. We worked together for many years. But he had a difficult personality. For a long time, we could ignore it because he was an effective chair, and very knowledgeable. Over time, though, his outlook diverged too far from everyone else's."

"Meaning?" Capone asked.

"He hated fundraising. It requires so much extra work—events, schmoozing, PR—all the things Edgar hated to do. There had been an offer of a substantial donation that came with strings attached."

"A donation from who?" Capone asked.

Isabel looked over her shoulder and lowered her voice. "The Criss family."

"As in Kennedy Criss?" Capone clarified.

"That's right," Isabel said. "Criss Communications has a publishing arm, and Kennedy's parents have pressured other libraries in Wisconsin to let them exercise curatorial control over the collections. To highlight or ban certain titles. They want to have input on which authors to invite for events and which types of community organizations we allow to use the space for free. Kennedy herself had attended public forums in the past and offered 'helpful' suggestions for monetizing certain aspects of our operations. The rest of the board and I felt that the conditions they wanted to impose were against the whole ethos of what a public library should be about."

"But Clemmons was in favor of accepting their conditions?" Capone asked.

"Not initially, but they won him over. They flattered him. Got him on their side. He pressured the board to take their donation so we could move forward with the renovation more quickly. Essentially, to skip to the end of the fundraising campaign," Isabel explained.

"And you weren't willing to go along with it," Capone filled in.

"That's right. Edgar's term as chair was up for renewal.

I nominated Pam to replace him, and she was unanimously voted in," Isabel said.

"Of course I knew he would be bitter about it," Pam said with a weary wave of her hand. "But I'm used to taking flak. And I'm passionate about keeping the library the way it is. I could've offered to bankroll the whole renovation myself, but I believe strongly that a library isn't one person's pet project. We need to do events like this and get wealthy donors involved. I'll write a hefty check, of course. But it's just as important that the local Girl Scout troop and the local church softball league are doing fundraisers, too. They may not be able to give on the same scale, but their gifts are every bit as crucial. Probably more so."

I cut in. "You said you're committed to keeping the library the way it is, but Edgar told me you were going to make big changes. Something about robot librarians?"

Pam and Isabel looked at each other and laughed.

"Edgar was a Luddite," Isabel explained. "He thought digital books were practically a sign of the end times."

"Is this something you and Clemmons fought about?" Capone asked.

"We didn't see eye to eye, that's for sure," she replied. "I explained to him many times that I see e-books as an environmentally friendly addition to the old-fashioned printed kind. So many people predicted that Invisible Inc. and other companies like it would drive publishing into the ground. But the opposite has happened. Year on year, the market just keeps growing. It's democratized publishing. Not only that, but e-books ensure that more money flows to authors. Think about how many times a paperback can change hands. An author sees those royalties only once."

"Edgar said the same things to me," Zaria agreed. "He and I shared a passion for print. But I didn't share his concern for the future of libraries." She shook her head in a graceful, almost balletic movement of her swan-like neck. "Poor Edgar. His fears were unfounded. You've seen Pam's library. She has such an affection for books. She's my best customer."

"You better believe it!" Pam replied.

"So he took issue with Pam helping to usher in the age of digital books," Capone said. "And he had a different vision for fundraising. Seems like there were quite a few potential flash points on the board. But I still don't understand—if Kennedy Criss was such a persona non grata, how did she end up with a seat on the board? It seems like Edgar didn't like change, and the Crisses wanted to change the library from top to bottom. Wouldn't he have objected to Kennedy's appointment on those grounds, even if he was tempted by their financial offer?"

"She'd been trying to get a seat for years," Isabel explained. "Edgar had always resisted as strongly as the rest of us. He called her a Neanderthal. She doesn't even like reading. To her, books are a 'knowledge commodity.'" Isabel's tiny hands made air quotes. "Knowledge commodity! She actually said that at a public forum! Can you imagine?"

Sonya shot me a meaningful look and mouthed the word "barbarian." I glared back at her in return.

"And yet, she's on the board," Capone pointed out.

Pam laughed again. Instead of her usual wholehearted guffaw, though, it was a weak and mirthless *ha*. "Edgar knew that Kennedy would make our lives difficult, so once he found out I was replacing him, he made sure she got a seat on the board, just to spite us. Kennedy was

Edgar's parting gift to us. A poison pill he slipped in on his way out the door."

"She's a pill, all right," Isabel said, removing her round, wire-framed glasses and cleaning them on the sleeves of her oversized black coat. "Edgar invited her to serve on the board without consultation and without a vote. Procedurally, that's not allowed. We could've blocked it, but he'd already put out a press release. Once he announced it, it would've created considerable ill will to undo the appointment. The Crisses are a powerful family."

"So she's a pill with clout and money," Sonya observed.

"Exactly," Pam said. "Edgar knew that, and he knew we'd be stuck with her."

"The way you're questioning everyone," Zaria said to Capone. "It's like you're trying to find a motive. You really do think he was murdered, don't you?'

Another boom of thunder ricocheted around the kitchen, sending the hairs on my arms to stand at attention and bringing an end to that topic of conversation. We all fell silent.

Lola Capone removed her satiny gloves and folded them into her handbag. "If what happened to Edgar Clemmons wasn't an accident," she said, "Zaria's right—it doesn't bear thinking about. There's nothing we can do about it, at least not tonight."

"Agreed," Pam said. "We might as well eat." She walked toward the center island, where the freshly rewarmed pizzas waited. As she arrived at the counter, she stopped short. "What are my books doing down here?" She continued over to where the two volumes lay. She shot a disapproving look at me and Sonya. "You should've asked before borrowing them."

"Those are yours?" I asked.

"Of course," Pam said. "From my library."

I reached for the books to hand them to Pam.

Zaria gasped. She rushed over and pushed my hands away. "Don't touch them! They should only be handled with clean, dry hands, and they shouldn't be anywhere near food or liquids."

"I thought Pam just said they were her books," I said, taking note of Zaria's overprotective reaction.

"I brokered the deal for Pam to buy them. These are the books Kennedy was upset about. The ones she wanted for her husband," Zaria replied. "They're extremely valuable."

"How valuable?" Capone asked.

"This is a rare 1930 first edition," Zaria explained, gazing lovingly at the cover of *The Maltese Falcon*. "I've never seen one in such good condition. It's valued at around thirty-eight thousand dollars."

Sonya let out a long whistle.

"I paid over fifty, but it was worth it," Pam said with a wink.

Given what I knew about their rivalry, I doubted Kennedy Criss would agree. What I'd previously understood to be a petty game between two rich ladies suddenly made a lot more sense.

"What about the other one?" Capone asked.

"The Man Who Knew Too Much by G.K. Chesterton. Also a first edition, valued around nine thousand dollars," Zaria said.

"Also with the original dust jacket?" Isabel asked, looking reverently from the volumes to Pam. "I didn't know you owned these. How did you even find them?"

"Victor knows a European collector with a very impressive library," Zaria replied. "Knowing the demand for detective fiction in the US market, I begged Victor to persuade his friend to let me sell these."

"I still don't understand," Pam said. "Why are these down here? Did one of you want to read them?"

"Edgar—" Sonya began.

Capone jumped in, cutting her off. "We came across them and didn't realize they were yours, or how valuable they were." He turned his back to the others and shot Sonya and me a look. He clearly felt that enough beans had been spilled for one evening.

"How strange," Pam said. "Well, let's get them out of the kitchen. Steam and heat and splatter aren't good for rare books."

"I'll be happy to take them," Isabel offered, taking a step closer. "I'd love to get a good look at them. It's rare to see first editions in mint condition."

"It's best not to handle them unless you've washed and dried your hands thoroughly to remove any dirt or oils," Zaria said.

"I know that," Isabel huffed. "I *am* a librarian." She walked to the sink and began to scrub her hands.

"I thought you were supposed to wear white gloves when you touch old books," Sonya said.

"A popular myth," Isabel explained. "Gloves make your fingers less sensitive, which makes it more likely you could damage the book."

"And gloves can actually attract dirt more easily than clean, dry hands," Zaria added.

"But your hands must be completely free of dirt, oils, and lotions, so you should wash them immediately before you handle the volumes and touch nothing else, not even your own face," Isabel said. She'd finished her elaborate washing ritual and was homing in on the books.

"You're not wearing nail polish, are you?" Zaria put her hands on her hips.

"Never," Isabel said. "Personally, I won't even risk clear polish."

"I remove all my jewelry, and put my hair back, too, although some people think that's overkill," Zaria replied, escalating their nerdier-than-thou back-and-forth.

"It's best if you leave the books with me for the time being," Capone said, moving between them and the counter.

Zaria, Pam, and Isabel eyed his ungloved, un-sanitized hands as if he'd just threatened to strangle a kitten. It struck me how casually I'd handled the books, having no idea I was stuffing the equivalent of an entire year's salary into my apron pocket. Then a further thought struck me. If Clemmons had spent his career handling rare books at the Newberry Library, why hadn't *he* taken more care with them? I could clearly picture his bare fingers running over their covers.

Turning my attention back to the conversation, I heard Pam say, "I really think they're safer back in the library."

Before they could resolve the standoff, Sonya raised her hand. "Does anyone else hear that sizzling sound? Like electricity crackling?"

We all stood silent for a moment. There was indeed a strange buzzing in the air, so low-pitched that I felt, rather than heard, it. Suddenly, a thunderous boom echoed through the kitchen, blinding light flashed, and then everything went dark.

CHAPTER 16

Another streak of lightning split the sky, briefly spot-lighting the rainswept landscape of turbulent trees out-side the windows. The only light in the kitchen came from a single gas burner, which I'd turned on low to warm the extra red sauce. Through the darkened space, a peal of thunder echoed.

"I think a transformer exploded." Lola's voice was a whisper, which seemed appropriate given how quiet it was.

"I was wrong before. *Now* it's a dark and stormy night," Sonya said, reaching out to take hold of my hand.

A stampede of footsteps rumbled down the hallway, and the rest of the house's occupants entered the kitchen. Jarka and the Count led the pack, illuminating the way with their phones' flashlights.

"What's going on?" Victor demanded. Zaria rushed to his side, insinuating herself between him and Jarka.

"Transformer explosion," I explained.

"The generator is supposed to kick in automatically to power the basics—the heating, the sump pump, and the fridge—but I don't hear it," Pam said. She opened the fridge door, and sure enough, the lightbulb didn't come on.

"So the generator doesn't power the lights?" Isabel asked.

"I'm afraid not. The wiring in this house is complicated, and it didn't seem worth it to me," Pam said. "But
there are plenty of candles around, and we can get the
fireplaces going."

Kennedy let out an exasperated grunt. "Well, this is
just great," she said. "Now we get to spend the night
in the dark with a dead man." She grabbed hold of her
husband's hand and stomped toward the dining room.
"Come on, Brian, I need a drink."

"Good idea," I said. "Daniel, could you get another
round of cocktails going? I think we're going to need
them." Dranger be damned. If we were going to get
through the night, our only hope was to get good and
liquored up.

Jarka set her phone inside a large metal sieve, which
peppered the room with faint, disco-ball speckles of
light. It cast a strange, pretty charm over the grim setting.

"I might need to go outside and start the generator
manually," Pam said.

"I'll come with you," Capone offered.

"Do you have a coat?" Pam asked. "The rain is ham-
mering down."

"I've got a winter jacket in the car," he replied.

"What should the rest of us do?" Melody asked.

"Well, we still have to eat," I observed.

The next few minutes passed in a flurry of activity. Pam
and Capone braved the storm to try to start the generator.
Melody and Sonya found candles and began illuminating the rooms. Victor led Zaria out of the kitchen by the
light of his phone flashlight, while Rabbit started a blaze
going in the dining room fireplace. Isabel helped Daniel ferry the drinks and Lola finished setting the table.
Meanwhile, Jarka brought out the rest of the food.

Little by little, the bustle slowed and everyone except

Pam and Capone drifted to the table. Without intending to, the group naturally separated, with me and my staff on one side and Lola Capone, the Huddleston-Crisses, Zaria, and Victor on the other. Isabel sat at the head, with empty places on the other end waiting for Pam and Capone. So much for forgetting about the upstairs-downstairs distinctions.

Dinner was a slightly more ramshackle affair than I'd originally planned, but at least the power outage happened *after* the food had a chance to warm through. With the glow of the candelabras, the flickering firelight, and the smell of garlic and baked bread filling the air, I was struck again by the incongruous hominess of the scene.

We laid on a feast of salad and appetizers, along with one each of the restaurant's signature deep-dish creations: the tongue-scorching Red Hot Mama; our umami-rific eggplant and sausage pizza; a tangy, creamy Curried Cauliflower calzone; and the Gouda and spinach masterpiece we called The Deep Dutch. I set Zaria's special free-from pizza at her place along with a dish of our green apple, pepita, and cranberry salad, the ingredients of which, by luck, met her exacting dietary standards. The spread contained enough food for at least twice the number of people in attendance, but without reliable refrigeration there was little point in trying to salvage it for yet another reheating.

"This looks amazing," Isabel said, lowering her face toward her plate to inhale the aromas. "And smells phenomenal."

"I could eat a horse," B.L. said, shoveling a large piece of Red Hot Mama pizza onto his plate with his usual showy bonhomie.

As the bowls and platters made their way around the table, I watched expectantly as Zaria cut into a slice of her free-from concoction. The peacock feather on her turban bobbed contentedly as she took a mouthful and slowly chewed. "Wow, this is actually really good."

"Don't seem so surprised," Isabel said.

"Especially since we bent over backward to accommodate your impossible request," I heard Sonya mutter.

"Oh, of course I didn't doubt you. I just don't know how you pulled it off," Zaria replied. "My diet can be very problematic. No gluten and all that."

"Are the nightshades an allergy?" Isabel asked, lifting a dainty forkful of food toward her mouth. "I've never heard of that one before."

"Yes. Sadly, I swell up like a puffer fish if I get any dairy, or gluten, or nightshades," Zaria said with a self-conscious laugh.

While I understood the reason for Isabel's curiosity, I personally didn't like to press people on the reasons for their dietary choices. As a chef, I wanted people to eat out as safely and comfortably as possible, regardless of their reasons for following a particular diet.

Sensing Zaria's seeming discomfort with the attention, Rabbit piped up. "My daughter's allergic to peanuts. It's a hard thing to live with. Real scary."

"One of my sisters can't eat shellfish, which is a terrible fate for a Puerto Rican," Daniel said.

"*Pobrecita,*" Lola said.

"I know exactly how that is, which is why I'm so grateful," Zaria said, with a relieved smile. "Would anyone else like to share some of this delicious pizza?" She pushed the pizza toward the center of the table.

"I wouldn't mind a slice," I said. "It's rare for me to serve something without practicing it a few times."

I had tasted each ingredient of the free-from pizza as I cooked, and was satisfied that I made my best possible attempt. Still, I wasn't totally sure what to expect as I lifted a slice and bit into it. Just as a cute dress, a well-tailored jacket, and a killer pair of boots don't always combine to make a flattering outfit, you can never be totally confident that a novel combo of ingredients is going to make a great dish.

This time, however, the result was runway-ready. Full of savory flavor, the nutritional yeast captured the nutty intensity of Parmesan, while the butternut squash and beet sauce was sweet and tangy. The gluten-free crust was standing strong despite being subjected to reheating and delayed service. I hesitated to call it a perfect specimen of pizza—the textures were less satisfying than the real deal and the faux cheese didn't stretch the same way. But it was a tasty dish in its own right. Maybe not a water-into-wine miracle, but certainly an example of turning lemons into lemonade.

"You know what I just realized?" Melody said. "If those trees had fallen a few minutes earlier, the entire party would be trapped here. How weird would that be?"

"This is plenty weird for me," Sonya replied, glancing around the table and then toward the drawing room where Edgar Clemmons still lay.

"Since we *are* trapped," Victor cut in, dabbing at his mouth with a napkin, "where will we sleep? Presuming we must remain here all night."

"Pam and I were talking about it earlier, but we didn't really settle on a plan," Isabel said.

"Well, there are nine bedrooms—six upstairs, plus the former servants' hall on the third floor, which has three additional bedrooms," B.L. said.

We all looked at him, surprised at his knowledge of the house's setup.

"That's right," Isabel said, tilting her head toward

him. "The original owners mostly used this house in the summer, and since heat rises, the upper floor was the least desirable."

"Why do you know so much about the house?" I asked B.L.

He and Kennedy exchanged a glance. "We looked at this house when it was on the market," he said.

"How should we decide who stays where, then?" Lola asked. "Draw straws?"

"Don't be silly," Kennedy replied. "Pam keeps her room, Isabel has another, then Detective Capone and his mother each have one, which makes four. That leaves me with Brian, and Zaria and Victor." She counted out each pairing on her fingers. "Then the bartender and"— she flicked her remaining fingers toward Rabbit—"*him* in one of the servants' rooms. The girls"—she indicated me, Melody, Sonya, and Jarka—"can sleep in the other two servants' rooms. Easy-peasy."

"That doesn't seem fair," Zaria protested. "If the top-floor rooms are less desirable."

"They're a bit drafty and spare, especially compared to the main bedrooms," Isabel affirmed. "I think we *should* draw straws."

Kennedy crossed her arms over her chest. "My plan makes sense. Besides, I'm not comfortable sleeping next to people I don't know," she said, eyeing my staff. "I heard about the restaurant people saying Edgar was murdered. I'm sure everyone has realized by now what that means?" She raised her eyebrows expectantly. When no one answered, she continued. "Someone in this room might be a murderer."

"Don't say that," Zaria snapped. It was the first time I'd heard her be sharp with anyone. "How do we even know he was murdered? And if he was, the person who did it could've come in from the outside."

Kennedy waved away the suggestion. "All the same, I don't think we should have to sleep on the same floor as people who don't move in our circle."

Rabbit shifted uncomfortably in his chair, no doubt glad that his criminal past wasn't public knowledge. Melody, too, seemed to shrink in her chair. Sonya and Daniel exchanged offended looks. Jarka continued eating with calm detachment.

I pressed my palms hard on the table. Kennedy's overt classism caught me off guard. One thing I loved about Geneva Bay was that it lacked the kind of entrenched snobbery you might find in ritzy destinations in Europe or on the East Coast. "Old" money here could be aged in decades, not centuries. That wasn't to say you never saw people flexing if their families owned one of the particularly noteworthy historic homes, or if they were part of one of the original "clubs" of wealthy Chicagoans who came to Geneva Bay looking for a spot where they could build side-by-side vacation cottages, replicating the social order of the city on a smaller scale. But it was uncommon for someone to pull rank based on money. And I sure as heck didn't like it. *Capone's mom probably won't be impressed by your potent right hook*, I cautioned myself.

"Look here," I said, seething. "Who says we're comfortable with *you*, either? I know my people, and I trust them."

"Well, *I* don't," Kennedy replied primly.

"You don't have to," I said. "We all have alibis, unlike you. Daniel was making drinks at the bar when Edgar was killed. Everyone saw him. Rabbit and Sonya were in the kitchen together. They didn't even know what happened until later."

"And Melody and Jarka were both serving," Lola added. "I saw them while I was singing."

"And I took canapés from each of them just before I went up to speak," Isabel said.

"What about you?" Kennedy asked, swishing her blond hair in my direction.

I paused, realizing that I'd been hidden away at the back of the room spying on Zaria and Victor when Edgar fell. Me vouching for myself wasn't likely to hold much water. For all the times Capone had told me to butt out of an investigation, this was the first time I wished he were here to shut down this highly uncomfortable line of questioning.

Luckily, Zaria swooped in to save me. "I was talking to her just before it happened, and then I saw her again when Edgar fell. She reached him just before Victor and I did."

"That's true. I saw Delilah standing at the back of the room when I got up to give my speech," Isabel said. "Out of curiosity, Kennedy," she continued, taking hold of the salad spoons nonchalantly, "where were you and B.L.? I don't remember seeing either of you when I was speaking."

Somewhere deep within the house, a door slammed.

CHAPTER 17

We eyed one another warily around the firelit table, startled by the sound of the slamming door.

"What was that?" Melody whispered.

"Probably Detective Capone and Ms. Philips," Jarka said coolly, marking the first time she'd interjected herself into the conversation.

I thought she was probably right, but still, as footsteps echoed along the hall, I took hold of my butter knife by the hilt. My jumpiness proved unwarranted when, a moment later, Capone and Pam returned from their mission, dripping wet and windswept, looking like they'd been at the helm of a fishing trawler.

Capone removed his puffy down coat and shook off the beaded rainwater. "I'll go hang our coats to dry."

Lola watched her son depart. "Any joy with the generator?" she asked Pam.

"Yes, thank goodness," Pam said, picking up a cloth napkin from the table to wipe the rain from her face. "The sump pump is on so the basement won't flood, and heat's kicked on so we won't freeze to death. Luckily, your son's as handy with machines as he is with the piano."

Of course he was. But who needed a guy who's smart,

good with his hands, musically gifted, and looked like a million bucks in a tuxedo? Not me. I had my cat—

No sooner had the thought crossed my mind than an orange mound of fur made an ungainly leap onto the table. Kennedy screamed and jumped to her feet, knocking over her chair. Isabel's drink went flying, her cocktail glass smashing against the floor.

"Butterball!" I scolded. I'd temporarily forgotten that he was marauding around the house. No doubt the smell of food had attracted him like a homing beacon.

"I'll get something to clean up the glass," Rabbit said.

"I'm so sorry," I said, scooping the cat up.

"Jangled my nerves a bit, but I'm okay," Isabel said.

Zaria rose to help Isabel mop up her drink. She switched on her phone's flashlight and shined it on the floor. "Watch out for broken glass," she cautioned.

"Let the restaurant people clean the mess. They're used to such things," Victor said. He took her by the wrist and pulled her back into her seat. "You should conserve your mobile's battery. You might need it." His hooded eyes regarded Butterball with disdain. "This is your cat, I take it?"

I nodded. Kind of hard to pretend I didn't know the furball who was pressing his forehead against my chin.

Pam pointed to the fireplace. "Oh, look, there's Gloria, too."

I turned to find a dainty little angel of a cat perched on top of the hearth. Although I loved my own cat deeply, I didn't have anywhere near an encyclopedic knowledge of cat breeds. When Capone described Gloria as a Ragdoll cat, I pictured some kind of tatty-furred stray. What I saw, though, was much more "doll" than "rag." Gloria was so snowy white she practically qualified for sainthood, and even in the semidarkness her sapphire eyes sparkled. I imagined everyone in the room comparing her to the furry chonkster writhing unhappily in my arms, trying to free himself so he could once again run amok on the feast table.

Daniel rose from his chair and laid a hand on Isabel's back. "I'll make you a fresh drink."

"Another double, please, dear," she said. "I could get used to having a bartender around all the time. You didn't answer my question, Kennedy. Where were you when Edgar fell?" Isabel asked, undeterred.

Kennedy looked at her husband.

"If you must know," B.L. said, "we stepped outside for some fresh air."

We ate in silence for a few moments. Capone returned to the table, and the rest of the meal passed quickly. Isabel, with her usual pep, tried to keep the conversation flowing, but most everyone seemed exhausted by the day's events and ready to put an end to the awkward togetherness of the forced dinner party.

As the meal wound down, Pam put her hand over her mouth and yawned. "Did we sort out the sleeping arrangements?"

"Yes," Sonya said. "The D and S crew will take the servants' quarters."

I opened my mouth to protest, but Sonya kicked me under the table.

"It's not worth it, *jefa*," Daniel whispered to me. "We could sleep in a pigsty and we'd still be better than her."

I knew they were right. While I found Kennedy's snootiness supremely irritating, her proposed arrangement kept me far away from her, which was my main, and in fact only, criterion for an acceptable sleeping place. It also meant I'd be on a floor with a group of people I trusted. I sipped the last of my drink—a South Side

Fizz—letting the alcohol mellow me out. Luckily, the gin seemed to have soothed everyone, and it was probably best if I didn't take it upon myself to start a socialist revolution.

"Well, I don't care where everyone sleeps, but I'd like you all to lock your bedroom doors," Capone said. "As a precaution."

Pam grimaced. "I'm afraid that's a bit of a problem. I'm in the process of having keys made, but they're not done. I'd have to use the master key and lock everyone in their rooms from the outside. The doors are restored from the originals, and they need keys to lock from either side. A locksmith in Philadelphia who specializes in antiques is making the keys, but it takes months to even get on his list. For now, I've only got one set of master keys, so I don't usually lock the doors. It's only me here, after all."

"Well, I'm not letting anyone lock me up like a common criminal," Victor said.

"Me, either," Kennedy said.

Capone frowned, but there didn't seem to be much he could do about the situation.

"Well, that's that, I guess. We'll just have to try to keep our wits about us," Isabel said.

We rose from the table and I began to clear the dishes. "I got this," Rabbit said. "You all look beat."

"Are you sure?" I asked. He wasn't wrong to sense that I was exhausted. Usually, I enjoyed scrubbing, scouring, and tidying up almost as much as I did cooking, but that night the mere thought of it seemed overwhelming. "It's a lot to clean up."

"I can help," Isabel said. "Least I can do in gratitude for that wonderful meal."

I nodded gratefully, leaving them to the task. I had no

idea what time it was, but by the time Butterball, Daniel, me, and the other "girls" made our way up the stairs to the servants' quarters, I was bone-tired and more than a little tipsy. Capone had an extra battery backup for his phone, but almost everyone else's cell batteries were hovering in the red zone. Mine was on four percent. Rather than drain it further by using the flashlight app, I switched it off to conserve what little juice remained. We opted to share the various flashlights, candleholders, and other portable light sources lying around the place to guide us upstairs.

I'd taken an antique oil lamp, the dim illumination of which revealed a long hallway. The rain and sleet had finally tapered off, and in the windows over the staircases at each end of the hallway scattered pinpricks of snow could be seen floating in the blackness.

On the right were two small and sparsely decorated bedrooms, joined by a Jack-and-Jill bathroom. Beyond was an additional bedroom and bathroom. An open doorway separated the hallway into men's and women's sections. In the olden days, the heavy door probably would've been locked to keep everything prim and proper, but it stood open now, revealing another set of stairs. We hadn't seen this area during our pre-party tour, but based on the location of the stairs, I guessed they led to the dramatic fourth-story observation room and widow's walk.

"Guess this is for me and Rabbit," Daniel said, walking to the far end of the hall. He threw up his arms and let out a yawn. "Good night, *queridas*. Will you be okay? I don't mind keeping watch in the hall."

"We're good," I said. "You look exhausted. Get some sleep."

"We've got a guard cat for protection," Sonya added, giving Butterball a pat on the head.

Daniel blew us a kiss as he staggered along the hallway toward the men's side of the hall.

Away from the roaring dining room fire, the house was every bit as drafty as you might expect. The nineteenth-century version of Kennedy Criss who'd built the place probably hadn't bothered to insulate this floor, thinking that the servants weren't worth the trouble.

"My eyes want to close," Jarka said, kneading the back of her neck with her fingertips.

I nodded in agreement.

The women's bedrooms were each furnished with identical, narrow twin beds and four-drawer dressers. I chose one of the rooms at random, plunked Butterball onto the bed next to the dormered window, and set the lamp down on the dresser.

Sonya flopped on the other bed, face-first. With effort, she rotated her body toward me. Her makeup had taken on a "walk of shame" smudged effect, exaggerated by the shadowy light.

"I don't know what Daniel put in those drinks," she slurred, "but I'm sozzled."

I slumped onto the bed next to Butterball. "Me, too. Isabel had two doubles. I don't know how she's still upright."

"I guess drinking too much is an appropriate ending to a Prohibition-themed party." Sonya kicked off her shoes and sighed. "Poor Edgar. He didn't deserve what happened to him."

"No," I agreed. "He didn't."

Melody ducked her head into our room, curls bouncing. She was a nondrinker, and I suspected that, come morning, we'd all envy her lifestyle choice. "Mind if I get into the bathroom real quick? I really want to change out of this dress and back into my own clothes."

"I meant to ask Pam about the rest of us borrowing some comfortable clothes to sleep in," I said. "Oh, well." The mere idea of tromping back downstairs sapped the last of my energy. "Can you turn out the lamp, Mel?"

As the room went dark, I pulled off my chef's jacket and work pants and piled them in a heap next to the bed. A camisole and underpants would have to serve as pajamas. Although the room was downright chilly, the feather-filled comforter felt as cozy as Cloud Nine. Without so much as a good night to Sonya, I curled up alongside Butterball's warm body, and my lights, too, went dark.

CHAPTER 18

Pat. Pat. Pat.

"Buuuutterbaaaaall," I groaned.

Mee-ow, he screeched in reply.

Pat. Pat. Pat.

The room was pitch black and silent. I rolled over, pulling the blanket over my drowsy head to block my cat's insistent paws. The unfamiliar, lavender scent of the linens stirred me to a gradual realization that I wasn't in my own bed. *Oh, yeah. I'm trapped in a remote mansion with a bunch of random rich people and a dead guy.*

Thump.

I threw off the blanket and wrapped it around me like a cape, wondering what Butterball had knocked over. Probably a priceless Ming vase or something. At least nothing seemed to have shattered this time. Groping along the wall, my hand found the light switch, but flicking it on had no effect. *Oh, yeah, no power.* The floor creaked.

"Butterball?" I called. "Sonya?"

All at once, a shadowy figure came thundering past me, knocking me backward into the wall. I cried out, and Butterball matched me decibel for decibel with a shriek of his own. Discombobulated, I took a couple of staggery steps after whoever had hit me. On the other side of the room, the door of the bathroom that connected the rooms flew open to reveal Melody. She was bleary-eyed and rumple haired, clearly just aroused from sleep. The retreating figure's footsteps thudded along the hallway and down the stairs. I closed the door behind them and leaned against it as Melody held her phone's flashlight aloft, using it like a spotlight to pan the room.

"What was that noise?" she asked.

"There was somebody in here," I whispered, my voice revealing more panic than I would've liked. I crossed the room and removed the glass top from the oil lamp, feeling around the table for the lighter. "Son, did you see anything?" I called over my shoulder.

Silence.

I turned just as Melody's flashlight beam found Sonya. My best friend lay in her bed, perfectly still. Her covers had been thrown aside, exposing her pale white body, still in its glorious beaded dress. Her arms lay limp at her sides. A pillow covered her face.

"Why isn't she moving?" Melody asked. She began to intone a desperate, terrified half prayer. "Oh my gosh. Oh god. Oh god."

The five steps it took me to cross the room were the longest distance I'd ever covered. I was traveling both too quickly and too slowly, my body divorced from my mind. In the shaking light of Melody's flashlight, I threw off the pillow that covered Sonya's face.

Sonya. Lovely Sonya. My favorite person. Blue-tinged skin. Closed eyes. Perfect stillness. I shook her by the shoulders, but she didn't stir. Her head with its glossy, wavy hair flopped from side to side.

"Jarka!" I called, my voice cracking. "Help me! Please!"

I laid Sonya back down, trying to feel for a pulse.

"Jarka!" I called again. Why wasn't she coming?

At last, heavy footsteps pounded in and Jarka appeared. She touched Sonya's neck and wrists.

"More light," she commanded. "She is not breathe."

Melody held her phone aloft as I hurried to light the oil lamp. In the seconds it took for me to return to them, Jarka, with Melody's help, had heaved Sonya onto the floor and started chest compressions. She pinched my sweet friend's nose and forced air into her mouth. Once. Twice.

Hhhhhhuh. A wheezy sound emerged from the floor. Then another. Jarka sat back and gently stroked her patient's head, whispering in Bulgarian. Sonya coughed and wheezed again. The rise and fall of her chest was the most precious thing I'd ever seen.

I slumped to the floor, nearly spilling the fluid from the lamp. Melody knelt beside me and raised her eyes to the ceiling. "Thank you."

We each clung on to a different part of Sonya's body, as if she were our life raft. As if we were the ones who'd almost gone under, instead of her. Little by little, the color returned to her skin.

"*Slava Bogu.* She is alive," Jarka whispered.

"What happened?" Sonya squeaked, her voice ragged. She freed her hand from Melody's grasp and pressed it against her forehead. "I have such a headache. Did I faint again?"

"If Butterball hadn't woken me up . . ." I swallowed hard, unable to give voice to the what-ifs. "I think someone tried to suffocate you."

Her eyes, already dramatically outlined by her period makeup and the strange lighting, widened in shock. "Who did *what* now?" She paused. "I had a dream. I thought it was a dream. That I was under the ice in a frozen lake. I was struggling to break through."

Butterball sidled into the crook of her hip, purring. I smooshed my face into his back. "You saved her life, Bud. You've got a free pass to eat off the table for the rest of your life." I turned to Jarka, realizing she'd played a somewhat more direct role. "And you, too."

Jarka gave me the rarest of gifts—her smile. "I can also eat off the table, yes?"

We all collapsed into a relieved mixture of tears and laughter, hugging one another and Butterball. When the paroxysm of emotion subsided, we fell silent, suddenly aware of the shift in our circumstances. The murder was no longer theoretical. No longer a case of waiting to see what the medical examiner would say. The killer wasn't a mysterious outsider or a nameless, long-departed party guest. Edgar Clemmons *was* murdered and whoever did it was still among us.

"I feel strange," Sonya said. She touched her own face. "Like I'm dreaming. I'm so tired." Jarka and I gently lifted her and got her settled back in bed alongside Butterball.

"It's probably the shock," Melody said. "Or the lack of oxygen."

"No." Jarka nodded vigorously. By now, we were all accustomed to the unorthodox way that Bulgarians nodded to mean "no" and shook their heads from side to side to mean "yes." She grabbed the phone flashlight from Melody and shined the beam into my face.

I squinted and blinked as she peered into my eyes.

"Do you not also feel this, what Sonya is saying?" she asked. "Very tired and like you're thinking with mud inside your head?"

"We all had a lot to drink . . ." I began. I stopped my-self. "But you're right. I was *so* tired after dinner. My head was spinning. I only had two cocktails, and I can hold my liquor better than that."

"Me, also," Jarka said, her features sharpened by the way the shadows crisscrossed her face. "I can drink very, very much more without such effects. And I am light sleep person, but tonight I'm in such a sleep, like coma."

"We were all like that," I said. "Sleepy. Did you notice at dinner how the conversation tapered off once everyone started eating? B.L. practically nodded off in his pizza."

"I feel fine," Melody said.

I drummed my fingers against my lips. "Isabel seemed okay, too. Which was weird because she had as much or more alcohol as the rest of us, and she's tiny."

Jarka looked around the room. "Why has no one come? We have made many noises and they are right below."

"It's a well-built house. Maybe they can't hear," Sonya said.

A lump formed in my stomach. "Or maybe we were all drugged."

"How would someone have drugged us?" Melody asked. "We didn't all eat the same food at dinner. Unless it was in every dish, or most of them?"

"I don't see how. At least one of us was in the kitchen the whole night," Sonya said. "We would've noticed if someone who wasn't one of us was going around sprin-kling fairy dust onto all the food."

"Still, I think it's safe to assume that if most of *us* were affected, the others were, too," I said. "We need to check on everyone."

"Oh, cripes! Daniel!" Melody jumped up. "And Rab-bit," she added.

I rose and yanked on my clothes. "You stay with So-nya," I called to Jarka.

I took hold of the oil lamp and inspected our door, hoping to lock it behind me. I tried the key I still had from the pantry, but it didn't fit. I sighed in frustration, recalling what Pam had said about not having keys to fit all the doors. The house's period charm had well and truly worn off. "Bar the door with a chair, okay? And don't let anyone in unless it's us or Capone."

Melody and I hurried along the hallway. The door be-tween the men's and women's sides had been closed, but thankfully it wasn't locked.

When we reached the door to the men's bedroom, Melody asked, "Should we knock?" But I was already opening the door. This was no time to stand on cer-emony.

Rabbit bolted upright in bed, squinting in the lamp-light. "Chef? Melody? What are you guys doing in here?"

"Are you okay?" Melody asked.

"Yeah, why?" he said.

In the other bed, Daniel's body lay motionless. "Oh, no," Melody whispered.

Before we could take two steps, though, our concerns were allayed by an almighty snore. The covers rustled as Daniel rolled onto his stomach, letting out another snort-ing breath. The blankets slipped, revealing his bare back and the side of his well-muscled rump. Apparently, Dan-iel slept in the nude.

Melody gasped. Her eyes were so big they could've filled a fourteen-inch pizza pan.

"We'd better wake him up," I said, dragging her toward the bed. "Make sure he's okay."

"What's going on?" Rabbit asked.

"Someone came into our room," I explained. "We're

all okay, but whoever broke in tried to hurt Son. And Jarka thinks somebody slipped us a Mickey."

"What's wrong with this place?" Rabbit muttered, pulling off his blanket and putting his shoes on. "I thought I was joking when I said before about this being a Halloween party. It is, and we're in a danged haunted house. I can't wait to get outta here."

"You were up later than the rest of us," I said. "Did you see anything when you came upstairs after you cleaned up?"

He furrowed his brow. "Only weird thing I noticed was that Sonya's knife roll was left open downstairs and the paring knife wasn't in it."

A good set of knives could cost well into the hundreds of dollars. Sonya and I were both meticulous about caring for our knives, and I couldn't see her casually forgetting about one.

"I don't like the idea of a stray knife," I said. "Not tonight."

"Other than that," Rabbit continued, "the house was dead quiet. Except for Daniel's snoring, that is. Lucky I'm a heavy sleeper."

"And you're feel okay?" Melody asked.

"Bright-eyed and bushy-tailed, all things considered," he replied.

Melody and I crossed the room. I plopped her down on one side of Daniel's bed and took a seat on the other. I raised the lamp and shook him gently. "Daniel, you need to wake up."

He let out a groan as his eyelids fluttered open. He looked from me to Melody and his mouth widened into a sleepy smile. He rolled toward me and by some miracle we dodged an X-rated display when the corner of the blanket fell modestly across his waist area. He waggled his finger toward Melody and then me. "I've had this dream before. But we were in a bigger bed."

I punched him in the arm. "I'm your boss, bub."

He clumsily swatted me away, protesting his innocence. "Hey, you're the ones who climbed into my bed." His speech was worryingly slurred. Although he had his wits about him enough to flirt, that didn't reassure me. Daniel could be stone dead in a casket and he'd chat up the undertaker. I held up the lamp. His pupils contracted, but slowly.

"Is he okay?" Rabbit asked, coming over to join us.

"I think it's safe to say he's been drugged, too," I said.

Daniel squeezed his eyes shut. "I can't say I'm feeling the best. And that's *really* saying something. Usually, when there are two beautiful ladies in my bed, I'm feeling very, very, *very* well."

"I'm sure." I gave him two quick pats on the chest and rose to standing. "Melody, you stay here with them. Give Daniel a nudge every few minutes to make sure he doesn't go comatose," I said. "I'm going to bring Sonya and Butterball over, too. Jarka and I will go downstairs and check on the others."

"Do you want me to come?" Rabbit asked.

"No. None of the doors lock. Since you and Melody are feeling okay, I think you should stay here in case whoever came into my room comes back. I don't think Daniel's up to playing the hero tonight."

We all looked over to see that our bartender had already rolled over and drifted back to sleep, bare buttocks on full display.

"I wish he was up to putting some pants on," Rabbit muttered.

Once Jarka and I had safely deposited Butterball and Sonya with Daniel, Melody, and Rabbit, we made our way down the stairs.

We moved slowly, acutely aware of each creak and squeak of floorboards. I couldn't decide which was creepier—the wan, flickering shadows cast by the candle Jarka held, or the wavery, shifting shadows cast by my oil lamp. All I knew was that I wasn't enjoying the combination.

"I don't like how quiet," Jarka said.

The second-floor hallway was indeed silent and dark. I knocked on the door that stood at the base of the stairs. No reply. I repeated the exercise. Nothing. It took two more rounds of knocking before a groggy B.L. Huddleston flung open the door, wearing a rumpled dress shirt and trousers. "What's going on?" he asked, scratching his head.

"Are you okay?" I asked.

"Why shouldn't I be okay?"

"And Kennedy? She's okay, too?" I asked.

He gestured into the room. "Of course. She's in bed right there."

"What's happening, Brian?" Kennedy's voice carried from within the darkened room.

He squinted and lowered his voice. "Is everyone all right?"

"We can talk about it in the morning," I said. "You should block your door as a precaution. Sorry to disturb you."

We continued along the hallway with similar results. Pam seemed perplexed, Lola befuddled, Zaria and the Count annoyed. Every one of them seemed dazed and out of it. None of them asked for an explanation, for which I was grateful.

It only took a single knock to rouse Capone.

"What's going on?" he asked, yawning as he ran his hand over his close-cropped hair.

I was momentarily struck dumb by the sight of his muscular physique clothed only in a white undershirt and snug boxer briefs. My face grew hot. Thankfully, Jarka had the presence of mind to bring him up to speed on what happened to Sonya.

"Is my mother okay?" he asked, once she'd gone over the basics.

"Yeah, we told her to bar her door," I said.

"Good. Wait here," he said, his face grim. He quickly pulled on his pants and shirt. As I saw him holster his handgun, the heat in my cheeks quickly dissipated, replaced by a creeping chill. He joined us in the hallway and said, "We need to gather everyone into one room."

"Shouldn't we search the house? What if there's someone else here?" I asked.

"I wouldn't rule anything out at this point, but it seems unlikely that a stranger could've killed Clemmons, drugged everyone's food, and attacked Sonya. They'd have to have been watching and listening very closely to find opportunities to do all that, and they'd have to move around with quite a bit of freedom—all of which makes it more likely it's someone from within the group who's working in plain sight," he said. "Besides, a house search would require everyone splitting up, potentially giving the murderer a chance to escape, destroy evidence, or worse." Capone straightened his spine. "This is the plan, okay? Get everyone in one place and wait it out."

"Shouldn't we be trying to find out who did it?" I asked.

"We will, but you said yourself you didn't get a look at the person who was in your room. We have nothing

concrete to go on until we can start a real investigation."
He looked around, thinking. "We'll need to find a place
to gather everyone that doesn't have ten different doors
and a bunch of staircases leading in and out, which lim-
its our options."

I shivered at the thought of passing the rest of the
night in the same room as the person who'd just tried to
murder my best friend.

"Hopefully the murderer won't try anything in front
of everyone," he continued.

He had a small LED flashlight on his key chain, and he
shined it down the hallway, along the line of closed doors
Jarka and I had already knocked on. When he shined the
light in the other direction, though, Jarka called out.

"Look," she said, raising her candle to reveal that the
door to the bedroom across the hallway stood ajar. "This
must be Isabel's room, yes? We didn't see her yet."

I pushed open the door. The bed linen was pristine
and untouched. "I know she stayed up to help Rabbit
clean, but she never went to bed?" I wondered aloud.

Jarka shrugged. Capone's frown deepened.

"Do you see that?" I pointed farther along the corridor.
A door stood open, a thin glimmer of firelight spilling out
into the hallway.

"That is the library, yes? Why the fire is going still?"
Jarka whispered.

We quickened our pace.

Capone peered around the edge of the doorframe,
poised to confront whoever might be waiting inside. The
sight that greeted him, though, caused his shoulders to
sink. He hurried into the room.

On the floor, lying on her side in front of the fireplace,
was the tiny, still body of Isabel Berney. A purple feather
boa tightly encircled her neck. Capone rolled her onto

her back and was greeted by a frozen grimace. Behind her broken glasses, unseeing ice-blue eyes stared. Little pinpricks of red dotted her skin, and her lips and eyelids looked swollen. Her lace veil lay on the floor beside her, and her black dress spread out gloomily around her, as if she were in mourning.

Jarka unwound the boa to check Isabel's neck for a pulse, displaying a garish red and black bruise. "She's cold and her small muscles have the stiffness of death." She sighed. "I believe she has died from strangling, I am sorry to tell."

My reaction was stronger and more profane than Jarka's sigh. After an initial gush of cursing, I shook my head. In my every interaction with her, Isabel had never been anything but cheerful and kind.

My voice broke. "What kind of monster would do this?"

Capone looked back toward the open door. "A dangerous one."

CHAPTER 19

The three of us knelt next to Isabel, inadvertently reenacting the scene that had played out with Sonya only a few minutes earlier. This time, however, the outcome was dreadfully different. Isabel Berney was not going to be miraculously revived.

I watched as Capone, more accustomed to interacting with the recently deceased, scanned the room. The murder weapon was obvious—the boa had been cinched tight around her neck. But why would anyone want to kill lively, bookish Isabel?

"You two stay here," Capone said. "I'm going to call the station. In light of what's happened with Sonya and Isabel, they need to re-prioritize getting us out of here ASAP."

Despite the adrenaline jolt of discovering Isabel's body, I still had a strange, disconnected feeling. His words washed over me as my attention flitted around the room. To the shelves of books, to the boa, back to Capone, Jarka, the comfortable furniture, the deep molten orange of the dying fire. Finally, my gaze came to rest on Isabel's body. "I wonder when she burned her hands," I said, half to myself.

Capone was halfway to the door but stopped. "What?"

"Her hands. They're both singed," I stated. I was something of an expert on the subject, having endured my share of kitchen mishaps. From what I could see of the irregular red patches, the burns were bad. The kind that would blister and peel and hurt like hell for a week or two. At least Isabel would be spared that pain.

Jarka leaned in closer and inspected the dead woman's fingers. "Yes, those look like burns. From the fire, perhaps."

Capone crossed back to us, sidestepping the coiled boa, and peered into the bottom of the fireplace. He did a double take and crouched down. "Is that what I think it is?"

Jarka and I squatted alongside him, looking closely at the ash and embers that had fallen below the fireplace grate. Fluttering in the minute updraft from the flames was a scrap of cinder-gray paper—a pallid image of a bird, faded by the heat of the fire. As I looked more closely, other remnants of printed paper became evident. Capone used the fireplace tongs to pull out the fragment and rake through the ashes. The books had been reduced to a powdery dust, but a few identifiable scraps remained intact. Enough to be sure that they were the same two volumes Clemmons gave me earlier that night.

"Was she burning the books? And the murderer tried to stop her? Or the other way around?" I asked.

"Good questions," Capone said. "Stay here until I get back, okay? Block the door, don't touch anything, and don't let anyone come in." He took a step away but then stopped and fixed his eyes on my face. "Don't trust *anyone*."

"You don't need to worry about us not being on our toes," I said. "Everyone is a murder suspect tonight, even Butterball."

Once we'd wedged a chair under the doorknob, Jarka and I settled into the leather chairs in front of the fire.

"I don't like for Miss Berney to stay here on the floor like this. Is not respectful," Jarka said. Her gaze was soft as it fell on Isabel.

"I know it's awful, but we shouldn't move her," I said. I wrapped my arms around myself. We sat in stillness for a few moments while the fire crackled quietly in the background. "When I was a kid," I said, "WGN, one of the local TV stations, used to run a broadcast of a fireplace every Christmas. The Yule Log. My sister and I would watch it, even though it was hours of nothing but a burning fireplace."

Jarka's forehead creased. "America is a strange place."

"Jarka," I said. "I know you're not really into sharing personal information, or talking in general, but I have to ask about the Count. Clearly you two have a history. We need to know more about who's staying here with us."

"Is true, I suppose." She glanced toward Isabel. "Although we cannot *know* other person. Not truly." She took a steeling breath and began. "Victor asked to marry me. Long ago." She looked away and tucked a strand of lank crimson hair behind her ear. "I wanted to leave behind that life, but it is found me."

She recounted her story of being born in Bulgaria to a single mother, never knowing who her father was. Her mother worked hard cleaning houses, while little Jarka excelled in school. I tried to picture Jarka Gagamova as a schoolgirl. Had she worn pigtails? Played with dolls? Hopscotched? The best my mind could conjure was a half-sized version of the woman before me, calm and serious, with garishly dyed hair, deep-set eyes, and a rumpled waistcoat and jacket.

"When I am sixteen, my mother died. She leaves

a letter, telling me a name of who is my father. He is very important businessman in Vidin, my hometown. Very, very rich man. She cleaned his house." She sat up straighter and uncrossed her legs. "I have nothing after my mother is dead, you understand—no money, and there are many bills that I must pay for doctors, apartment, and other things. I did not like to beg, but this news of my rich father is like a miracle to me. I went myself to this man and say, 'I am Jarka Gagamova, your daughter from Blaguna who cleaned your house. I need please two thousand leva for paying these bills, and then I will go.'" She looked at me intently. "I did not want nothing from this man, except that I must pay these bills for my mother."

"I understand," I said. And I did. I, too, had nearly bankrupted myself paying for useless therapies when my father was dying of cancer. And I, too, had a white knight to bail me out of my financial hole in the form of my wealthy ex.

"I was surprised by how my father does not send me away and he does not either give me only two thousand leva. He says I should come live with him. He has no child other than me and he is old, and, I think, lonely." She cast her eyes down. "My father is not a bad man. He thought to help me, but I could not be happy. He wishes for me to be so very different from myself. He buys me clothes and send me to the rich girl school. But I do not speak French nor either English and already I was almost seventeen. I cannot ride horse like other girls, or laugh at things that are not funny as they do."

She explained how she couldn't stand the parties, the excess, the circles her father moved in. She didn't want any of it. "But, for him, I try. And because I love school. I wish to be a doctor, and a poor orphan cannot do this so easily. So, I take his money and I go to his parties." She clasped her slender hands together and laid them in her lap. "At one such of these parties, I see Victor."

Jarka described how she and the Count formed an instant connection. "I was so alone in that life, and Victor seems to understand me. He is an artist, painting and sculpting, so full of passion. We become lovers. Like Pascin, he has made close study of the female body. Victor is a very powerful, yet tender, lover."

I nodded, trying to arrange my features into a neutral expression even as I pictured their bony limbs intertwined, their lipless mouths interlocked. I *had* asked for her to share details about her past. Maybe next time, I'd specify in advance where to draw the line.

She continued to detail her tempestuous, years-long affair with the Count. "I know Victor loves me, but he has no wish to be—what do you say?" She frowned, searching for the right expression. "A starved artist. For him, he cannot imagine a life without luxury."

"I thought you said he was rich, though. Wasn't his ancestor some kind of nobility?"

"Yes, his family long time ago had great fortune, but little by little it has been lost. Now he has only his name. His friends buy his paintings and he lives from this money, but it is not enough. He cannot imagine how to get up early and go to hospital every day and work as I did. I did this, you see, even though my father and Victor did not like it. I became doctor and I worked in hospital for poor people, helping people like my mother. My father and I are fighting about this many times. I tell him, 'I will pay you back all the money you have given me if just you stop asking me to give up my work.' But this is not what he wants. He wants me to take his money when he dies. Live in his big house. Marry Victor. And many times Victor and I are fighting about this. He tells me we cannot be happy without my father's money."

"And you thought differently?"

"Yes, both of them want me to leave hospital and accept inheritance of money, each for a different reason. I refuse. This situation is so paining for me." She pressed her balled fists to her heart. "I love both of them, but I see no way for to solve this. So I ran away to America. Here I know is land of free." She hung her head. "I am a coward to do this, I know."

"Did Victor follow you to Geneva Bay?" I asked. "To try to change your mind?"

She considered. "I don't think so, no, but is possible. Some years ago, friends of my father at one of his parties are talking about this place. I liked how it sounds with lake and trees and snow. So I come here. Perhaps Victor would guess this? I don't know."

"What did he say to you outside, when he first saw you?" I asked.

"He was surprised, I think, to see me here," she said. "He tells me my father has not very long to live and if I do not return to Vidin, he will give all his money to cousins who he does not know even at all. He tells me it is shame I am working as waitress, even worse than doctor. He says that we could live together and be happy with my father's money, if only I will take it. Most of all, he says he loves me still, and knows I love him still." Her mouth twisted into a bitter smile and her eyes glimmered with unshed tears.

"And do you?"

Her shoulders curled forward over her chest, and suddenly she looked as small and fragile as an injured bird. "My heart is a mystery. Even to myself. I now have my new boyfriend, sweet, sweet Harold Heyer, who is so kind. But Victor holds me by my soul. You must think also that I am crazy for to give up that life and not take my father's money, probably."

I smiled. "If anyone understands self-defeating stubbornness about love and money, it's me. You know my ex had to trick me into taking the house, right? The whole Butterball caretaker setup is his way of forcing me to accept some kind of alimony since we weren't married. I've never wanted anything that I didn't earn myself."

There was a soft rap on the door, followed by two short knocks. Then the pattern repeated. I rose and crossed to the door.

"It's me," Capone said quietly, from the other side.

I unbarricaded the door and let him in. "All quiet on the Western Front?" I asked.

"Yes," he said. The two of us stood near the door, while Jarka stayed seated by the fire, lost in her own recollections. "After I got off the phone, I did a quick patrol outside around the house. There's a dusting of snow on the ground, enough that I would've been able to see any footprints that were made within the last hour or two. I didn't see any. It's dark, mind you, but based on that, I believe whoever attacked Sonya and Isabel is still in the house."

CHAPTER 20

We were silent for a moment, letting the implications sink in. Little by little, all the theoretical possibilities had fallen away. Now we were left with the reality that a killer lurked close at hand, somewhere inside the walls of Bluff Point.

"Well, after this, maybe Pam will think about investing in some security cameras and a more heavy-duty generator," I said. "Did you talk to anyone at the police station? Did they say how long until someone can get here?"

"About two hours yet. We're the top priority now, but all the county's heavy equipment is on the other side of the lake," he explained. "They asked if we could walk to the road, now that the storm has died down."

"Why walk? Can't we drive as far as the place where the road's blocked? That's what Zaria and the others did earlier," I said.

"Afraid that's not an option anymore. There's a massive pine tree down just at the bottom of the driveway. All of our cars are blocked in. I noticed there's an ATV parked by the lake, though," he said.

"I thought of that, too, but it would take forever."

His expression darkened. "Besides, I don't see how we could ferry people two by two, knowing that one of them is very likely a murderer. I don't know why I even considered it."

I pressed the bridge of my nose with my fingers. I still felt floaty, but my brain was starting to settle back into my skull. "It's like that riddle, how to get the fox and the chicken and the bag of grain across the river with nothing getting eaten."

"Right," Capone agreed. "Only we don't know who the fox is."

"And we're sitting ducks, not chickens," I said. "Which is why we've got to figure out who the killer is."

"We don't need to do anything except stay safe until help arrives. We'll investigate once everyone is out of here," he said.

"I don't want to just sit around." I threw my hands up. "Maybe we *should* walk out, like they said?" I suggested. "The wind is calm, so we don't have to worry about falling trees."

"I already told them that's a nonstarter. It's pitch dark, and nobody has the right clothing or shoes to walk almost four miles in the cold," he said.

"I suppose you're right. Besides, if I have to listen to Kennedy Criss yammer on for that length of time, then you'll end up with another murder on your hands." I chewed on my thumbnail. "Can't they send a police boat? They operate in bad weather."

"More bad luck on that score," he said. "I walked down to take a look at Pam's pier when I was outside, to see if an intruder could've come up by boat. Part of the dock is floating about twenty feet from shore. It looks like a log rammed into it during the storm."

We were silent, our eyes trained on the flickering fire. "So we have to survive two hours and we're home free," I said, trying to smile.

The sound of someone's throat being cleared came from the hallway just behind us. Capone and I spun toward it. His hand flew instinctively to the side of his chest where I'd seen him holster his weapon.

Pam stood in the doorway, hair in a silky head wrap, a fluffy yellow bathrobe over her pajamas. She clutched the base of a three-stem candelabra. "I'm sorry to intrude," she began, "but I saw you from my window looking around the house with your flashlight. I've been awake since Delilah and Jarka knocked, wondering what's going on. When I saw you coming back, I couldn't wait any longer. I can tell something's wrong."

"Very wrong, I'm afraid. It's Isabel. She's been killed." I stepped aside, allowing her a clear view into the room.

"Isabel?" she gasped. She clutched the fleece material of her robe with her free hand. She took a few steps forward and then stopped, searching our faces.

Capone gave the slightest of nods.

Pam took a few more halting steps and then wavered. Capone clasped her under her arm. I took hold of the candelabra, fearing she'd drop it.

"I need to sit down," she said.

I looked at the available chairs, all of which stood in close proximity to Isabel's body. "Maybe back in your room?" I suggested.

"Stay here," Capone called to Jarka. "And don't forget . . ."

"Yes, yes," Jarka said, waving us onward. "I will bar the door and let no one enter."

We led Pam back into the hall and steered her to her room, settling her onto the edge of her bed. Pam's shoulders slumped, her chest caving in. Her usual self-assuredness seemed to have leaked out of her, like air from a helium balloon. There was a scattering of candles on the dresser, and I lit them, filling the room with a soothing light and the scent of vanilla. Gloria, who'd been asleep on a furry poof bed at the foot of Pam's mattress, stirred.

Pam, though outwardly calm, took a shaky breath. "This feels like a nightmare." Gloria, sensing her distress, nuzzled her owner with her delicate head. "I knew," Pam began, her voice cracking. "I *knew* something terrible had happened." She drew another slow breath, trying to stifle her emotions. "Oh, Isabel."

"You said you *knew* something bad had happened," Capone said. He moved a wide bench from the dressing table next to the bed so that he and I could sit on it. "Just a sense? Or is there something you want to tell me?"

Ignoring his question, Pam pressed her eyes closed. "I feel so tired. I don't understand how I can want to sleep after everything that's happened, but I do." She yawned, and then quickly covered her mouth in embarrassment. "I'm so sorry. Please don't think I'm insensitive. I'm just exhausted."

"It's not your fault. Jarka thinks someone drugged us," I said.

Her eyes flew open. "What?!"

I nodded. "Someone attacked Sonya, and she and I both almost slept through it." I swallowed hard. It would be a long time before I could think about the incident without my stomach clenching with the horror of what almost happened to Sonya. What *did* happen to Isabel. "I'm guessing the killer slipped something into our food."

"This is unreal." She closed her eyes and shook her head. "I really hoped it was someone from the outside who snuck in and killed Edgar. Horrible as that is to imagine, it's worse to think anyone that I actually know could be capable of it."

Capone nodded. "Looks that way, though. We could

all be in danger. So anything you know, you need to tell me, okay?"

"Of course." Despite her words of agreement, her tight posture told me she was withholding something.

Turning to Capone, I asked, "What happened to the two books after the blackout? They left the kitchen somehow and got up to the library."

"They were still on the counter when Pam and I went outside to check on the generator," Capone said. "I should've locked them back up. I can't believe I didn't secure them."

"There was a lot going on," I pointed out.

He shook his head in disgust. "That's no excuse for a mistake like that."

I felt a pang as I recognized Capone as a fellow Perfectionists Anonymous member. Not a fun club to be in.

"Why do you ask about the books?" Pam said.

"You didn't see the books after that?" I prodded her.

She shook her head. "Detective Capone and I went straight out to start the generator. I assume they're still down in the kitchen unless Zaria or Isabel brought them upstairs." She picked up Gloria and cradled her in her lap. "It's crazy to think that I could lose track of fifty thousand dollars' worth of books." Her face took on a wistful expression. "But if anything goes to show that money doesn't buy happiness, it's tonight. Now I wish we had just let the Crisses bankroll the entire library renovation. Or that I'd done it myself. If I hadn't thrown this party, none of this would've happened." She squeezed Gloria tighter, and a soothing purr rose from the cat's chest. I envied the animal's obliviousness.

"You can't know that," Capone soothed. "This could've happened some other place, some other way."

"Maybe," Pam said. Then, turning to me she asked, "Why did you ask me about the books?"

"We found them, or what was left of them, destroyed in the library fireplace," I said.

Her head drew back. "What?"

"Isabel's hands were burned," I explained. "We don't know if she was putting them into the fire or taking them out."

"She must've been trying to pull them out. Isabel would never burn a book. Never. She loved books, knew them like they were people," Pam said firmly. "But I don't understand. Why would anyone destroy such valuable books?"

"Clemmons gave them to me earlier," I explained. "That's how they ended up downstairs. It must've been one of the last things he did before he was killed."

Capone frowned at me. "Delilah . . ."

I held up my palm. "I know, I know. You want to keep all the evidence in your vest pocket, but we still have at least two hours stuck here, all right? And I'm not okay with sitting on my hands. This isn't a typical investigation where you can take your time and organize the evidence and question each suspect down at the station. We're *living* in the crime scene, and *all* of us are the suspects. Sonya almost died. Isabel and Clemmons did die."

"I don't understand," Pam said. "Are you saying Edgar was trying to steal them? Why would he do that?"

"I don't think he intended to steal them. I think he was using them as part of some kind of coded message," I said. "Maybe he didn't realize how much they were worth."

"I doubt that," Pam replied. "He worked with rare books his whole career."

"The books have to figure into all of this somehow. Either the books themselves or a secret message in the books, or a combination of the two," I said. "When you heard me talking about the coded message in the kitchen before, that's what it was about. But we still don't understand what he was trying to say."

Capone shot me another "hush up" look.

Noticing it, Pam shook her head. "No, Delilah's right. Our best hope is to catch the murderer dead to rights, ideally before they kill anyone else."

"I know. If we could just get them to expose themselves. Force them to make a mistake . . ." I began.

"Absolutely not," Capone said. "The investigation is on ice until backup arrives. Keeping everyone safe until then is the top priority. I'm looking at this the same way I would if I were responding to a motor vehicle collision. When there's a wreck in the middle of the highway, you don't start interviewing witnesses about who caused the crash. You secure the scene. See that nobody else gets hurt. My job is to make sure this doesn't turn into a twenty-car pileup."

Although I understood the sense of his plan, I didn't like the sound of it. In my opinion, this already was a twenty-car pileup. Idling away two hours cheek by jowl with a murderer who'd just attacked my best friend? Not for me, thanks. Patience may be a virtue, but it's not one of mine.

"You're the one who's always saying that the first few hours of an investigation are the most critical," I countered.

I turned back to Pam, sensing she and I were on the same page. I knew I should be more wary of her. After all, I barely knew her. But of all the strangers in the house, she was the one I felt the most kinship with.

"I wonder if Isabel figured it out," I said. "And whatever it was would reveal the truth about what happened to Clemmons. The murderer must've guessed that. *Something* happened this evening that made the killer reckless. Everyone here would have to know that they'd be suspects, so keeping your head down would be the safest option. But Clemmons's killer became desperate enough that he or she felt the need to silence Isabel as quickly as possible."

"And if someone attacked Sonya, well, the thing you said earlier in the kitchen—about Sonya being the intended recipient of Clemmons's message—maybe they had to kill her, too, before she figured it out," Pam said, picking up on my line of thought. She grew quiet before turning her attention to Capone. "You asked me before if I had some information, or just an inkling that something bad would happen."

Capone leaned forward expectantly.

"There's no easy way to say this," she began, and looked down at her sheepskin slippers. It was unlike her to be indirect, and I suspected that whatever info she was about to spill would be a dam breach rather than a trickle. She lifted her eyes back to me. "I wasn't telling the truth when I told you earlier that I didn't cross paths with Clemmons."

I nodded, remembering her comparison of her house to a game of Clue.

"It was true that I didn't actually *speak* to him," she continued, "but I did find him. Earlier tonight, before the party, I went up to the library to meet him. He'd told me on the phone this morning that he'd come early and wait for me there. But he was already with someone, so I didn't go in." She swallowed.

"Yes?" Capone prompted.

"They were arguing," she said. "It got very heated. From what I could tell, Clemmons was threatening to expose a secret. And she said she'd see to it that Clemmons got what was coming to him."

"*She?* Did you see who it was?" I asked.

Pam nodded, her face growing resolute. "It was Lola Capone."

CHAPTER 21

Capone sat so still, I half wanted to check him for a pulse.

Pam lowered her voice. "Of course, I don't think your mother is guilty of anything. I want to be clear about that. There's bound to be a good explanation for why she said that, but I think it's time to find out what that good explanation is, don't you?"

In the flickering candlelight, I saw a single muscle in Capone's eyelid twitch.

I thought back to Clemmons's insinuation that Lola Capone had loose morals. "Not to speak ill of the dead, but Clemmons could be kind of a jerk," I said. "He probably provoked her."

"He had a very definite worldview. Right and wrong were clear cut, in his opinion," Pam agreed.

"Why didn't you say anything earlier?" Capone asked. "Instead of telling Delilah you hadn't seen him?" His tone was carefully controlled.

"It was a white lie, or so I thought at the time. I didn't technically *see* him. And what I overheard didn't seem worth going into then," she said. Gloria, who'd been reclining on her owner's lap, meowed in agreement. "But now things have changed. I agree with Delilah. I don't want to sit around twiddling my thumbs. I've always been the type of person who'd rather have everything out in the open, even if it isn't pretty." She paused. "From your expression, I take it that you didn't know about your mother's run-in with Edgar?"

"No, I did not." The words were clipped, and I got the impression the cork on his suppressed emotions could pop at any moment. "She said she didn't know him."

"She said she'd never met him *before tonight*," I pointed out. "Maybe that was a white lie, too? It's possible that whatever went down between them just happened tonight and she was telling the truth that she didn't know him before."

"White lies don't belong in my murder investigations," he snapped. "If her integrity is in question, she knows very well that mine is, too, by extension. And that's something I can't tolerate." He rose. "I need to have a very *direct* conversation with her."

"You're right to be mad," Pam said, rising along with him. "I would be, too. But don't let it make you say anything you'll regret. She's your mother."

Capone shot her a dark look. "I know. Believe me."

I was well versed in every shade of anger, from merely seeing red to seething, white-hot fury. And heaven knew family drama was my second language. Biz could get my goat like no one else. Capone's quieter, internalized anger, however, felt more potent somehow. And more ominous.

"You know, I think you were right about gathering everyone in one place after all," I said. "How can we help prevent the twenty-car pileup? We can't leave everyone barricaded in their rooms all night."

Up until then, I'd seen Capone as a stone tower. I knew I caused him aggravation on occasion, but I figured he could handle the tiny arrow slings of my interference and nay-saying. After all, he'd always remained calm, cool, and collected. Seeing this chink in his emotional armor, though, I suddenly felt protective of him and decided to throw my weight behind his plan.

Capone remained impassive and silent, his gaze fixed on a shadowy corner. I shot Pam a look that I hoped conveyed that this wasn't the time for arguing with him.

"Yes, how can we help? I bet everyone is worried and wondering what's going on," Pam said. "Not to mention that one of those rooms has a killer in it."

Capone nodded crisply, his thoughts snapping back into his body. "We need somewhere that's not easy to get in and out of, where I can contain people and see what everyone is doing," he said. "Somewhere comparatively small like the library, although we can't go there for obvious reasons."

Although I didn't say it out loud, I was thinking that we were lucky it was a big house, because we were running out of rooms that didn't have dead bodies in them.

"Any ideas?" Capone asked Pam.

"The observation tower on the fourth floor is the best option. There's enough seating for everyone and it has just one way in and out," she said. "The only other door leads out to the widow's walk. The external staircase from the patio stops at the second floor, so you can't access it from there. We should be able to see the road from there so we'll know when the police are finally on their way."

"Okay, let's do it. Delilah, you and your team can start moving people while I talk to my mother." Turning to Pam, he asked, "Do you have any guns in the house?"

Pam and I shared a quick look, slightly thrown by

his mention of guns right after he stated his intention to question his mother.

"Not in the house, but there're a couple of hunting rifles in the groundskeeper's cottage," she replied.

"Great. Daniel's ex-military," Capone countered. "He'll know how to handle them."

"I'm not sure Daniel can handle walking in a straight line right now, much less shepherding a group that very likely includes a murderer. Whatever drugged the rest of us hit him especially hard," I explained. "Plus, it's one thing for you to have a concealed gun for protection. But everyone sitting around with a rifle out in the open? That would feel like we're being held hostage."

"Maybe that's a good thing? I expect everyone's as jumpy and suspicious as I am," Pam said. "That's why I brought up the run-in between Clemmons and your mother. Now is the time to get things out in the open."

Capone heaved a breath in and out of his lungs and turned to me. "Can we talk in private?"

The two of us stepped into the sitting room that adjoined Pam's bedroom and shut the door. Capone had brought his flashlight, but he clicked it off, seeming to prefer the privacy of darkness for whatever he was about to say. I could just discern the outline of his body in the faint moonlight that streamed in through the windows.

He leaned toward me and took hold of my arm at the elbow. "*You* need to question my mother," he said.

I did a double take. "What?"

"If what Pam is saying is true, my mother was lying." He let go of my arm and let out a hiss of disgust. "I knew something was off with her when the three of us were in the library. If she were anyone other than my mother, I would have pushed her harder about it, especially after what you told me Clemmons said about her character.

Clearly, he knew enough about her to form an opinion. But I let it go." His tone had a slow-roasted, baked-in bitterness.

"She *is* your mother, though," I said.

"She's my mother," he responded.

"Why do you want me to question her then?" I asked.

"You're the only one here I'm sure I can trust. I'm making mistakes. Having her here is clouding my judgment. You were right to remind me that keeping everyone safe is the most important thing. If Daniel's out of the picture, I need to be the one to get everyone where I can see them, and quickly. I'm already uncomfortable with how much time has passed. I don't want to do anything that could compromise the investigation, but if my mother knows something, I'd like to know it, too. Sooner rather than later. I don't want to create an appearance of bias or have people think there's some kind of cover-up." He'd been speaking with urgency, but he suddenly paused.

"What is it?"

He lowered his voice even further. "I'm also not sure I can ask her the questions that need to be asked. At least not in a neutral way." He fell silent for a beat before picking up again. "My mother . . ." He paused again.

"What?"

"She dated a lot of men when I was young. When it comes to men, she always jumps in headfirst without thinking. When I was a kid, she'd bring a new 'uncle' home a couple times a year."

"I'm sorry. That must've been hard."

I touched his chest with my fingertips. I hadn't meant it to be a flirtatious gesture, but the dark, quiet space amplified the intimacy. For a moment, the connection between us felt like a completed circuit, electricity coursing back and forth. I quickly drew my hand away. We'd discovered a dead body only moments before and were still in danger, so the whiff of romance felt out of place.

"She's a wonderful mother, don't get me wrong, and a good person, too. She'd give her last dime to anyone who asked. But with men, she has bad taste. Some of the men she brought home weren't good people." The hushed rumble of his voice deepened. "A lot of them weren't."

"Sonya's exactly the same. Her girlfriends are a rogues' gallery. And no matter how they treat her, she's always halfway down the aisle in her mind before the end of the first date," I said. "It's hard enough to handle as her friend. I can't imagine it happening with my mother when I was a kid. Is that still the way things are?"

"Honestly, I don't know. I drew a line a few years ago. She knows her boyfriends won't get a warm reception from me, so she doesn't try to get me to meet them anymore. I don't ask about her private life, and she doesn't talk about it with me," he said. "I doubt she's changed her ways, though. She's always on my case to find someone. I don't know how to tell her that *she's* the reason I won't. After C.J.'s mom left, I swore I wouldn't do that to him. No kid should walk into the bathroom at two a.m. and find a stranger brushing his teeth at the sink."

"So you haven't dated since then?" I asked.

I didn't know the ins and outs of Capone's relationship with his son's mother, but I knew they'd been apart for at least a decade. It seemed crazy to me that he'd spend his prime years alone in order to compensate for his mother's mistakes.

"There've been women, if that's what you're asking. I'm a human being. But, no, I haven't had anything long-term or serious. Definitely no one worth bringing into my son's life."

"But C.J.'s a grown man," I said. "He'll be a doctor in a few years. You don't have to protect him from the realities of life."

"Old habits die hard. Besides, with my granddaughter living with me during the week, and my mom, and my job, it's not easy to find space in my life." Perhaps he realized that the conversation had veered further from the investigation than he intended, because his voice became firm. "Now that Pam has raised this, it's especially important not to make it seem that I'm letting my mom get a pass. If she has information that can help keep everyone else in the group safer, we need to know it. But I don't want to risk everyone's safety while I get to the bottom of this, either. The more I think about it—someone needs to talk to her, and I don't think that someone is me. I'm not thinking clearly." He huffed out a bitter exhalation. "Feelings are a weakness if you're a cop. You can't fall apart."

"It's not a weakness to feel things," I said. "Or so Sonya tells me." The irony of me telling someone else that it was okay to get emotional wasn't lost on me. "O'Learys don't cry" was our unofficial family motto. "I'm glad if I can help, and I think you're right that it might look better if you're not the one questioning your own mother."

"It probably doesn't matter at this point," he said. "This is already the sloppiest case I've ever worked."

"I guess you've never had a crime scene that you and all the suspects and all the witnesses *and* all the victims had to live inside?" I said.

"Thankfully, no. This is a first." He exhaled. "I can't even imagine the report I'm going to have to file about this."

CHAPTER 22

As Pam and Capone began the process of herding the remaining guests to the observation tower, I gave a gentle knock on Lola Capone's door. I expected Capone to leave me with some kind of detailed best practices primer on questioning witnesses. Instead, his one and only instruction was, "Get the truth out of her."

If I'd held any hopes of getting on the woman's good side, they were out the window. Shaking down my crush's mother about how she covered up her potential role in a murder wasn't likely to endear me to her.

I knocked again, harder this time.

"Yes?"

"It's me. Delilah," I said. "It's safe to open the door."

She slid something heavy away from the door, and cracked it open, her round, dark eyes peering into the gap. Once she seemed sure that I wasn't an axe-wielding maniac, she opened it all the way, reached for my wrist, and pulled me inside. The room was comparatively well lit, Lola having lucked out with a battery-powered camping lantern that Pam dug out of a storage closet. Not exactly a full-on interrogation spotlight, but certainly enough to allow me to observe her facial expressions.

"What on earth is going on?" she asked. "First you

and Jarka tell me to barricade myself in my room. Then I heard Calvin's voice in the hall, and saw him through my window, looking around outside. Did someone break into the house? Or escape from it? I've been beside myself wondering."

With zero experience in formal interrogation techniques, I walked into the room with no particular strategy for the conversation. However, I had reams of "transferable skills" to draw upon. I'd grilled suppliers who tried to price gouge or swap in subpar ingredients. I'd caught servers shorting the bussers and runners on their tip-out percentages. And I'd had my share of very *direct* conversations with diners who harassed the front-of-house staff. Bluntness had always been my tactic of choice.

"There was another murder," I said.

Her eyes widened in shock and she staggered over and collapsed into a brocade-covered chair. "Oh my god. Who was killed?"

"Isabel."

"Oh, no. She seemed like such a nice person," Lola said. "And you *know* it was murder?"

"There's no question this time," I said. I decided to throw a little guilt trip lure into the water and see if I got a bite. "Maybe it could've been prevented if we'd found out sooner who killed Clemmons and why."

"Where's Calvin? Did he catch the person who did this?" She made half a move to stand but then collapsed back into the chair and pressed her hand to her forehead. "I feel all fuzzy."

"I'm afraid no one's been caught. He's gathering everyone together upstairs in the observation tower so he can keep them safe until help arrives," I explained.

"Well, I better get changed then, so we can join the others." She rose, and for the first time, I noticed that she was wearing a sumptuous, eggplant-colored silk pajama set. It fit her perfectly.

"Did you borrow those pajamas?" I asked, glancing down at my rumpled chef's outfit.

"No, I always have my overnight bag with me. I can't tell you how many times over the years it's come in handy when you end up sleeping somewhere you didn't expect."

"That happens often? That you sleep somewhere . . . you didn't expect?" I loaded the words with innuendo and leveled a meaningful look at her. Now that I had brought her up to speed on the main events, there was no reason to beat around the bush.

Her posture stiffened. "Excuse me?"

Okay, Delilah. Time to flambé this bridge. "Why did you pretend you didn't know Edgar Clemmons? You told me and your son you'd never laid eyes on him before tonight. Yet, someone heard you threatening him in the library." I took a step closer, positioning myself above the smaller woman. "Right before he was killed."

Her eyes darted from side to side, seeking an escape route from my pointed gaze.

I pressed her. "Don't you think that your son had enough on his hands without you lying in the midst of an investigation?"

She shook her head rapidly. "What I said was true. I'd never met the man before tonight," she said. "That conversation was the first and only time I spoke to Edgar Clemmons. I didn't even know Clemmons had been murdered when I said those things to Calvin. Remember? When you, me, and Calvin talked in the library, we still thought he tripped over your cat. What would've been the point of bringing it up?"

"You made it seem like he and I were crazy for even thinking it could be foul play," I reminded her. "And yet you, apparently, had just told the man to his face that you wished . . . What did you say? That he 'got what was coming to him'?"

"Clemmons was awful to Brian. He was going to ruin his life," she said.

"Brian? You mean B.L. Huddleston?"

"Yes." She lowered her eyes and sat down on the bed. "Clemmons caught him"—she corrected herself—"caught *us*."

"Caught you doing what?" This wasn't a time for delicacy. I'd been fixated on the mysterious books, but suddenly, B.L. and Lola were smack in the middle of this thing.

"Kissing. I hadn't expected to see Brian here tonight," she explained. "But I ran into him downstairs when he and his wife arrived. I didn't know he was married. We've been seeing each other for months. I thought it was serious. When he introduced Kennedy as his wife, I was shocked and upset. I came upstairs to collect myself. Brian followed me."

"How did you end up kissing him right after you discovered he lied to you about being married?" I asked.

She closed her eyes and waved her hands around her head. I was struck again, as I'd been when I'd seen her perform, by how beautifully her gestures could express emotion. In this case, the whirling irrationality of love.

"He told me he thought I knew he was married, and I realized he was right. I should've known. All the signs were there, in plain sight. I suppose I had my suspicions, but I played them down. He said he was sorry if he hurt me." Her eyes popped open and she looked at me. "He doesn't love his wife, you know. Even meeting her for five minutes, I saw that. He wants to divorce her and marry me."

Now *this* I had experience in. Believing an adulterer was going to leave their partner for you was straight from my dog-eared copy of the Sonya Dokter romance playbook. If Lola believed that B.L. was going to throw away his millionaire's lifestyle for love, I had a nice little bridge in the New York City area I could sell her. But my experience with Sonya told me there was no use in trying to argue the logical points.

I softened my tone. Continuing my hard line would run the risk of upsetting Lola to the point that she'd shut down. I still hadn't gotten to the bottom of her argument with Clemmons. "Do you *want* to marry B.L.?"

"I know my life looks glamorous to some people, but it's lonely. Brian is charming and romantic. It's been a long time since a man paid that much attention to me."

"So Huddleston came after you and apologized. You forgave him, and you kissed and made up. Then, what? Clemmons saw you?" I asked.

"Yes. We were in the library and Clemmons walked in. He'd been eavesdropping. He came in riding his high horse. Like some sort of avenging angel with a mission to enforce his own personal moral code on us." She opened her hands toward me, pleading for my understanding. "Can you imagine? What kind of grown man butts into someone else's private business like that? He said he was going to march downstairs and tell Kennedy right then and there. How about that? When there's a party starting and I'm supposed to go onstage, this man I don't know from Adam comes out of nowhere and says he's going to take it upon himself to break up a marriage."

"Did Clemmons try to blackmail you?" I thought of

the stolen books. If Clemmons was having money problems, maybe that figured into his murder somehow.

She shook her head. "No. Blackmail, I could've handled. Brian offered him money, but Clemmons took offense to that. No," she said again. "That man was a crusader. He said he 'couldn't countenance' adultery."

"What did B.L. do then?" I asked.

"I thought he handled it well. He stayed calm."

"But you didn't?"

"No. I slapped the man, and I don't regret it." She jutted out her chin.

That explained the welt I'd seen on Clemmons's cheek when he came downstairs to give me the books. "Sounds like he had it coming," I said. "Was B.L. mad, too?"

"Of course, but he held me back. He picked up on Clemmons's sense of honor. He's very good at reading people."

I managed not to say what I was thinking, which was, *No kidding? The gigolo leading the double life is good at manipulating people?* Biting my tongue was a heroic accomplishment.

"He convinced Clemmons to let him talk to Kennedy himself," she continued. "Something about owing it to her because of their marriage vows."

"And Clemmons left it at that?" I asked.

She shook her head. "He told us he'd be keeping an eye on Brian to make sure he held up his end of the bargain. And that if he didn't, Clemmons would make sure Kennedy found out what her husband was up to."

"B.L. kept his cool through all of that?" I asked, surprised. If it'd been me, despite Clemmons's disability, and even if I was the one in the wrong, I would've been right there with Lola, smacking the J. Edgar Hoover right

off of that nosy old man's face. "Did he know Clemmons? Maybe Kennedy hired him to spy or something?"

"It didn't seem like he and Kennedy had that kind of
relationship," she said. "Clemmons said he knew Kennedy through the library board, but I don't think she'd
hired him or anything like that. In fact, he said that he'd
come upstairs to meet Pam Philips."

"And when exactly did you threaten Clemmons?
Seems like his plan to break up their marriage would've
worked out well for you, especially since B.L. said he
was going to leave her anyway," I observed.

She fidgeted with the hem of her pajama top. "After
Brian went back downstairs, I gave Clemmons a piece
of my mind. I didn't like the way he interfered in our
private business. He made it clear that he thought I was
some kind of temptress. What was the word he used?
Trollop, I think. Like we were in an old-fashioned novel
and he was a fire-and-brimstone preacher. Honestly, I
wished Brian had stood up to him a little more. I'm glad
he kept his cool, so things didn't escalate, but he walked
away and left me there with that horrible man looking
down at me all superior. I lashed out. I told Clemmons I
thought he was a hateful person and that I hoped something terrible would happen to him because he deserved
every bit of what was coming to him."

"And you went straight downstairs after all of that and
started your show?" I asked, a little incredulously.

"I'm a professional," she said, straightening her spine.

"What about after 'Mack the Knife' finished?" I asked.
Her answers had cleared up a number of small mysteries,
but the main question—who killed Edgar Clemmons—
remained. "You took a break just before Clemmons fell
and then didn't reappear until after everyone else had
rushed over."

"I was looking for Brian. He went outside, though, with his wife. I waited near the door to try to catch him when he came back in, but Kennedy came in first without him. She walked right past me." She paused. Her voice quieted as she explained. "I hid behind a lamp so she wouldn't see me."

"Did you see B.L. come back inside?"

She shook her head. "No, I heard the commotion and came back to the drawing room." She rubbed her hand against her chest. "So you must see why I couldn't tell Calvin any of this, especially in front of a woman he respects. He'll be so disappointed in me." Her eyes glistened. "I wish he could understand my life a little more. I was only nineteen when he was born. A silly, nineteen-year-old girl who got her head turned by a famous mobster's name. I was trying to make it big as an entertainer. I was never going to be a nun. How could I be?" She brushed away a teardrop. "After the things Clemmons said to me, I couldn't handle another scolding from Calvin. I guess it's all out in the open now, though. Tell him not to think too badly of me, will you?"

I nodded. "I will."

"And you, you must think I'm a terrible person," she said.

To think that I'd started the night so worried about what she'd think of *me*, obsessing over things like whether or not the appetizer course would come out on time. And here she was, being forced to lay bare her most intimate secrets in front of me. Of course I didn't condone her actions, but a wave of sympathy washed over me.

"I don't think that. My parents are both dead. Do you have any idea what I'd give to have someone look at me the way you look at your son? I can tell how proud you are of him, and I think he knows it, too," I said.

She brushed away another tear and tried to smile. "I can't have everyone see me like this. I'm a mess." She tried again to force a smile, but her breath juddered uneasily in and out of her lungs. She rose and walked to her bedside table, where she opened her purse and drew out a prescription bottle. She turned back to face me as she unscrewed the top.

"I suffer with my nerves sometimes, and this night has me rattled worse than I've been in a long time. I usually wouldn't take two in the same night because they can make me sleepy," she said. She tipped the bottle upside down into her hand. When she pulled the bottle away, though, her palm was empty. Not believing her eyes, she tried again. Once again, the bottle yielded nothing. She held it to the light. "This was full. I just filled the prescription last week."

I took it from her hand. "'Alprazolam,'" I read. "What's that?"

"It's the Sunday name for Xanax. For my nerves." She looked at the bottle again. "I don't understand. I took one earlier, right before the power went out, and the bottle was full. I would've noticed if I'd spilled them. What could've happened to a whole bottle's worth of pills?"

Unfortunately, I had a pretty good idea.

CHAPTER 23

I made my way into the hallway, leaving Lola alone to change out of her pajamas and gird her loins. I decided not to share my suspicions about the whereabouts of her missing medication with her. It wasn't that I didn't trust her. In fact, my conversation with her had inspired a considerable degree of sympathy. If Capone's Mr. Perfect exterior left *me* a little perturbed sometimes, I could only imagine how his mother, an emotional, slightly delicate woman, must have felt. I emerged, expecting to find a dark, empty hallway. Instead, I came upon Capone leaning against the wall next to the door.

"Listening at keyholes?" I asked.

"Trying to, but these doors are thick." He made a single short rap on the frame with his knuckle. "I'm also waiting because the two couples are taking their sweet time getting ready. Kennedy is putting on makeup, if you can believe that, and Zaria and the Count are arguing."

Now that he mentioned it, I could hear the sound of angry voices carrying along the hallway from one of two open doors.

"Can't you invoke the power of the law or something?" I asked.

"I'd like to, but I need to strike a balance. There are

thirteen living people in this house, and twelve of them
are most likely innocent. I can explain to them what they
need to do for their own protection, but I can't compel
them at gunpoint. I can't separate the innocent from the
guilty, either. If I come on too strong, I risk acting in
a way that forces the murderer to lash out." He looked
down the hallway to where Jarka and Pam lingered just
outside the open doors, in plain view of the rooms' inhabitants. "I let Zaria, Victor, B.L., and Kennedy know
that we can wait for them as long as it takes and then
help them upstairs," he said. "And that we're going to
keep the doors open to make sure we know where everyone is, so we can make sure they're all safe."

"You mean you let them know you and your spies are
keeping them under close watch," I said.

A wry gleam crept into his eyes. "Tomato, to-mah-to.
I don't want anyone to have a chance to dispose of evidence or make a break for it, and I can't be everywhere at
once," he explained. "This is an instance where instilling
a little paranoia isn't a bad thing." He flicked his eyes
toward his mother's room. "How'd it go in there?"

I summarized the things I'd found out as quickly as I
could, including the bombshell about the missing pills.
"I'm sure they were stolen from her," I added, not wanting him to think I was accusing her.

His face was a stone mask.

"Of the people who are here," I continued hastily,
"B.L. Huddleston and your mother were the only ones
I didn't see right after Clemmons fell down the stairs.
You were still at the piano in plain sight of everyone.
Victor and Zaria were next to me, and came over shortly
after he fell, and Isabel and Pam were right behind them.
I remember seeing Kennedy standing by herself a little
while later," I said. "B.L. wasn't there."

"Sonya and Rabbit also weren't there at all. They stayed in the kitchen the whole time and didn't know what was going on until later, or so they said," Capone observed. "The dead man gave Sonya fifty thousand dollars' worth of books that he'd stolen from Pam's library right before he died, and Rabbit is a convicted criminal with money problems and a long rap sheet."

I grunted in exasperation. "You think Sonya and Rabbit snuck upstairs and clubbed Clemmons during service and then covered for each other?"

"No, I don't. I'm pointing out that you often conveniently forget your own people when you're making lists of suspects." He cast a bitter look at the closed door of his mother's bedroom. "In an investigation like this, you can't be blind to any possibilities."

"First, my cat's the killer, and now it's my friends," I huffed. "Why are you ignoring the obvious new suspect—Brian Huddleston? So far, he's the only one we *know* had a good reason to kill Clemmons during the party. He knew that the countdown was ticking, and any minute his affair with your mother was going to blow up in his face. Kennedy would dump him, and he'd lose everything because of their prenup. And he doesn't have an alibi. What are you always saying? Means, motive, opportunity? Well, *boom*. With B.L., we have all three."

"What about killing Isabel and trying to kill Sonya? Why would Huddleston take such a big risk in going after them? And what about the books? How does he fit into that?" he asked.

"Maybe one of them witnessed something and didn't realize it," I began. No sooner were the words out of my mouth than a memory flitted through my mind. "Or maybe *I* did."

Capone gave me the "go on" eyebrow raise.

"At the party, just before Clemmons died, Kennedy asked Zaria about some books she'd wanted for her husband. She was really upset about it because they'd been sold to Pam instead," I said. "That's a link between the books and B.L. and Clemmons. Or maybe it has something to do with the town library or Pam's book collection. Clemmons said something about those two books being part of a larger collection."

"B.L. Huddleston doesn't have anything to do with the library, though," Capone pointed out.

"Not directly, but Kennedy is on the library board, snuck in through the back door by Edgar. And now two of the board members are dead."

"Are you suggesting Kennedy put her husband up to committing multiple murders so she could gain more power on the town library board?" Capone asked.

I shook my head. "I'm not saying that." I paused. "Although honestly, she seems like she'd be willing to commit murder if someone cut her in line at Trader Joe's." I snapped my fingers, suddenly recalling a detail that had slipped my mind. "Plus, they were wet."

"Who was wet?" His forehead creased in confusion.

"Kennedy and B.L. When they came over after Clemmons fell, they were both wet like they'd been outside in the rain. There's an external staircase that goes from the veranda to the hall outside the library. They could've snuck up that way and killed him without anyone seeing."

"So now you're saying they were in it together?" Capone asked.

"Maybe B.L. *did* tell her about the affair and convinced her to cover for him?" I tapped my finger against my lips. "Although that doesn't make a ton of sense. She'd just dump his ass, right? They have a prenup. Unless she hated the idea of people knowing he cheated on her?"

He sighed. "Look, Delilah, I appreciate you getting the information out of my mother," he said. "Based on what you discovered, I agree that Huddleston is a suspect, and I'll be having a good, long talk with him back at the station once we get out of here. We'll get to the bottom of Kennedy and the books. Until then, we should watch them closely. All of them. But this is the end of the investigating for now, okay? The odds of us solving this thing here and now are slim. The more we poke around, the more we increase the odds of screwing up the investigation or, worse, of somebody getting hurt."

"I know," I said, but my earlier resolve to support Capone's "no investigating" plan was crumbling. "But it feels like we're so close."

"Delilah," he said sternly. "I'm revoking your deputy badge as of this minute, hear me? Help will be here in less than two hours. My only job is to keep everyone safe until then. If you want to be useful, help me with that."

I nodded, trying to push aside the feeling that we were right on the cusp of breaking the case wide open.

"Good," Capone said. "I'll take reluctant agreement as long as it's agreement. Is Sonya well enough to move?"

"I think so. I'm more worried about Daniel. He's heavy."

"Do you think you, Melanie, and Rabbit can manage them between you?" he asked.

I nodded.

"Get your crew wrangled then. We'll meet you in the tower as soon as the second-floor crowd can be extracted from their rooms."

I mounted the stairs, holding the oil lamp in front of me. Even though I knew that everyone's whereabouts were accounted for, I couldn't help but be jumpy. I felt a sense of relief when I finally reached the bedroom where

I'd left Sonya, Rabbit, Daniel, Melody, and Butterball. I knocked.

"Who's there?" Melody's tone was nervous.

"It's me."

"You're not being held at gunpoint by the murderer or something, are you?" Rabbit asked.

In the background, Sonya said, "If she was, how would she tell us? We can't exactly do a 'blink once for yes' thing through a closed door." I could almost hear her roll her eyes.

"I'm alone, I promise." I hesitated. "Isabel is dead, though. The killer is probably still in the house, so I'd feel better inside than out here."

The door flew open. Melody and Rabbit stood framed in the doorway, their mouths agape.

"Ms. Berney is dead?" Melody asked.

Rabbit pulled me inside and shut the door. "Killed?" he asked. He was already using his back to push a sturdy-looking wooden dresser in front of the door.

"Yes. Someone strangled her. Jarka and I found her in the library." I set the lamp I was carrying on top of the dresser.

Sonya, who'd been sitting on Rabbit's bed with Butterball in her lap, stood up and hurried over to enfold me in her arms. Butterball plopped onto the floor, screeching his disapproval at being suddenly displaced. "Oh, Dee. That must've been awful." She pulled quickly away and held me by the shoulders. "Hold on. Where's Jarka? Is she okay?"

"She's fine. She's downstairs helping Capone." I paused. "Mel, where's the feather boa Pam gave you?"

"I hung it up in our bathroom with my dress. Why?"

I rose. "I'll be right back."

My crew exchanged puzzled looks as I pushed aside the dresser that Rabbit had just used to block the door.

"You want me to come with you?" Rabbit asked.

"I'll be okay. I just need to get that boa," I said.

"She picked an odd time to finally get in costume," I heard Sonya mumble as the door closed behind me.

I hurried through the bedroom Jarka and Melody had shared and into the bathroom. Sure enough, Melody's sparkly dress hung from a hook on the wall. Her purple feathered scarf, however, was missing. I returned to the men's bedroom.

"I thought you were going to get the boa," Sonya said.

"It's not there," I replied.

"I don't understand. It was there when we went to bed," Melody said. Her forehead wrinkled in confusion. "Do you think the person who attacked Sonya took it?"

"What would anybody want a big, feathery thing like that?" Rabbit said.

"To use it as a murder weapon, apparently," I answered. "We found it wrapped around Isabel's neck."

CHAPTER 24

A collective gasp rose from the room when I delivered the news about the missing boa. "Where's Pam's half?" Sonya asked. "Didn't you say she cut her boa in half to split with Mel?"

"I remember her taking it off right before the black-out," I said. "When everyone was arguing over the books. And then she didn't have it on during dinner. I guess it's still in the kitchen."

"It wasn't down there when I was cleaning up," Rabbit said. "Maybe Miss Philips took it back upstairs with her when she went to bed."

Melody, who'd been making a nervous circuit of the room, stopped her pacing. "What if it was my half, though? Detective Capone doesn't think I did it, does he?"

Sonya rubbed the young hostess's back. "Of course he doesn't." Turning to me, she asked, "Does he?"

"Well, he just had me interrogate his own mother, so who knows what he thinks. But we don't have time to worry about it now. We need to get moving. We're supposed to meet everyone in the observation tower," I explained. "So we'll all be in the same place."

Melody wrapped her arms around herself. "What?

Why? You said the killer is still in the house, so it's probably one of those people, right?"

Daniel, who'd been lolling against the pillows, sat up straighter. I was relieved to see that somewhere along the way, someone had gotten him dressed. "What else can Capone do?" he said. "If he leaves everyone in separate rooms, the killer could escape, or have his run of the house and destroy evidence. Anything could happen. This place is a nightmare if you're trying to secure a scene. Multiple ingress and egress points. Poor lines of sight." His voice lacked its usual vivaciousness, but at least he seemed coherent and rational. He turned to me. "He has his service weapon, yes?"

"Yeah," I said, remembering how, earlier in the night, the presence of a gun seemed excessive.

"Good. I wish I'd brought my gun." Daniel shook his head. "It would help to have two people armed so we could separate the groups, or in case the person who did this is also armed."

"What is this, the O.K. Corral?" Sonya asked.

"We already nixed that plan anyway," I said. "Someone would have to go out to the groundskeeper's cottage to get a rifle, and I don't think you're in any shape to be wielding a weapon."

"I could do it if I had to. In the military, you push through." He put his hands to his temples. "But I suppose it would help if I could sit up without seeing stars."

"Daniel's still a little worse for wear," Sonya explained. "He's so dizzy he can barely stand."

"We've been thinking about the drugging," Melody said. "We think there must've been something in the gin."

Daniel nodded. "Remember how I told you about the bathtub gin? How Prohibition-era cocktails were designed to have strong flavors to hide bad batches?"

I felt a pang as I recalled Isabel's enthusiastic portrayal of Carry Nation. "I remember," I said.

"He gave that same spiel to everyone, so everyone would've known that would be an easy thing to spike," Sonya said. "Someone could've put something in the drinks and we wouldn't have tasted it."

"And it makes sense. Melody's okay 'cuz she never drinks. And I didn't have any because I'm in recovery, and I'm okay, too," Rabbit said.

"I didn't see Capone take more than a sip," Sonya said. "How's he?"

"Fine," I said, leaning down to pick up Butterball. Just having him in my arms felt like a talisman of protection, a furry, orange shield. "How can you be sure it was the gin, though? Isabel had two doubles."

"That's true," Rabbit said. "She stayed downstairs and helped me clean up. She seemed real good."

"She must've been unaffected," I said, "at least until she was killed. If she'd been as zonked as the rest of us, she would've gone straight to bed."

Our guessing game paused as we considered.

Melody bounced on her toes and shook her hands. "She didn't get to drink the *first* round of cocktails," she said. "Butterball spilled hers."

"That's right," I said, remembering the scene.

"And I opened a fresh bottle after that," Daniel said. "So whatever they used had to be in the original one. It also explains why I feel worse than everyone else. I was tasting as I went along, since I couldn't see well in the dark to measure. Plus, everyone else only had one cocktail from that bottle, but I had two. Usually, that would make me *un poco alegre*. But *no estoy alegre*."

"The drinks are definitely not going to make you

alegre when they're spiked with *Dios* knows *qué*," Sonya said, mirroring his Spanglish.

"I have a high tolerance for alcohol, but I'm not good with medications. I don't even take Tylenol if I can help it," Daniel explained.

"Well, who had access to the bottle?" I asked. "It must've been spiked after the power went out." My crew didn't know my deputy badge had been revoked, so maybe I could get a little sleuthing done on the sly.

"How do you know that for sure?" Melody asked.

"Because Lola Capone took a Xanax right before that," I replied. "And now her pills are missing. We'd need to ask Jarka to be sure, but I think the uber-relaxed feeling a lot of us had is what you get from Xanax. Only more so, because we had an unusually large dose."

Rabbit cocked his head. "You think Mrs. Capone slipped you guys a Mickey?"

"No, I don't think she would've taken the empty pill bottle out in front of me if she's the one who drugged us. We have to think about who knew she had the pills. She took one in full view of me and Son, plus Isabel, Zaria, Capone, and Pam, and then set down her purse right before the power cut happened," I said.

"So any of those people might've seized the opportunity," Sonya said. "At least that eliminates the suspects who weren't there."

I shook my head. "I'm not sure it does. Zaria could've mentioned it to Victor, and B.L. would probably have known because he and Lola . . ." I pressed my lips shut, hesitant to air Lola Capone's dirty laundry.

Sonya's mouth dropped open. "OMG, was there something between Lola Capone and B.L. Huddleston?" So much for discretion. Sonya had a bloodhound's ability to sniff out romantic intrigue.

"Yes," I conceded. "I guess we might as well have everything out in the open now. They were having an affair. Clemmons saw them together in the library before the party and threatened to expose everything to Kennedy."

"Huh," Rabbit said. "I wonder if that's what Mr. Huddleston and Miss Criss were fighting about."

"What do you mean?" I asked.

"I saw the two of them go outside. I wondered why they were going out in that weather," he said. "Looked like she was giving him hell about something."

"You saw B.L. Huddleston and Kennedy Criss arguing during the party? That backs up what Lola said, and explains why they were wet from the rain. Why didn't you say anything about it?" I asked.

"Why would I?" he replied. "You think this is the first time I seen something I probably wasn't supposed to see? You've worked in this business longer than I have. How many times you seen somebody out for dinner with someone they shouldn't be out with? Or seen somebody have one too many drinks and make a fool of themselves? What other people do ain't none of my business, and nobody's gonna thank me if I try to *make* it my business."

He had no idea how true his words were. Clemmons, the avenging angel, thought differently. He believed it was up to him to call out other people's behavior, and look where that got him.

"If they were outside, doesn't that mean one of them could've killed Clemmons while the other one was the lookout?" Melody said. "There's that staircase outside that leads up to the second floor."

"Seems possible," Sonya said.

"I thought of that, too, but I can't see them working together," I said.

"I could. It seems like she'd do anything for him," Melody said.

"Don't seem like he feels the same if he's running around on her with Mrs. Capone, though," Rabbit replied.

"Geez, what a night." I began to enumerate the events on my fingers. "Jarka's run-in with the Count. Clemmons's murder. The message and the books. The bloody cane. The spiked drinks. The attack on Sonya. Isabel's death. Burned books. Missing pills. B.L. being a man-whore with Lola Capone. And B.L. and Kennedy fighting. This case was already a big bowl of tangled spaghetti. Now I don't even know how anyone's going to begin to pull the strands apart. It's like . . ." I searched for the right descriptor.

"Orzo, because it's too small to pick up the individual pieces?" Daniel suggested.

"Or cannelloni, only it's stuffed with lies instead of ricotta?" Melody ventured.

"Or like gluten-free, dairy-free, no-nightshade spaghetti Bolognese, because it's completely impossible." Sonya threw her wrap on the opposite bed. "*Ugh*, this is so frustrating." She groaned, scooching closer to Daniel. He put his arm around her and she leaned into him. She looked toward the window. The clouds had mostly cleared, revealing a sliver of moon that dangled in the black sky like an open wound. "How is it still dark?" she asked. "This is the longest night *ev-er*. When is it going to be morning?"

"I know right how you feel," Melody said. "World's worst sleepover."

"More like purgatory," Daniel said.

We heard voices in the hall outside.

"I guess that's everyone else going up to the observation tower," Sonya said. She wrapped her arms around herself. "I hate the idea of sitting around with a murderer."

I paced up and down the small room, mindlessly running my hand along Butterball's spine. "We've *got* to be close to solving it. If we don't count ourselves or Capone or his mom, that leaves only five possible suspects. Setting aside everything else—the books, Clemmons, the cane, Isabel, and everything—surely we can figure out which of them could've drugged the liquor. If we can figure that out, we've got our killer." I sat down on Rabbit's bed and faced Daniel. "Think about the gin bottle. There wasn't very much time between when Lola took her pill and when the drinks were served. She said the bottle was full at that point. The drug must've been in our drinks twenty or so minutes later when we all sat down. Who had access to that bottle?"

"Not Detective Capone or Ms. Philips, right?" Melody chimed in, moving to take a seat alongside me. "They went straight outside to fix the generator and didn't come back until we were all sitting down. Everyone else was in and out of all the rooms downstairs. Lighting the fire, finding candles, setting the table, bringing out the food."

"Maybe two people are working together?" I guessed. "All this murder and mayhem is a lot for one person to pull off on their own. It would make more sense if there were two of them. Neither of the couples seem to actually like each other, though."

"Right," Sonya said. "Rabbit said Kennedy was pissed at B.L. when he saw them, and B.L.'s having an affair. And Zaria and the Count . . ." She waved her hand. "I can't even begin to guess what's going on there. One second she's rushing into his arms and the next they seem to hate each other."

Thinking back to Jarka's description of her passionate relationship with Victor, I shrugged philosophically. "Who's to say what people in love should act like?" I turned back to Daniel. "So no idea who had access to that bottle?"

"I wish I could think clearly. Six years of military training out the window with a few little cocktails." Daniel squinted and rubbed his temples. "Let's see. It was very dark. I only had my phone flashlight . . . Isabel helped carry in the drinks . . ." he trailed off.

"Well, sadly, we know she's not the killer. And she was about to drink her cocktail when Butterball knocked it out of her hand," I said. "She couldn't have planned that that would happen, which means she wasn't aware there was anything wrong with the drinks."

Daniel snapped his fingers. "B.L. and the Count came in right after the power went out. I made them their drinks before anyone else's. I probably turned my back on them a few times, since the other things I needed were behind me . . . The rest of the cocktails, I put on a tray for Isabel to bring in, but there were too many, so Zaria helped her." He sank back down. "That's practically everyone, isn't it? I'm not sure that gets us anywhere. Everyone is still a suspect."

We fell into dejected silence.

Rreee-oww, Butterball said.

I gave him a squeeze. "That's right, Butterbutt. Everyone except you. You've been exonerated."

CHAPTER 25

"Are you sure you want to bring Butterball?" Sonya asked as we trudged up the stairs to the observation tower. "He's not good with other cats. If Pam brings Gloria, they might fight."

"Maybe you could put him in a cat carrier," Rabbit suggested. "Ms. Philips probably has one you could borrow."

I shook my head. "You might as well suggest I put him into an iron maiden and torture him with flaming pokers." His hatred for his own carrier was so intense, he could practically melt it. No way could I convince him to get into a carrier that smelled like another cat. "I have to bring him. I'm not leaving him shut up in a room in a strange house all by himself," I said firmly, shifting my cat's weight to the other arm. "Not an option."

"You're totally right," Melody said.

"I'm glad somebody agrees," I said.

"I mean, what if he got out and started wandering around?" she continued. "I read that if an owner passes away, their cats start eating their eyeballs, like, the day they die. It doesn't even matter if they're hungry. And there are two dead bodies in the house."

"Butterball would never eat me, or anyone else," I protested, nuzzling my cat into my neck.

Sonya cleared her throat, and Daniel, who had his arm slung over Rabbit for balance, said mm-hmm in a way that didn't sound like agreement.

My rebuttal was halted by the sound of voices trailing down the staircase. The rest of the party, it seemed, was already in the tower. My muscles tightened. I'd just about convinced myself that Capone's plan of herding us all into the same room was the best move, but the reality that I was going to pass the next hour plus in the company of a cold-blooded killer was deeply unsettling. We reached the top of the landing and stood for a moment.

"Ready?" I asked.

Sonya, Daniel, Melody, and Rabbit nodded in unison.

I pushed open the door and a draft of cold air washed over me. The large, lighthouse-like room was glazed with 360-degree windows, which allowed what little moonlight the night afforded to trickle in. The windows also, apparently, let in frigid currents from every direction. The candles that dotted the room gave off a wavery, flickering light that seemed in danger of being extinguished by the vacillating movements of air. Luckily, I had Butterball to cuddle for warmth.

"Where have you been?" Capone asked, concern furrowing his brow.

"We took a detour before coming up," I explained apologetically. I gestured to my crew, who held boxes, bags, and thermoses. "Down to the kitchen for refreshments."

"I told you to come straight here," Capone scolded.

"We figured everyone could use a pick-me-up. Even once the cops and whoever else get here, they'll probably

210 Mindy Quigley

want to take statements, right? Maybe conduct a search? And then we still have to get back home on slick roads. Even though this ordeal is almost over, it'll be hours before it's *really* over."

Capone gave a half nod, but his frown didn't lessen.

I scanned the room, looking for somewhere to set down our offerings. As the name suggested, the observation tower was designed for looking out, rather than conversing, and thus was furnished with an enormous C-shaped, red velvet sofa whose seats faced out. On the lake side, the windows revealed the black void of water and the faintly visible lights of the town of Geneva Bay beyond. It felt unreachable, like looking at the reflected glow of Mars.

The south side of the room looked out over the forest, and even in the predawn gloom, it was clear that last night's windstorm had scraped the surrounding trees clean of their leaves. Their newly bare branches waved in the breeze like skeletal fingers. Judging by the temperature in the room, the unpredictable violence of the earlier storm had given way to the more insidious power of the Wisconsin winter. Near the door, a substantial telescope pointed up into the sky full of faintly twinkling stars and paper-thin clouds.

Inside the room, the assembled company looked like they were posing for a photo to accompany the dictionary definition of the word "jittery." Taking note, Sonya muttered, "Guess the chill pills are wearing off."

Jarka and Victor stood together at the far end, near a door that led out onto the widow's walk. Victor leaned toward Jarka, speaking to her in a low, fervent voice. Jarka stood stiffly, her hands clasped at her waist, gazing out the window. Zaria perched on the edge of a window seat on the opposite side of the room, watching them with a strained look on her face. She'd wrapped herself in a blanket against the cold, and her restless hands worried the edge of it.

On one side of the enormous sofa, Kennedy was seated next to B.L. While he sat in unnatural stillness, she shifted every few seconds as if she were being swarmed by fire ants. There was a bar cart next to the door, and Pam and Lola had availed themselves of the large selection of whiskeys. As Lola reached for her glass, her eyes flitted from her son to B.L. and back again. I noticed a slight tremble in her hand as she took hold of her drink. Capone, meanwhile, stalked around the room, avoiding even the slightest glance in his mother's direction. The only one who seemed calm was Gloria. The majestic feline perched in one of the widow seats looking like a porcelain sculpture.

While Rabbit got Daniel settled onto the couch, Sonya, Melody, and I arrayed the pick-me-up sweets on a circular table at the center of the couch. I'd had to improvise a bit, given that we still had no electricity, so I concentrated on foods that required no preparation—homemade Cracker Jack, plus the Italian wedding cookies and tiramisu cream bar cookies we'd been planning to serve for dessert. I figured that sweet things are always good when you're running on no sleep.

I set out a platter and began to lay out the spread. First, the Italian wedding cookies, perfect little snowballs of buttery crisp dough flavored with almond and coated in confectioners' sugar. Next, the tiramisu bar cookies, a portable, mini version of the famous Italian dessert. It consisted of an espresso-and-rum-flavored cookie base layered with Kahlúa and mascarpone cream, and sprinkled with chocolate.

Finally, I opened the large thermos flask and began

to pour out cups of steaming hot java. At the restaurant, we ground coffee to order and hand-pulled each coffee drink on our fancy espresso machine, but given the power outage, we'd instead boiled teakettles and made pour-over coffee. For catering gigs, I always used a crowd-pleasing roast—not too bitter, and heavy on the nut and fruit undertones. The scent wafted from the thermos and into my nostrils, caressing my brain. In the cool air of the tower, it smelled even more fragrant, so much so that it was all I could do not to guzzle the flaming hot liquid straight from the thermos, like a frat boy doing a keg stand.

The guests gradually converged on the table. Lined up, huddled in coats and blankets against the room's chill, Geneva Bay's wealthy resembled a photo from a Depression-era breadline. Apt, maybe, considering that the Great Depression followed close on the heels of the Roaring Twenties.

I regarded each of them in turn as I served them. I'd almost convinced myself that B.L. Huddleston was the culprit, with his obvious motive to silence Clemmons. If his affair came to light, he risked losing his very hefty meal ticket. But I still couldn't think of a firm connection to Isabel, Sonya, and the destroyed books.

Although I hated to think ill of her, Lola Capone couldn't be ruled out. She'd hidden the truth about both her relationship with B.L. and her whereabouts during the time of Clemmons's murder. Plus, her medication was used to drug us. Capone himself said that Lola lost her bearings when it came to romantic relationships. If B.L. and Lola were working together, they had more opportunity than almost anyone else to pull off the series of crimes. But the idea that Capone's own mother could be capable of going on a murderous rampage at the bidding of her paramour seemed way beyond belief.

As Kennedy Criss and B.L. Huddleston took their turn for coffee, I noticed how she clung to his arm. How much did she know? Was her continued devotion to him an act, a desperate attempt to win his love, or something else? B.L., for his part, picked up a tiramisu cookie and took a sizable bite, chewing with relish.

"That's a killer cookie, Chef," he said to me.

I smiled tightly. He didn't seem appropriately uncomfortable, nor did he balk at his unfortunate choice of words. Was that because he knew who the killer was? The man was either a highly proficient actor or completely amoral.

I rested my gaze on Kennedy. She clearly hated the idea of being embarrassed, and poured considerable energy into maintaining a perfect façade. Rabbit saw her and her husband arguing. Maybe B.L. had come clean to her about his affair. Could the possible exposure of her husband's womanizing have been enough to drive her over the edge? Her connection to the burned books seemed tenuous, but she and her family had designs on imposing their will on the Geneva Bay Library. And while Clemmons had been the one to secure her board appointment, they'd been uneasy allies. Maybe there'd been a quid pro quo involved that she wanted to ensure never saw the light of day.

Zaria and Victor's alibi for Clemmons's death seemed fairly ironclad, given that I'd had my eyes on them when he fell, but I wondered if they could be part of some larger conspiracy. I'd suspected the Count from the moment I laid eyes on him, and the background Jarka provided hinted at the possibility of a financial motive—he clearly valued the finer things in life. Plus, two or more people working as a team made the startling breadth of the evening's criminal activities more plausible. But I couldn't see how Clemmons's or Isabel's death would benefit Victor financially. What did he have to gain?

Zaria would no doubt feel threatened by the possibility of Victor rekindling his romance with Jarka. But I couldn't see how her jealousy could lead to her flying into a murderous rampage. And the books once again seemed to rule them out. If they were greedy or in need of cash, why not steal the books instead of burning them? Of all the suspects, Zaria had the most obvious connection to the books, but why would she want to burn Pam's novels when she seemed to care so much about them?

As Zaria came for her coffee, I saw her survey the dessert offerings with a downcast expression. It must be difficult to go through life like that, watching others enjoy things that you'd never be able to. Never being able to eat a slice of pizza after a football game or a chocolate buttercream cake at your birthday?

I smiled apologetically. "I'm sorry. I'd planned to do a honeydew sorbet for you for dessert with one of Daniel's melons, since you can't eat any of this stuff." I smiled to myself at the memory of my bartender's shocked face when he saw Melody in her *hubba-hubba* dress. "But with all the craziness I didn't have time."

"Don't worry," she said. "No one expects you to be my personal chef under the circumstances." She took a black coffee and retired to one of the window seats.

Pam came next. When I thought about it, she seemed to be at the center of everything. She'd helped engineer the coup to take over the library board, and was passionate about books. Had that passion been twisted into something more sinister? She owned not only the mysterious books Clemmons tried to smuggle out of her library but also the house where the cascade of evil had rained down. Was that happenstance or proof that she'd been behind the whole thing? She was familiar enough with the house to move around undetected and attack Sonya and Isabel. But she was one of only two people who didn't have the opportunity to spike the drinks. Capone was her alibi during the time that had happened.

Next in the queue for coffee came my own crew, whose possible involvement Capone told me again and again not to rule out. I tried to push aside my fierce sense of loyalty to them and look at the facts. Sonya was out. If Clemmons was indeed trying to steal the books, he'd involved her in the failed heist, but she had no reason to want him dead. She had a firm alibi for Clemmons's murder as well—Rabbit was with her when Clemmons was killed. And she certainly hadn't tried to smother *herself* with a pillow. Most importantly, she was Sonya, and my BFF was no killer.

Rabbit and Daniel, too, had alibis for the time of Clemmons's killing and had no discernible relationship to the victims. Melody's alibi was a little squishier. No one could say for sure where she was at the exact time of Clemmons's death, and she'd been one of the few people unaffected by the drugging. Plus, her boa had been used to kill Isabel. Despite all of that, there was no way I could believe that my Wisconsin farmgirl housemate had masterminded a one-woman crime wave.

Jarka? As Sonya said, the woman was a dark horse. Plus, I knew far less about her than I did about the other members of my team. She was one of the only people present who had medical knowledge, meaning that she'd be well aware of the effects of the pills on whoever ingested them. She had ready access to Melody's boa, and likely could've crept downstairs unseen to kill Isabel.

Given her physical fitness and the multiple staircases to
the servants' hallway, it was even possible she could've
attacked Sonya, run away down one set of stairs, and
then been able to come back up the other set of stairs
to rush in when I raised the alarm. And she sure had a
long, strange history with Victor. Was there enough history there for him to draw her into some evil scheme?
Even with all of that against her, I couldn't picture her
acting so maliciously. She'd rushed to try to help Clemmons and Isabel, even when it was hopeless. She'd saved
Sonya's life. All in all, she demonstrated a willingness to
tell the truth, even if it was ugly. For all her idiosyncra-
sies, I believed she was, first and foremost, a doctor, and
would stay true to her "do no harm" oath.

I finished pouring out the last of the coffee and sidled
over to the spot near the door to the widow's walk, where
Capone stood alone. He hadn't queued up for a cup with
the others, so I brought one over to him, along with a
tiramisu cookie.

"Black with one sugar, right?" I said, holding up my
offerings.

He took the coffee and set the dessert down on the
window seat. "Thanks."

Sonya approached me and tugged my arm toward the
bar cart. "Come on, let's get a real drink."

I put my hands up. "Tempting, but I'm going to stick
to the coffee I made with my own two hands. I'm not eating or drinking anything unless I know exactly where it
came from," I said.

"Well, *I* need some liquor to warm my cockles," Sonya said, pulling her iridescent wrap more tightly around
herself.

"At this point, I prefer to have cold cockles. I'm not

taking any chances," I said. "I can't believe you're rolling the dice. You almost died."

She shrugged. "You know what they say. Fool me once, shame on you. Fool me twice, and make it a double."

I walked over to the lakeside windows, near enough to Jarka and Victor to hear what they were saying. If I'd been hoping for some intel, though, I was disappointed. They were speaking rapidly in Bulgarian. If it were Spanish or French, I'd have had a fighting chance of understanding, having picked up a significant amount of both languages in the restaurant kitchens where I'd spent my career. Bulgarian, however, was as foreign to me as, well, Bulgarian.

Jarka broke off their conversation and came to stand with me. Victor stalked across the room to stand alone. Zaria rose and came over to him, taking hold of his arm and whispering something I couldn't hear. He rebuffed her with a flick of his wrist and she skulked back to her window seat.

Watching them, I asked Jarka, "What did he say to you?"

"He tells me I am a fool," she said. Outlined in the dim moonlight, her cheekbones looked sharp as razor blades. "Because I refuse to take the life that should be mine. He asked why should I choose struggle when I can live in comfort? He asks why I do not wish to carry on two noble houses of Europe. He tells me to come away with him."

"He propositioned you right in front of his fiancée?" I looked toward Zaria, who'd disappeared into the shadows, wrapped in a blanket, not fifteen feet away from us.

"He is very passionate man and must say how he feels.

And also she doesn't speak Bulgarian." She glanced at Victor and shook her head. "It's madness, how obsessed is he to carry on the . . . what is the word? The bloody line?"

"Bloodline?" I offered.

"Yes, bloodline. Like I am a dog to be breeded. Having such blood does not promise that you will be beautiful or smart or free of pain. What does it matter if I marry a king or a common man if I am not happy? I must live my own life. Victor thinks money will make me more free, but I am free because I make my own choices." She grunted. "Still, my heart cannot break free of him. With such sex as we had, so splendid that anyone would weep to witness its beauty. With many, many climaxes. Such passion is rare." She shook her head. For a moment, her lip trembled, and I thought she might break down. I reached out and laid my hand on her pointy collarbone.

"I'm sorry. Do you still love him?" I asked.

She lowered her eyes. "It is better that he marry Zaria Singhal. They can live the life he wants," she said quietly.

Jarka and I walked over to join the rest of the D&S crew on the couch. I could hardly believe the audacity of the Count, trying to reunite with Jarka in front of his fiancée. Whether or not Zaria spoke Bulgarian, she had clearly picked up on the intense chemistry between Victor and Jarka. And from what she'd said earlier when I'd overheard the two of them arguing behind the folding screen, she knew of their past romance and felt threatened by their unfinished business.

While all this was playing out, Capone halted his caged-lion pacing, coming to a stop at the lakeside wall of windows. He clapped his hands loudly together to get the group's attention. Everyone shifted positions to face him.

"I appreciate your cooperation in assembling up here," he began.

"I don't recall being given a choice," Victor snapped. He turned back toward the windows and flicked up the collar of his coat with his thumbs.

"I just spoke with one of my colleagues," Capone continued, ignoring the Count's peevishness. "We have a little over an hour until help arrives, so hang tight."

"Sorry it's so cold in here," Pam said, moving to stand alongside Capone. "I wasn't thinking about how poorly insulated these windows are when I suggested this room. There are space heaters, but of course, they're electric. There are more blankets in the chest over there."

"It's only for an hour. We'll live," B.L. said.

"You sure about that?" Sonya, who sat next to me, muttered into my ear.

Capone carried on with his speech. "The most imperative thing is that we all stay safe until then. From now on, nobody goes anywhere alone. Not even to the bathroom. I want a buddy system for everything. Got it? It's for everyone's safety."

"So you're in charge now?" Kennedy said. "Do I need to remind everyone that there've been two murders on your watch? Guess we shouldn't expect too much from Detective Calvin *Capone*." Turning to Victor, she explained. "His great-grandfather was Al Capone, you know, the FBI's Public Enemy Number One."

"Only in America would such an absurd thing happen," Victor scoffed. "Here, there is no appreciation for the importance of coming from a good family."

I narrowed my eyes at them and set Butterball on the couch. Even if Capone and I weren't going to become a couple, I counted him as one of *my* people. Sure, I might give him a hard time in all sorts of ways, but that was because I respected him. I certainly wasn't going to stand idly by while he was insulted by the likes of Kennedy Criss and Count Victor Blah-de-Blahstein-Whathisbutt.

"Who are you to talk smack about Detective Capone?" I asked. "Two brats born into the lap of luxury who throw their weight around to make everyone else feel bad? Capone came into this world with this giant albatross of a family legacy dragging him down. But he's built his entire career, his entire life, to redeem the Capone name by being an honest, hardworking, and brave public servant. All he's done all night is think about other people."

Sonya, who'd risen to stand when I did, held her arm backward across my chest, the way you might instinctively do to keep someone from flying through the windshield. I hadn't realized that I'd taken several steps toward the two of them with balled fists.

"I'm just saying," I said, tucking my hands into my armpits.

"Well, you looked like you were going to start 'just saying' with your knuckles," she whispered out of the corner of her mouth.

Lola rose and wrapped her blanket more tightly around her shoulders. On her, the tartan fabric draped as elegantly as a queen's robe. "Thank you, Delilah. None of this is my son's fault. He's a good man, and he's trying to keep you all safe, even though one of you is a murderer."

"One of *us*? Maybe it's you!" Zaria said, becoming animated for the first time since we entered the room.

"How dare you!" Lola countered.

Capone held up his hands. "Everyone, please." He shot me and his mother a pointed look. "Sixty more minutes of calm. That's all I'm asking. Sixty minutes."

Kennedy glared at him. "Whatever. With this 'buddy

system'"—her air quotes billowed with sarcasm—"what about Delilah and her employees? They all know each other, so how can we rely on them to police each other?"

"Well, the same goes for the couples, then," I said.

"And me and Calvin, I suppose," Lola said.

Thirteen sets of untrusting eyes scanned the darkened room. Each, no doubt, wondering the same thing I was—which one of this room's inhabitants was a cold-blooded killer?

CHAPTER 26

Pam was the first to break the tension. She picked up Gloria and walked to an old-fashioned, freestanding wind-up gramophone that stood in a little nook between the lakeside windows. She set the cat on the floor and pulled open the doors of the gramophone cabinet. Bending down, she selected a record from the collection stored under the machine.

"I think we should all settle in and wait this out, and be as pleasant to each other as we possibly can." She patted the case of the record player. "This is an antique Victrola phonograph from 1920. It works with a hand crank—no electricity required." She carefully slipped the record from its case and placed it on the turntable. As she wound the crank, the strains of a Jazz Age dance hall song crackled through the room.

It's three o'clock in the morn-ing,
We've danced the whole night through.
And daylight soon will be dawn-ing,
Just one more waltz with you.

While the part about the dawning daylight was true, we certainly hadn't danced the whole night through.

Unless you counted careening blindly from dangerous crisis to dangerous crisis.

I settled back onto the couch next to Sonya, still seething from my verbal confrontation with Victor and Kennedy.

"That was quite the display of emotion for someone who *isn't* in love with Calvin Capone," she said. She kept the volume of her voice low enough to be masked by the sound of the music.

"Capone didn't deserve their criticism, especially not after all he's been through," I said. I glanced sideways at him. He sat in a window seat, facing the group. His sentry post was directly opposite his mother, who'd settled alone at about three o'clock to our position on the giant velvet circle of sofa. For a nanosecond, he and I made eye contact. All I could hear was the old-school vibrato of the singer on the record. All I could see were the beautiful contours of his face in the flickering candlelight.

"Dee . . . ?" Sonya said, following my eyes.

"Somebody needed to tell them off, and I knew he'd be too much of a professional to say they should shut their snobby little face holes." I looked over again, but he'd turned his attention away. *Dammit. I needed to get a grip. He'd as much as told me it was never going to happen.*

"Speaking of professionalism, weren't you the one who told us all how crucial tonight was for making a good impression on the who's who?" she said.

"I think that went out the window somewhere around the second murder," I replied. "I wouldn't cater another party for these people if they offered me ten brand-new catering vans. I don't imagine this gig is going to generate good word of mouth no matter how delicious the food was anyway."

"It *was* good," she said. "Even the free-from pizza.

You outdid yourself, even though it meant that you almost caused me a stress heart attack by leaving me to do everything else."

I put my arm around her and gave her a squeeze. "You rocked it. You could be a head chef, you know. You're wasted as a sous."

"You and I both know I'd hate the pressure of running a kitchen. Plus, I like the second banana role."

"You *are* pretty bananas," I said, laying my head on her shoulder.

"That's why we're *prime-mates*," she quipped.

I groaned. "That was maybe the worst joke I ever heard."

"I'll be here all night, folks. Don't forget to tip your waiters." She waved to an imaginary crowd, sighed, and leaned her head against mine. "Seriously, though, I'm glad we were able to do a favor for Isabel, and make Zaria happy, too. I can't tell if I even like her, but I feel sorry for her. I think Mel's right about Victor not being in love with her. It seems like he's never gotten over Jarka."

Pam put on another record, something classical with a warbly soprano voice accompanied by a violin.

"Have you given any more thought to the message from Clemmons?" I asked.

Sonya nodded. "I've been racking my brain. I know Capone's going to question me about it again when we get out of here."

"Any epiphanies?" I asked.

"I've been over and over it. He said I needed to keep the books safe." She let out a bitter chuckle. "So much for that. Maybe whatever he wanted me to know went up in flames. If Pam is right that the killer burned the books, *they* certainly thought that they were incriminating."

"But maybe they were wrong? If we're right that the

first part of the message, about *The Man Who Knew Too Much* referring to Clemmons himself having potentially dangerous info, then the destruction of the book wouldn't matter." I recalled again how casually Clemmons had handled the valuable books, with nowhere near the care displayed by Zaria, Isabel, and Pam. He hadn't flinched when I shoved them into my apron pocket. "That book, at least, would only be a vessel for his message, not the message itself. So what did he know too much about?"

Our eyes both traced a line between B.L. Huddleston and Lola Capone. "Seems plausible that Clemmons was referring to knowing too much about them," I said.

"Could be," Sonya agreed. "Although you said there was some other thing he was worried about even before he saw them together, right? The thing that was 'amiss' in the house?" Sonya pressed her finger to her chin. "What was the rest of the message? That the plot of *The Maltese Falcon* was more realistic than you might imagine, and that the books were a small part of a larger collection?"

While Sonya and I were talking, Butterball curled up on the back of the couch just over my shoulder. I suddenly noticed how Gloria had gradually pawed her way along the upper radius of the giant velvet expanse until she came face-to-face with my cat.

"Uh-oh," I said, swiveling around to sit on my knees facing them.

Butterball had a reputation for catfighting, and though I was never sure how he'd respond to a new feline, it was a safe bet that it wouldn't go well. As far as I knew, he and Gloria had given a wide berth to each other all night. They'd been in the same room during dinner, but with his attention occupied by all the food on offer, I doubted he'd taken much notice of her.

As Gloria edged closer, Butterball rose. He assumed

a wary stance, his tail swishing back and forth like it
was trying to start a Mexican wave. Gloria paused and
cocked her head to the side. She gave him a long, probing
look and slowly blinked. I searched the room for Pam,
wondering if this encounter would be as worrying for her
as it was for me. Probably not. Little miss perfect Ragdoll
beauty queen cat probably never threw down with other
felines. Pam was on the opposite side of the room with her
back to us, demonstrating the room's telescope to B.L.

"*Meee-ooow?*" Gloria suggested, bringing my attention back to the scene playing out in front of me.

Rrrow, Butterball replied, seeming unsure how to in-
terpret her apparent friendliness.

I moved to scoop Butterball into my arms. Before I
could reach him, though, his posture relaxed as Gloria
took a few steps closer to him and kneaded the back of
the sofa with her paws. She performed a dainty pirouette
and lay down, with her back facing him. She cast a few
come-hither glances over her shoulder.

Butterball, seemingly hypnotized by her display, took
a cautious step toward her, as if he were creeping out
onto the edge of a cliff. She turned again and planted
herself a fraction closer to him. Amazingly, the two
moved closer, one minute movement at a time.

Sonya gasped. "Oh my god, is Gloria flirting with the
Big Man?"

"I think maybe."

The two cats met and dragged their bodies alongside
each other. My heart filled. I was the mother of a cat who
lacked social graces, and the prospect of him making feline friends was more than I could've hoped for. I'd never
had a pet before Butterball, and I had little experience in
the development of kitty friendships. Still, this looked
promising.

The two cats paraded back and forth for several turns of their intricate tabby tango. Just before I could chalk it up in the win column, however, Gloria hip-checked Butterball and sent him flying off the back of the couch. He landed heavily and meowed his dissatisfaction from behind the couch.

"That was a low blow, Gloria," Sonya chastised, leaning over the back of the sofa to retrieve an annoyed-looking Butterball.

Gloria, for her part, moved a few feet along the sofa's top and sat upright like catnip wouldn't melt in her mouth.

A shadow loomed into view and I looked up to find Capone standing over us. "Everything all right? I heard something fall."

"It was Butterball, poor thing. Gloria laid a honey trap for him," I said, squinting distrustfully at Pam's cat as I helped Sonya right herself and returned Butterball to his rightful spot on the couch. "I swear to God she just laughed at him."

"All right." Capone pivoted to return to his seat near Lola, but his eyes stopped on my face. "You've got that look," he said. "That 'investigating a crime' look. Did you forget that you're not wearing your deputy badge anymore?"

"Well, I've gone rogue," I replied. "We have an hour to kill. You can't expect us to switch our brains off and stare into space."

Sonya looked around to be sure that no one else was in earshot, then pulled Capone down on the couch between us and brought him up to speed on our theory about the first part of Clemmons's message.

"B.L. Huddleston is definitely near the top of my suspect list," Capone said, once he'd heard our line of reasoning. "But the fact that Clemmons knew a damaging secret is an incomplete explanation. Without all the witnesses being questioned or the evidence and the victims properly examined, you'll only ever narrow it down to a best guess. I can't make an arrest on the cryptic words of a dead man."

"He's right," I said.

"Nice to hear you say so for once," he replied.

"I mean, the part about the title of *The Man Who Knew Too Much* only explaining part of the message. Why would he say the rest of the message unless it meant something important? 'The plot of *The Maltese Falcon* is more realistic than you might imagine.' What would that have to do with B.L., or with Clemmons knowing a secret? And the thing about those books being part of a larger collection? Did he mean there's something fishy about Pam's whole library? Or the town's whole library?" I asked.

He sighed. "That's not what I meant. I meant taking a flying leap at Clemmons's clue isn't the way to systematically solve the case."

I gestured to the room. "Oh, I know what you meant, but I don't see a mobile crime lab or a bunch of uniformed officers taking statements, and we still have about"—I checked my watch—"fifty-four minutes left to kill."

Sonya winced.

I reached across Capone and squeezed her hand. "Sorry. Poor choice of words."

Capone sighed again, even more deeply. He rose and pulled over a stool so that he could sit facing the room and still be close enough to us to hear over the gramophone's music. "Fine. I can play your game while I keep watch. What's the plot of *The Maltese Falcon*? I've never read it."

"Don't look at me," I said. "I'm a barbarian, remember? Son's your woman for culture."

Sonya scooted closer to us. "Let's see. The movie's from the forties, but the book is set in the twenties. Sam Spade—Humphrey Bogart in the movie, but we're talking about the book so that's irrelevant—anyway, Spade's a private investigator who meets a client. She's gorgeous, of course, tall, great figure, red hair and blue eyes. My dream woman, in fact, and I once dated a woman who looked just like that."

"Helen from that doomsday cult?" I asked.

"Yeah." She sighed.

"She *was* pretty," I assured Capone.

"Maybe not relevant to the story, though," he said.

"Right," Sonya agreed, launching back into her retelling. "Anyway, the hot redhead says she's looking for her sister and the man she—the sister, that is—ran off with. Spade and his partner take the case, but that night his partner is murdered, along with the man the alleged sister allegedly ran off with." She looked from my face to Capone's. "You following?"

I wobbled my hand back and forth. "Ish?"

"Well, the murder of Spade's partner is just the beginning. Spade figures out his client has a fake identity and her real name is Brigid O'Shaughnessy. Total femme fatale archetype, of course, played by Mary Astor in the movie, but again, we're talking about the book. So, Spade discovers the whole sister-running-off story was bogus."

While Sonya was talking, Melody and Jarka had moved to take seats on either side of me and Sonya.

Butterball, too, moved from the top of the couch to nestle in between us, ears perked attentively.

"What are you guys talking about?" Melody asked.

"Son's telling us the plot of *The Maltese Falcon*," I explained. "So far, we've learned that Sonya's perfect woman is a femme fatale type who's also a serial liar, which sounds about right."

Sonya glared at me. "*As I was saying*," she continued, "on the back of that fiasco, Spade takes another case to find a valuable statue of a bird, the Maltese Falcon. It's bedazzled with jewels and from ancient times, so it's worth beaucoup bucks. That turns into a whole mess because the guy who comes to him about the statue is just a front man for another, way worse, crook called Mr. G, or, in the movie, the Fat Man, which is really size-ist, but it was the forties, so what are you going to do? Spade goes to meet Mr. G, but during the meeting, Spade's drink is spiked and he's knocked out cold."

"Spiked drinks?" Melody said. "Do you think Mr. Clemmons predicted that?"

I turned to Capone. "Your mother's missing Xanax pills—my crew figured out they were in the first round of cocktails. The gin bottle was spiked."

His surprised expression morphed into one of understanding.

Jarka tilted her head thoughtfully. "This makes sense, I think. In hospital, we use this class of drugs as sedative, and also for anxiety. How many pills Mrs. Capone did have?"

"A whole bottle," I replied.

"Yes, this could be enough to affect so many of us. Mix with alcohol, this can be dangerous and cause very much of sedation. Sometimes patient becomes ataxic—

dizzy like is Daniel. Can also cause some people to say or do not appropriate behaviors. Each person can have different effects," Jarka explained.

"It's too big a coincidence if anything else was used." I quickly filled in the details of our process of elimination, since Jarka and Capone hadn't been there when we'd gone through the whole thing.

Jarka agreed. "These pills, they have a moment of sweet taste, then turn to bitter. This would be covered by gin."

"So whoever did it acted sometime between the blackout and the time we sat down to eat," I explained. "The only people who were likely to count on having access to tranquilizers tonight would have been you"—I indicated Capone—"your mother, and most likely B.L. Huddleston since he's been dating your mother for a while. Maybe Clemmons somehow knew that and was trying to warn us by telling us to think about the spiked drink in the book's plot?"

Sonya crossed her arms over her chest and shot a smug expression at Capone. "And you said we wouldn't be able to figure this out without a full-on investigation."

"Okay, okay, you did some good work," Capone granted. "But spiked drinks are in practically every film noir movie, not to mention countless murder mysteries. It's not the main plot, so I'm not sure that's the plot point Clemmons would have meant. Besides, I can't figure how he could've predicted the whole chain of events that led up to the spiked drinks."

Melody twirled one of her blond curls. "He has a point. Plus, if the killer planned all along to spike our drinks, wouldn't they have brought their own drugs?"

"They probably didn't plan it," I said. "Drugging

everyone only become important so they could get to Sonya and Isabel during the night without anyone waking up."

"Which only became important when everyone found out about the coded message—when you announced it to the world in the kitchen," Capone finished.

I grimaced, realizing that my loose lips may well have triggered the killer to strike again.

Capone paused. "A quick, opportunistic decision to drug everyone fits with the profile I have in my head of this suspect. Assaulting Clemmons with his own cane feels like an opportunistic decision, too. Possibly something that was only decided a short time in advance, or even in the moment. I don't think Clemmons could've predicted all of that. If he had, presumably he wouldn't be dead at the bottom of the stairs."

We were all silent for a moment, granting the point.

"Finish the story," Melody urged. "I want to know what happens."

"Right." Sonya slapped her palms on her thighs and continued. "After the drink spiking, Spade randomly receives a mysterious visit from a ship's captain. The captain's been wounded but manages to give Spade the Maltese Falcon statue before he dies. Spade's like 'oh, snap!' because he realizes that everyone's going to be after it, so he hides it. Spade meets with Mr. G and agrees to give the statue to him, but when he does, it turns out that *duhn-duhn-DUHN*"—she widened her eyes dramatically—"it was a fake the whole time. And they all start to wonder if there ever even *was* a real statue."

"Just like Jules Pascin," Jarka said. She gestured to her outfit. She'd lost the bowler hat at some point during the night, but the rest of her "most famous" Bulgarian artist getup remained intact. "My father owns several of his paintings. Some years ago, he hired someone to say how much are they worth, for to get insurance. And this person, he tells my father the paintings are fake."

"Whoa, that's wild," Melody said. "What happened to the real paintings?"

"Even to this day, the real paintings are not found any-place," Jarka said. "It causes great sorrow to my father. Not for the money. For him such money is *pffftt*." She blew a raspberry and waved her hand. "But these paint-ing are important part of history for my country. Pascin is most famous Bulgarian since Khristo Botev."

We all nodded, although I suspected I wasn't the only one who hadn't the faintest clue who Khristo Botev was.

Melody turned back to Sonya. "Okay, how does *The Maltese Falcon* end?"

"Mr. G peaces out of there before the fuzz can catch up with him," Sonya said, "and Spade figures out that Brigid O'Shaughnessy killed his partner. And he's like, 'You're hot and all, but I'm turning your lying, murder-ing ass in to the cops.' And he does. The end."

Melody frowned. "That's awful. So it's not a happy ending for *anyone*? Not even the good guy?"

"Nope," Sonya said. "That's what film noir is all about."

Jarka fixed her eyes on Victor. "No happy ending. Like life."

CHAPTER 27

Capone, Melody, Jarka, and I sat quietly for a moment, absorbing the details of Sonya's tale. Double crosses, fake statues, fraught love affairs. Why couldn't Clemmons have conveyed his message with something a little more straightforward like, say, the plot of *The Very Hungry Caterpillar*? I stroked Butterball's back, listening to him purr as I stared out into the still-dark sky. His face was smooshed against my thigh, his long tail waving lazily back and forth. It had been a long night for everyone. Whatever you wanted to call this experience—purgatory or the world's worst sleepover—if I had to be here, I was glad I was with Butterball and the rest of my crew.

Capone seemed as lost in thought as I was, but suddenly his attention sharpened. He bent down, looking under the couch. "What was that?" he asked.

"I saw something, too," Sonya said.

The jazzy tune that had been playing on the gramophone ended, replaced by a staticky *thup, thup, thup*.

"I think it was Gloria, trying to play," Melody said. She pointed under the couch. "There she goes again."

I leaned over just in time to see the blur of a white paw take a swipe at Butterball's tail. Butterball rolled over but didn't fully awaken. "That little booger," I said.

"I don't think she means any harm. Our barn cats mess with each other like that all the time," Melody said.

No sooner were the words out of her mouth than Gloria's little white diamond of a face popped out from under the couch. She zeroed in on Butterball's tail, eyeing it like it was a runaway gerbil. A lightning-fast series of kitty karate chops ensued, followed by a full-on pounce onto Butterball's recumbent body.

Screeeeeeee.

Butterball sprang up, yowling.

All the human inhabitants of the couch arose en masse as the two cats began to tussle. The people arrayed around the room, hearing the commotion, hurried over.

"Are they playing or fighting?" Lola wondered aloud.

Pam and I answered simultaneously.

"Fighting," I said.

"Playing," Pam said, our words overlapping.

Whichever one of us was right, the events of the next few moments played out with dizzying rapidity. The two cats wrestled and swiped their way up and down the couch, caterwauling loud enough to wake the dead. Which, in that house, was saying something.

Then, Gloria took off at maximum speed around the top of the round couch with Butterball in hot pursuit. They made the circuit once, both managing to leap across a several-foot-wide chasm where the C shape of the sofa opened. For the first few moments, the humans stood helplessly, watching the two pursue each other like Olympic speed skaters. It quickly became apparent, however, that the far more agile Gloria was about to lap her ungainly opponent.

"Grab them," I said, fearing what would happen when she caught him. She clearly had more feistiness in her than her outward appearance suggested. More than that, though, I was worried that Butterball, who probably weighed double what Gloria did, could badly injure her if he struck out in self-defense.

The scene unfolded like a slapstick comedy, with various people unsuccessfully attempting to intervene and corral the wound-up felines. Rabbit, who'd been spared the sedative cocktail, seemed to have the best chance at grabbing Butterball, moving quickly to head him off by the closed door that led into the house. He positioned himself like a baseball catcher at the gap between the two sides of the sofa.

Just when it looked like Butterball would run straight into his waiting arms, though, the cat pulled off one of the most astounding displays of athleticism since Michael Jordan led the Bulls to a second three-peat in 1998. Butterball, my graceless mound of feline flesh, somehow careened past Rabbit and mounted the tower's large telescope. It had been fixed at a steep upward angle, and Butterball scampered up it like it was a ramp. A transom window, which I'd failed to notice before that moment, had been left open over the door. Butterball launched himself through it like a kitty cannonball. We heard a telltale, sandbag-heavy *thunk*, followed by scampering sounds that let us know he'd survived his feat of derring-do. While we all stood marveling at the impossibility of what we'd just witnessed, Gloria followed him up and out.

"What the actual hell?" Sonya breathed. "Since when can he move like that?"

"Did you just see that?" B.L. said, pointing and grinning like a kid at the circus.

After a moment of shocked paralysis, I tore across the room and flung open the door.

"Where are you going?" Capone called, rushing after me.

"To get Butterball," I replied.

"No, you can't go running all over the house. It'll only be a few minutes until help arrives," he said.

"I *have* to get him," I said desperately. "He could get lost. He could get hurt. He may already be hurt! What if he gets outside somehow? This estate is how many acres? I'd never find him."

Energized as Butterball was, there was no telling what he was capable of. We'd all just witnessed him practically take flight.

"How're you gonna find him in the dark in this huge house?" Rabbit asked.

"I don't know, but I have to try," I said.

By now, Pam had come to the door. "Delilah's right," she said. "Even if they were playing, they might get hurt. You never know with cats."

"The door to the library is closed, so we don't have to worry about Ms. Berney, but what if they get curious about Mr. Clemmons's body?" Melody said. "It's laying out in the open."

"Oh, gross," Sonya said. Even in the candlelight, I could see the color drain from her cheeks.

A collective look of disgust passed across the faces of the congregated people as they processed the unspoken implications. I, too, shuddered as I remembered Melody's earlier comment about cats feasting on the eyeballs of their dead owners. It had been hours since Butterball had eaten, and he usually started rooting around for nom-noms just before dawn. I didn't think the eyeball thing was true, but I wasn't in the mood to find out.

Seeing Capone's resolve waver, I pleaded, "It would break my heart if anything happened to him, or if he hurt Gloria or if"—I dropped my voice—"God forbid, he did something to a dead body. Please, he's my baby."

Looking into my eyes, he nodded. "Okay."

Kennedy stepped over, her arms crossed over her chest. "What about the buddy system?"

"I'll go," Sonya said, stepping over and taking me by the hand.

"We agreed it would be *unrelated* people," Kennedy interjected.

"Pam, you'll come with us, won't you?" I asked.

"Of course," she said, giving me a sympathetic pat on the arm.

The three of us started out the door before further objections could be raised. I was surprised to find Capone following us onto the landing. He pulled the door behind him, leaving it open only a crack. "Delilah, can I have a word?"

Sonya looked from my face to his. "We'll wait for you at the bottom of the stairs," she said, leading Pam along.

Once they were out of earshot, Capone leaned toward me and spoke low into my ear. "Be careful." There was almost no light on the landing, just a dim yellow seepage around the doorframe that led into the observation tower. He pressed a large metal object into my hands. A flashlight. I heard a click, and a circle of illumination played across the ceiling. "It's for light, obviously, but also in case you *need* it."

He didn't need to elaborate. I slapped the hilt into my palm, taking stock of its ability to double as a truncheon. "Got it," I said. I pointed the beam downward, casting mine and Capone's faces once again into shadow.

"Does your phone still have any juice?" he asked. "It would be good if we could reach each other."

"No. I think pretty much everyone's batteries are empty," I said. "Rabbit's phone is ancient, Daniel and Jarka burned through theirs while using their flashlight apps, and Sonya's was already dead. Melody's is still hanging in there, but we want to save it in case Biz needs to reach us."

"You have a watch?"

I raised my wrist to show him that I did.

"Twenty minutes, then, okay?" he said. "Like Rabbit said, this is a huge house. If you can't find Butterball in that amount of time, just come back. I don't want to have to come looking for you. We can have a thorough search once help arrives and it's daylight. Remember, you don't really know Pam Philips, and we can't completely rule out someone else hiding in the house. Anything is possible."

"I have to take the chance," I said. "Besides, if Sonya and I get murdered while we're downstairs and then Pam comes back whistling nonchalantly, it's going to make solving the case a whole lot easier. So you're welcome in advance for that."

He took hold of my forearms. "Delilah, please don't joke. I'm serious. I don't want anything to happen to you." His voice was husky and intimate.

I clicked off the flashlight. I was worried sick for Butterball, frightened for myself, wrung out from the hours of endless anxiety and horror, running on too much adrenaline and too little sleep. And yet, as I stood with him in the dark, so close I could almost feel his heartbeat, I knew it was now or never. I wrapped my arms around Capone and pulled him toward me. His lips met mine and I let myself be swept into his kiss.

I'd imagined this moment so many times. In my dreams, I thought I'd feel some magical zing of passion. And I did—as his strong arms enfolded me, a chemical reaction coursed through me from the tips of my toenails to the ends of my hair. This didn't feel like the consummation of my months of lusting after him, though. Instead, the passion was coupled with an unexpected emotion, a deep bass note striking, like a gong sounding in some hidden corner of my soul. I clung tighter, the solidity of him rooting me to the earth.

I love you, I thought. *To me, you're perfect.*

Who knew if I'd ever be brave enough to say the words out loud, but I hoped he felt them. I pulled away quickly, stunned by my own boldness and frightened that he'd push me away. After he'd rejected my obvious hints and overtures so many times, I couldn't stand that. Not now, when I'd laid my bare heart on a silver platter for him.

"Twenty minutes," I said. With that, I turned and hurried down the stairs.

CHAPTER 28

I caught up with Pam and Sonya at the bottom of the staircase, my heart still booming in my chest. *Had I really just kissed Capone?* I recalled what Jarka had said about Xanax making some people do reckless or impulsive things. That must be it. *You're not in love with Capone. Your drug-addled brain made you do something crazy.* So much of what had happened over the last few hours felt like a nightmare, and the line between reality and mirage felt even more questionable now.

"Everything good?" Sonya asked.

"Yep." I kept my reply as curt as possible and shined the flashlight's beam away from myself, trying to keep my face in shadow. Still, I was pretty sure Sonya would use her telepathy to divine what just happened.

Pam looked down, "Oh, good, Detective Capone gave you the heavy-duty flashlight. This thing is pretty dinky." She clicked her little key chain LED off and on. "I wish I'd put some lights on a generator backup, too. It seemed unnecessary. I always liked power outages when I was growing up. I'd sit under a blanket with a camping lantern and read all night. But then, I grew up in a little five-room bungalow in Milwaukee. Nothing like this."

"That sounds cozy," Sonya said. "When I was a kid, I lived in an apartment in downtown Chicago. We almost never lost power, and when we did, all I remember is having to climb up twelve flights of stairs because the elevator was out."

"Butterball must be terrified," I said. "He hates unfamiliar surroundings, and this place is huge."

"Try not to worry," Pam soothed.

"Well, let's get started with the big-game hunt," Sonya said.

I nodded.

We walked along the servants' hallway, shining the flashlight into each corner of the rooms. I'd hoped he might retreat to the place where'd he'd slept with me, but no dice. Next, we made our way down to the second floor.

"Should we split up?" Pam asked. "We could cover more ground."

"I'd rather stay together, to make sure we're being systematic," I said. In my mind I added, *And so you can't sneak up and murder us.*

"I suppose that makes sense, since I know the house better, and I know Gloria's usual hangouts," she said. She let out a long sigh. "I guess I'll have to move now."

"I'm sorry. I know how much time and money you poured into the renovation," I said.

"The money doesn't bother me; I just don't know if I can live with all these bad memories. I can't help feeling like there's bad karma here," Pam said.

"One of my exes offers cleansing rituals," Sonya said. "Sage burnings, exorcising evil juju—she does it all. I'm sure she could hook you up."

"That's very generous," Pam said.

"You should definitely *not* take her up on that," I cautioned.

Sonya waved me off. "Delilah's a skeptic, but if you're interested, as soon as she gets out of prison, I can put you in touch with her."

I shot Pam a "see what I mean" look. Aloud, I said, "Just don't sell it right away. Not after all the work you've put into it. Bad things can happen anywhere."

"I suppose I could rent it as an Airbnb or give tours if I wanted to. People seem to be drawn to this sort of thing," Pam said.

I nodded, thinking about the mob tours in Chicago that took sightseers to the place where the Saint Valentine's Day massacre went down. The same fascination had brought Geneva Bay's wealthiest residents together the previous night, to reenact that era of lawlessness. Little did any of us know that the pantomime of violence and mayhem would overlap with the reality of it.

"Before tonight," Pam continued, "I didn't mind the loneliness of this place. I liked it, actually. I like my own company."

We continued our search of the dark, silent bedrooms, calling out the cats' names. The downstairs bedrooms were spacious, and stuffed with furniture—chaise lounges, canopy beds, armoires—a veritable wonderland of hiding places for pair of fugitive cats.

"This seems hopeless," I moaned. I checked my watch. "I promised Capone we'd be back in twenty minutes." I shined the flashlight along the hall. "Buuuuutterbaaaaall."

"Still three more bedrooms, plus all of downstairs, plus the basement to search," Sonya pointed out.

I sighed. "Maybe it would help if we had some food. Butterball responds to the sound of an anchovy tin opening a lot better than the sound of his own name."

"That's not a bad idea," Pam said. "If there was any food left out in the kitchen, they might've gone there."

Sonya took a few steps toward the main staircase and I followed along, nearly reaching the landing.

A firm hand on my shoulder startled me. "Probably best if we take the servants' staircase," Pam said. "Edgar's still at the bottom of this one."

I stiffened at her touch, realizing I'd completely let my guard down. Pam had been right behind us at the top of the stairs, just as Clemmons's killer must've been right behind him. Had he and his murderer been casually chatting until the moment he or she pulled his cane away and struck the fatal blow? My heart beat faster.

"Oh, right," I said, turning back to head the other way.

I tried not to let my eyes rest on the door of the dumbwaiter as we passed it. The killer had opened that door only a few hours before and slipped the cane, still wet with Clemmons's blood, into the dark shaft.

You don't really know Pam Philips. Capone's words echoed in my ear. I stole a quick glance at the woman next to me. With her duckling-yellow robe and matronly physique, she looked about as murderous as a feather pillow. Then again, hadn't a feather pillow almost killed Sonya? Could Pam's buoyant exterior be hiding a more sinister interior? She was a supremely intelligent woman with vast resources. Had she engineered this entire scenario somehow? I was so caught up in our kitty quest, I'd forgotten to stay alert.

As we rounded the corner to the servants' staircase, I squeezed the flashlight, feeling the reassuring heft of its heavy metal shaft. "After you," I said to Pam.

Pam blazed a path forward with her tiny key chain flashlight. Sonya went next, and I entered the stairwell just behind her, realizing for the first time how claustrophobic the small, enclosed space felt. The thick carpeting deadened sound. In the daylight, the carved patterns on the stairwell's wooden panels showed cornucopias brimming with fruits and flowers against a background of swirls and braids and fleurs-de-lis. My flashlight's harsh beam, though, played a macabre trick of the light with my eyes, revealing strange patterns that looked like ghoulish faces and screaming souls.

Keep it together. You need to find Butterball.

Pam turned the final corner and disappeared from sight. I heard a gasp and watched the light from her flashlight pinwheel in all directions before disappearing. Pam stumbled backward, falling hard onto her rear end. Scrambling back to her feet, she barreled past Sonya toward me, her eyes wild. She was on me in an instant, her flailing body knocking the flashlight out of my hand. It landed facing the wall, snuffing out the light. Everything around us plunged into darkness.

CHAPTER 29

I struggled to keep to my feet as Pam fumbled past me. Clutching at my arm, she attempted to pull me up the stairs.

"What are you doing?" I demanded, tugging my arm free from her grip. I pressed my back into the banister, unsure if the greatest threat to me was Pam or whatever had frightened her.

"*Shhhh.*" She spoke in an urgent whisper. "There's someone down there. Waiting at the bottom of the stairs."

"What happened to your flashlight?" Sonya asked in a low voice.

"I dropped it. It must've rolled underneath something," Pam replied, her voice shaking.

As my eyes adjusted, I could make out a small arc of illumination that revealed where my own flashlight—still lit—was wedged against the wall. I leaned down and picked it up, feeling a smidgeon more secure with it in my hands. The outlines of the space came back into focus. Pam, who was already halfway up the stairs, turned back, startled by the light. She looked past us to the turn in the staircase, beyond which lay the person she'd seen. Sonya was pressed against the wall, her outturned thigh peeking out of the slit in her flapper dress. With her head turned dramatically to one side and her eyes and mouth making matching O shapes, she looked like she was ready to start belting the opening number from the musical *Chicago*.

I looked from Pam looming above me to the darkness looming below Sonya. Was this some kind of ruse, designed so Pam could rush past us and claim the high ground? Clearly, whoever killed Clemmons and Isabel liked to sneak up on their victims from behind. But Pam was frozen, statue-still, her eyes fixed on the abyss of blackness the flashlight couldn't penetrate. I tried to slow my juddering heart and shaky breath so I could listen for movement from below. Nothing. Not the slightest shifting of position, not the merest creak of a foot upon a stair tread.

I glanced back up at Pam. "You're sure you saw someone?"

She nodded. "A tall man with a hat on."

"Who's down there?" I called out.

No reply.

I played out various scenarios in my mind. Maybe our rescuers had come while we were conducting our search.

And decided to stand completely still.

In the pitch dark.

Okay, maybe not.

Maybe the murderer had been hiding in the house this whole time, a stranger creeping around in the shadows, picking off his victims one by one. But how could we have missed him? And how could an outsider have moved around freely enough to steal Lola's pills and slip them into the gin bottle? Even in the blackout gloom, surely Daniel would've noticed a tall mystery man creeping close enough to spike the bottle? Who could be down there? Suddenly, an image popped into my mind.

I took a few cautious steps downward.

"What are you doing?" Sonya said, her voice raspy with fear.

"What kind of hat was the person wearing?" I called up to Pam.

"What?" she asked. "I don't know. Why does that matter?"

"Just tell me," I said. "Was it a bowler hat?"

She seemed taken aback. "I couldn't see clearly, but possibly? How did you know that?"

I exhaled, walking forward with more determination, fairly certain I knew the identity of the mystery man. Still, I held on to the flashlight with both hands, not ready to start taking any chances.

I moved past Sonya and rounded the blind corner slowly. I was greeted by the sight that had scared the wits out of Pam Philips a moment earlier. A thin man in a bowler hat standing perfectly motionless just to the right of the base of the stairs. When I shined the flashlight directly on him, however, he morphed into his true identity—a coatrack, hung with Capone's puffy down jacket and topped with Jarka / Jules Pascin's bowler hat.

I'd noticed how earlier, when he'd come back from restarting the generator, Capone had splayed the jacket across two arms of the coatrack for maximum drying effect. At some point during the evening, Jarka's hat ended up there as well, creating the scarecrow image that had sent Pam fleeing up the stairs.

"It's okay!" I called up to her and Sonya. "It was just a coatrack with a hat and coat on it."

I heard hesitant steps creeping down the stairs. Pam's face popped around the corner, looking as if she still expected an axe-wielding murderer to be lying in wait. Sonya's face appeared alongside hers a moment later. At the sight of the now-illuminated coatrack, Pam clutched her chest.

"Oh, sweet baby Jesus in the manger," she said. The gleam of her relieved smile stood out in the darkness. She dismounted the stairs and walked over to the coatrack, grabbing it between the top of Capone's coat and the bottom of Jarka's hat. She wrapped her hands around its "neck" and pretended to strangle it. "You scared the living daylights out of me, mister," she said. She turned to me. "I'm sorry for overreacting."

"I think we can all be excused for being a little jumpy," I replied.

As if in response, a heavy clang sounded from the direction of the kitchen, causing us to startle again.

"What was that?" Sonya asked.

Another clatter sounded, followed by a familiar feline voice.

"Butterball," I said.

Pam sighed with relief. "I swear I don't know how my body can make any more adrenaline. You'd think I'd be tapped out by now."

We hurried toward the kitchen, where we caught up with our two fugitive cat burglars. Pam and I shined our flashlights on the cats. Two pairs of eyes—one on the counter and one on the floor—mirrored the light back at us like reflectors on a highway sign.

"What in the world . . . ?" Pam said.

Judging by the looks on the cats' faces, we'd caught them in the act of committing the crime of the century. Gloria stood on the counter, front paw aloft, having apparently just succeeded in knocking a large metal box onto the floor. Butterball stood below, swiping at the thing.

"What do they have?" Sonya asked, crossing the kitchen toward them.

"It's a bread box," Pam said. "The old-fashioned punched tin and wood kind. There's only bread in it, though. What kind of cat eats bread?"

"There's not much Butterball won't eat. He's been known to eat packing peanuts if he's desperate enough," I said. "I guess bread is the best he could do."

I played my light across the countertops. As I suspected, Rabbit had done his usual meticulous job of cleaning up. Not a speck of food remained for Butterball to feast upon. Clearly, he'd had to improvise.

Pam crossed the room and scooped up her cat. She tsked her tongue against the roof of her mouth. "You're a regular Bonnie and Clyde, you two. Butterball must be very persuasive to have convinced Gloria to take part. She's a finicky eater."

"He probably bribed her," I said, picking up my own feline and pressing my face into his body. I had the twin urges to reprimand him for his antics and cradle him against my chest for the rest of his natural life. "When it comes to food, I wouldn't put anything past him. You probably promised Gloria her weight in catnip or something, didn't you?" I asked him.

He meowed his claim of innocence, but I didn't buy it for a second. We'd caught him red pawed. I took a moment to breathe in the comforting scent of his fur. He was a scoundrel, but he was *my* scoundrel. Plus, it looked like Pam and Melody had been right about the two cats playing, or at least cooperating. This orange maniac had been in fights so often, I had no idea he was capable of friendship.

I glanced at my watch. "Our time's almost up. We should get back upstairs," I said, cradling Butterball against my hip.

As we headed out, I stole a look at Pam, who carried

Gloria in her arms like a baby. It was hard not to like the woman. She seemed like a straight shooter, definitely my kind of person. But I was doing my best to channel Capone's always-suspicious posture. No reason to let my guard down now, when we were so close to rescue.

We retraced our steps through the dining room and back to the servants' stairs. As the flashlight caught the coatrack scarecrow, Sonya remarked, "It does look just like a person."

Pam nodded. "Took a year off my life when I saw it in the shadows. But I guess if we've learned anything tonight, it's that appearances can be deceiving." She looked around. "I wonder how it ended up all the way back here. I guess someone moved it during the party."

I hadn't thought about it before, but now that she mentioned it, I realized how odd it was to have a coatrack so far from any doors. "Where do you usually keep it?" I asked.

"Near the front door in the main hall. Isabel probably moved it to get it out of the way," she said with a shrug. "She rented collapsible garment racks for all the coats. Those are still in the front hall."

I stopped, suddenly immobilized. I walked over to the coatrack, mesmerized by its humanlike proportions. It was a few inches shorter than I was, putting the top of Jarka's bowler hat right at my eye level.

"Dee?" Sonya asked.

I could barely hear her. My pulse had only just returned to normal after the false alarm earlier, but now it began to quicken. I took hold of the coatrack and rocked it gently from side to side, doing a slow-motion dance. Capone's coat waved its arms and Jarka's bowler hat nodded in time to the silent beat.

I took a step back, not taking my eyes off of the rack. "Can you jiggle this for me while I watch, Son?" I asked.

"Jiggle it?" she asked.

"Yeah, move it around like I just did."

Her face creased into a "Have you lost your mind?" frown, but she obliged. We swapped places. "*Da-da-da-dum-dum-dum-wah-waaaah*," Sonya sang a few bars of a bump-and-grind burlesque-style air as she moved the rack from side to side. Her "dance partner" quivered and shimmied as she swung her hips.

"Should I leave?" Pam asked, her tone echoing Sonya's concern for my sanity.

"What do you see?" I asked her.

"Two women who've left their senses dancing with a wooden hatstand," Pam replied.

Ignoring her answer, I turned to face her. "What about that folding screen? The one we used to shield Clemmons's body? Where do you usually keep that?" I asked.

Pam tilted her head to one side, examining my face. "It's usually in the drawing room," she said slowly. "The rental company probably moved it when they delivered the tables and chairs. I noticed it was out of place, but the hallway seemed a good spot for it so it wouldn't block anyone's view during Lola's performance."

I checked my watch. Only two more minutes until Capone's twenty-minute time limit was up. What would happen if we didn't make it back in time? Would he send out a search party? If my theory turned out to be true, I didn't want the group splitting up. I set Butterball on the floor. "Please don't run away, B-man. Okay? Just be a good boy this one time."

He stared up at me and gave a single *mewrrrr*, making no promises. Was there such a thing as a cat obedience class? I'd be sure to google it when and if we ever got back home.

I crossed into the drawing room, beating a beeline toward Clemmons's body. The room was chilly and silent, its huge windows revealing the first predawn inklings in the form of a colorless gloom. Jarka and Rabbit had cleaned up the abandoned food and drinks earlier, but the room still gave off the eerie, suspended-animation vibe of a submerged shipwreck.

"I know this seems crazy, but there's something I have to try," I called back over my shoulder. I took hold of one side of the screen and began to fold it in on itself.

"I don't understand what's going on," Pam said, shuffling in her slippers to catch up. She was holding Gloria in her arms, with Sonya and Butterball padding along next to them.

When Sonya realized where I was headed, she skidded to a stop a few feet short of the folding screen. "What are you doing? Is that where Edgar is? Oh god." She gagged.

Butterball hissed, his back arched. Apparently, he also wasn't a fan of the idea of getting this close to a dead body.

"I know. I'm sorry. Believe me, I don't want to be doing this. I need to move the folding screen back over by the stairs. Son, you should go back to the other room. Take Butterball. I can't have you fainting on me. Pam, can you hold the flashlight? There's something . . . Just don't look at the body. Point the light away." The words tumbled out of my mouth so quickly I wasn't entirely sure I was speaking English.

Without Pam's assistance, dragging the screen back to its position by the stairs was no easy feat. I accomplished it, however, in short order, propelled by my dawning understanding.

The coatrack, so convincing in its imitation of a person, had opened a new possibility to me. What *had* I actually seen during the party? The top of Victor's head, yes. But I hadn't *seen* Zaria once she disappeared behind the screen. I'd seen the top of her turban, its adorning peacock feather waving. Just the turban.

In less than a minute, I'd arranged the coatrack and screen back in the positions where they'd been just after Clemmons fell down the stairs. I hurried into the dining room, plucked an ostrich feather from one of Melody's glorious centerpieces, and positioned it under the hatband of Jarka's bowler. I came out from behind the screen and inspected my work. The crown of the bowler hat, decorative feather aloft, arched over the top of the folding screen. The screen itself was angled perfectly to shield the bottom of the staircase from the view of anyone on the drawing room side.

"This is how it was set up during the party," I explained. "I told Capone that Zaria and the Count were behind here, right next to me, when Clemmons was killed. I'm their alibi. Except, I'm not sure anymore that I am."

CHAPTER 30

Pam took a few steps to stand next to me. The coatrack and screen stood just where they had in the moments before Clemmons fell. The top of Jarka's hat, with the stand-in feather, peeped just over the horizon of the screen. From the angle where I stood, there'd be no way to know if the hat sat atop a person's head or a coatrack, and the entrance to the stairs was shielded from the view of anyone casually passing by. With the props fully set, Pam, who'd been watching my furniture-arranging efforts with increasing interest, finally understood what I'd been driving at. Her eyes widened. "You think they put Zaria's turban on the coatrack so she could slip upstairs to kill Clemmons?"

Sonya, who'd been reclining on a hall chair with her eyes closed, popped up, her wooziness forgotten. "Wait, what? How can that be? Wouldn't you have noticed?"

"I could see Victor's head and hear him, so I don't think he could've left. But Zaria? She could've slipped upstairs," I said.

"But if they were talking, didn't you hear her voice, too?" Pam was warming to the idea, but her tone still held a note of skepticism. "I can't imagine they'd have been clever enough to record a whole conversation in advance.

And even if he'd been moving the coatrack around to make Zaria's turban move, you would've noticed if he suddenly started carrying on a five-minute monologue."

I played the memory back in my mind. They'd definitely both been speaking at the outset, but then Zaria had lapsed into silence when Victor started to steamroll her. "I'm not sure I would've," I said. "Haven't you noticed him talking over her and bossing her around? He did the same with Jarka earlier. He was doing most of the talking, and it didn't strike me as out of the ordinary. Zaria was crying. I remember hearing a bit of that and then they seemed to make up and started kissing."

"Crying would be easy to fake," Pam said. "Much easier than imitating someone's voice." She let out a few sniffly sobs, first in a low register and then in a higher one, to demonstrate.

"So would the make-out session," I said.

Sonya gave the back of her hand a few noisy kisses. "Like when I used to practice in junior high," she said.

"Exactly. If Zaria snuck upstairs during the singing or when Isabel started talking, I wouldn't have noticed. When she ran over after Clemmons fell, her face was flushed and her chest was heaving. I thought she was upset because of what happened. But maybe she was out of breath from running up and down the stairs."

"Do you really think Zaria ran upstairs and killed Edgar while Victor covered for her?" Pam said. "It seems crazy."

"It *is* crazy." I squeezed my eyes closed. "Right? Maybe I'm just tired. If this is right, it would mean that they'd planned it all on the fly, including having me standing there as an alibi witness. Or maybe they planned the killing, but figured out all the stuff with the screen and coatrack when they arrived. And then there's the whole matter of Isabel's killing and the attack on you," I said to Sonya. "I keep thinking it would be more plausible if it were a couple working together, since they could serve as lookouts for each other and cover more ground." I pointed to the screen. "This makes me think twice about what's possible."

I half expected Pam and Sonya to dismiss the turban-on-the-coatrack scenario out of hand. Instead, Pam turned thoughtful. After a moment she said, "Zaria is a smart woman. But I don't understand why she would want to kill Edgar. Nearly everyone here, including me, had more of a reason to dislike him than she did. And why would anyone kill Isabel? Zaria and Victor don't seem to be hurting for money. Her business is certainly very profitable. So why risk all that over a few thousand dollars' worth of books?"

I tapped my finger on my lips. "How did you meet Zaria?" I asked.

"Word of mouth. When I was buying things for the house, someone put me on to her, knowing how much I love books. She has a big clientele in Geneva Bay."

Sonya sprang up. "It's got to be something about those books. Remember how Clemmons said they were part of a much larger collection? He could've meant Zaria's inventory. What if the books are fake, like the statue of the Maltese Falcon?"

"They can't be," Pam said. "I had them examined by an expert for insurance. I'm sure other collectors have done the same."

"I just want five minutes to question them and I feel like I could get a confession." I held my watch in the flashlight's beam. "We're already two minutes late, though."

"What should we do?" Pam asked.

"Capone can't exactly tie them up or beat a confession out of them," Sonya said.

"Is this enough to arrest them?" Pam asked, indicating the coatrack. "Probable cause or whatever the term is?"

"No way," Sonya said. "My uncle Avi would have a field day with Delilah's little sock puppet theater if these were his clients."

"I wish we could just nail them, but we can't risk enflaming the situation," I said. "At least not until reinforcements arrive. We've got to keep everyone calm. Capone will already be guarding against anyone trying to make a break for it. *Ugh.*" I struggled to cork up my surging frustration. Now that I was confronted with the practical realities of taking action, I understood why Capone had been so keen to bide his time. "I can't believe it's me saying this, but we have to cool our jets. There's nothing we can do without the risk of provoking something bad. Our best bet is to go back upstairs and pretend like we don't suspect anything."

Pam nodded. "You're probably right, but we have to at least try to say something to Detective Capone so he'll be on guard."

"I will."

"I guess we don't have a choice," Sonya sighed. "But don't give the game away, okay? You have a terrible poker face."

"What do you mean?" I said.

She crossed her arms. "As if I don't know that you kissed Capone on the stairs before."

"I don't know what you're talking about—" I began.

She raised her hand to still my futile denials.

"Even I suspected something," Pam admitted.

"Fine. Let's get back," I said, defeated. "Be on your guard." I looked around. "Oh, no. Where's Butterball?"

Pam shined the flashlight back and forth around the hallway, stairs, and drawing room. We hurried back to the kitchen, but he wasn't there, either. Gloria, of course, had stayed obediently by her owner's side, while my cat had gone walkabout once again.

"Do you want to look for him?" Sonya asked.

"Yes, but let's go back upstairs and check in first." I exhaled in exasperation, my chest heavy with self-reproach. Maybe if I'd trained Butterball properly, he'd be more compliant. I'd never read a single book on cat behavior. Instead, I'd spoiled him, thinking my love was all he needed. Was he even a normal cat? I didn't know. I had nothing to compare him to other than the outdoor cats he brawled with and little-miss-perfect Gloria. Now he'd run off, and he could be in danger. "It's not fair to worry Capone. Everybody else will be wondering where we are, too."

"Well, now you don't have to worry about him cat-fighting at least," Sonya consoled.

"I'm sure he'll be fine," Pam said. "Gloria's never gotten into trouble here. The house is actually pretty well cat-proofed."

"For Gloria," I said. "Not Butterball." I glanced toward the room where Edgar Clemmons now lay, with only a tablecloth to shield him, and hoped to God that if Butterball got hungry, he would fill up on bread.

The three of us hurried up the stairs, where we found things much as we'd left them, although the crowd was a bit more subdued. Dawn was finally breaking, the eastern sky filling with a burnt-orange brilliance. Although the light was still weak, the observation tower had brightened to the point where we could turn off our flashlights and extinguish the candles. Daniel, Rabbit, Melody, and B.L. were all fast asleep on the couch. Kennedy stared out the window. Lola perched alone in a window seat. Jarka sat perfectly upright in another. Zaria and Victor hunched next to the door to the widow's walk. Capone once again did his pacing lion imitation. There was no music now, just the heavy silence of waiting.

Capone crossed the room toward us, his face a mixture of annoyance and relief. He tapped his watch. "Twenty-four minutes."

I nodded, unsure how to arrange my features into an acceptable expression or to form my words into coherent sentences. *Remember how we kissed twenty-four minutes ago?* I wanted to say. *Can we do it again sometime? And P.S.., I think Zaria and Victor are the killers.*

"No Butterball?" Capone asked, his forehead creasing in concern.

"We had him, but he slipped away," I explained. "I didn't want to stay away any longer in case you were worried. Not that you'd worry about me. About us. I mean, any more than is normal to worry, given the circumstances."

Sonya looked from me to Capone and back again, mouthing the words "poker face."

I clenched my lips together and shook my head rapidly from side to side. I took a step toward Capone, intending to tell him about my theory.

"Look!" Lola said, hurrying over and pointing toward the road that wound through the forest. Down below, glimpses of emergency vehicles appeared in the trees. Their lights and sirens were off—I supposed they didn't need them in the middle of an isolated forest. The rest of the assembled guests rushed over and watched as a line of vehicles snaked toward us, coming to a stop at the massive pine tree that lay downed across the top of the driveway.

"Oh, thank god," Pam sighed.

Capone flicked his chin toward the window. "Rettberg just texted to say that all they have left is to clear the tree that's in the driveway."

I grabbed his arm and pulled him to the other side of the room, away from everyone else. "I think it's Zaria *and* Victor," I whispered.

"Did you find something?" he asked.

"There's this coatrack downstairs—" I began. "It looks like a person."

"And that proves that Zaria and Victor committed two murders?" he asked. "An hour ago you were convinced it was B.L. Huddleston."

"Okay, but I *really* think it's Zaria and Victor, working together. Remember how Victor told her to conserve her phone battery during dinner? By then, they knew they were going to try to kill Sonya and Isabel, because that's when they decided to drug everyone. I bet they wanted their phones working so they could see what they were doing and communicate with each other," I said.

"I appreciate that you're trying to help, and you could well be right, but I'm not going to be able to make an arrest based on this," he said.

"I know," I sighed.

"Once everyone is safely away from here, we'll conduct an actual investigation, analyze the cane and feather boa for fingerprints and DNA, do an autopsy on Clemmons and Isabel, question the witness, check backgrounds, confirm alibis, et cetera. We'll make sure that neither they, nor any of the other suspects, leaves our sight. And when the case is good and tight, we'll make an arrest. In other words, we'll do our jobs."

"This is so infuriating!" I said, glaring at Zaria and Victor. "I know you can't do anything. I *know*. But I'm telling you, he's the guy. I bet he forced her into it. Look at him, for heaven's sake. He's got evil eyebrows."

Capone clamped his lips together and looked at the floor.

I crossed my arms. "This isn't funny."

"You're right, but I'm glad you understand why I have to behave this way. We can't expect anyone to make a confession at this point," he said. "Often getting someone to confess means exerting extreme pressure. Either catching them red-handed in a lie or manipulating them emotionally or backing them into a corner. Almost always, you're pushing a violent person close to the edge in some way, which is a dangerous thing to do. That kind of volatility can be managed in an interrogation room, but it's not something I'm interested in trying in a room full of civilians."

"What if they try to run?" I asked.

"Do you see how many police vehicles are down there?" he asked. "They've all been fully briefed on the situation, including the possibility of someone else being in the house. I've even cautioned them to be careful not to let Butterball out."

"It's a big estate," I argued. "If Zaria and Victor make it to the ATV, they could head off through the woods. Heck, they could zoom away across the lake on Pam's Jet Ski now that the water is calm."

He placed a hand on my back. "If it's them, we'll catch them. We will. But for now we did the most important thing. We made it through the night. Let's round everyone up to go downstairs."

The sound of chainsaws from below seemed to lend credence to his promise. Help had arrived. Rescue was imminent. Capone announced the departure plan to the guests, who began to collect their belongings and shuffle their way toward the door. I looked around. He was probably right. With all of us up here together, anything could happen. Better to let the noose close around Zaria and Victor once we were safely away.

"Hey, what are you doing?" Melody's voice cut across the otherwise silent room.

Capone and I turned to find my young hostess pointing an accusatory finger toward Zaria, who was standing at the refreshment table.

Zaria edged backward. With her cheeks full, she looked like a shocked chipmunk. She chewed and swallowed.

"What'd she do to you?" Daniel asked. He had been leaning heavily on Rabbit for balance, but suddenly he stood up to his full height. His voice was strong and protective.

"She *ate* a tiramisu cookie," Melody said.

Confused glances pinged back and forth around the room.

Sonya shot a tense look across to me. Even though she hadn't heard Capone's "let's not mess with violent people" speech, she seemed to be tuned into the potential danger. She put a calming hand on Melody's shoulder. "Just let her be. Come on, let's go downstairs."

Shaking her off, Melody continued. "I saw her eat a cookie. A gluten-y, buttery, chocolatey cookie. I don't understand why she'd make such a big deal about her diet if she isn't strict about it. I thought she said she was allergic to all of that stuff. It's not like we're starving or stranded on a desert island. We all just ate a few hours ago."

Zaria's eyes narrowed. "I don't know what you're talking about."

"No, I saw you," Melody said.

"Lay off of her. It's just a cookie," I said, shooting meaningful looks at Pam, Capone, and Sonya.

A thundercloud formed behind Victor's eyes and he edged toward the door.

Just a moment ago, I'd been laying out the case for arresting Zaria and the Count, but now the consequences of prematurely lighting the fuse on this powder keg were laid bare before me.

"I don't understand why you want to give her a free pass," Melody continued. She turned back to Zaria. "Prep was super stressful because Delilah was busy making that pizza for you. Sonya almost had a meltdown. Butterball got kidnapped and brought here, all because Delilah and Jarka had to go get the extra stuff to make that pizza. Poor Butterball was accused of killing Mr. Clemmons for heaven's sake!" Melody held up her hands, looking around for support.

"Mel's got a point," Daniel said. "We bend over backward to accommodate dietary restrictions all the time. There are real people with real allergies and intolerances. It's not right to fake something like that."

"My daughter could die if she eats a peanut," Rabbit said.

"This is true," Jarka agreed. "You say to Isabel that you swell big like a puffy fish from gluten or dairy. But you are not puffy one bit. Why you have lied?"

CHAPTER 31

I grimaced. Melody had caught Zaria in a lie, and she wasn't going to let it go. Usually Melody was a people-pleaser, but when something violated her sense of morality, she could combust like a Roman candle. Here she was, once again choosing a particularly inconvenient time to dig in her heels, and she'd recruited my entire staff to her cause.

Zaria backed up farther, looking like a cornered animal. "I don't know what she's talking about."

"Melody wouldn't make that up," Daniel said firmly. The color had returned to his face and he was standing up under his own steam.

"You fool." Victor spat the words at his fiancée.

Zaria wheeled toward him. "*Me*, the fool? That whole free-from pizza thing was your idea. You should've been the one to do it. I hate black coffee!" She flung the half-full coffee cup she'd been holding at his head. It sailed wide of its mark and hit Kennedy, splashing hot black liquid down the front of her clothes.

Kennedy stood shaking for a moment, like a rocket just before takeoff. "How dare you!" she shouted.

"Don't get involved," Lola began.

"Don't speak to me, you hussy," Kennedy snapped.

"Kennedy, honey, calm down," B.L. said, using his handkerchief to mop her off.

"*Me*, calm down?!" She wheeled on him. "I let you parade around like a big shot, spending *my* money. I bought you anything you wanted. I quit my job because you didn't like it that I had a career and you didn't. I turned a blind eye, even when I knew you were cheating on me with that . . . that . . . *lounge singer!*" She leveled a finger at Lola.

Lola's mouth dropped open. Capone looked like he'd swallowed a stick of dynamite.

"Oh, snap," Sonya said, her eyes growing round.

So much for keeping everything calm. My stomach knotted. Had Kennedy lost it? It seemed like she was on the cusp of something. A confession, maybe? Had I been wrong about Zaria and Victor? Angry as Kennedy was, I could easily see her as a murderer.

"You *knew*?" Lola gasped.

"Of course I knew," Kennedy growled. "Brian's too much of a numbskull to get away with an affair. Don't think you're the first."

My thoughts scrambled to catch up with the revelations. "You knew he was having an affair, multiple affairs, and you stayed with him?" I asked.

"He always comes back to me." Her tone was defiant, but I saw the pain in her eyes.

"But I saw you guys, you and Mr. Huddleston, arguing during the party," Rabbit sputtered. "That wasn't because you found out about the affair?"

"No." B.L. shook his head. "Well, yes and no. Kennedy knew about Lola, but she didn't like the idea of other people knowing about our arrangement. I'd promised to keep my"—he cleared his throat—"*activities* out of the public eye."

"But you didn't, did you?" Kennedy's pale complexion had developed a worrying resemblance to one of Auntie Biz's beets. "I love you!" she screeched. "Why. Don't. You. Love. Me. Back?!" With each word she pummeled her husband's chest with her balled fists.

Pam, who was standing next to them, attempted to pull her off.

"Don't touch me," Kennedy said, pushing her away. She wheeled to face Pam and rammed her pointed finger in the center of the other woman's chest. "If it hadn't been for you, Brian wouldn't have cheated on me."

Pam shook her head, baffled. "How do you figure that one?"

"You knew I wanted to buy this house for him, and you stole it from us."

"I *saved* this house from you. You would've destroyed it," Pam said. "You were going to gut it and make it into another modern monstrosity. Geneva Bay has enough of those."

"I would've improved it. You didn't even put in a pool! Or a media room!"

Pam threw up her hands and looked at the rest of us. "See?"

"And what about the books? Every time I tried to buy a book for him, you outbid me!" Kennedy continued. "You didn't even really want them. Brian actually likes books."

"I love books. I devoted my whole career to making them more accessible," Pam countered.

"But you didn't want those particular books, did you? Or any of the other ones you bought from Zaria. You only bought them to spite me," Kennedy said.

"That was because of what you and your family were planning to do to the library," Pam said.

"I care about this town," Kennedy said. "And so does my family. We want to improve it. I grew up here, unlike you. I attended those public meetings for years. Then, Isabel and the rest of those tyrants on the board wouldn't take our money just because we wanted the library to work better. Would they listen to us? No!" She pointed at Pam again. "Where were you while I sat through all those meetings and offered my helpful suggestions? You didn't even want to be on the board and yet somehow you're chair."

"Helpful suggestions?! Like charging kids for story time?! Your plans would wreck the library!" Pam shouted. "You wanted to control it. Make it your own little fiefdom, keep out the riffraff."

"I was *helping*," Kennedy screeched.

Apparently, micromanaging the library's content and exercising unilateral control over the exchange of ideas that went on there was her idea of helping. I was reminded of an old adage—every villain is the hero of their own story. While I doubted any of us were likely to set aside Kennedy's behavior just because she was playing the poor-little-rich-girl card, it was hard not to feel a smidgeon of sympathy for a woman who seemed to have no clear sense of her own motivations. No ambition beyond what other people wanted *from* her. Kennedy thought she could buy her husband's love. Instead, the man flagrantly cheated on her. From her point of view, her ambitions were continually thwarted by others. While most of the world saw her as a stereotypical mean girl, she saw herself as a victim.

"Every time I turn around," Kennedy continued, "you're doing something to mess with me. First you keep me from making my parents happy by trying to keep me off the board; then you keep me from making Brian happy by buying this house and the books he wanted."

"I was only . . ." Pam began. She paused and frowned. "Actually, you're right. I was being petty. I hate to admit it, but it's true. I don't like you. I don't agree with you. And I did it because I could."

"I knew it! If I'd been able to give Brian what he wanted," Kennedy said, "he'd still love me, and *you* prevented it."

"Well, maybe if you didn't act like such a banshee, you could keep a man," Lola muttered. "And maybe if you weren't so mean to everyone, they'd be nicer to you."

Kennedy took a few steps toward Lola, clearly intent on taking out her rage on *someone*. Her husband's mistress, a woman about her size, must've seemed like a pretty good target. She cocked her arm back and took a swing at Capone's mother, who recoiled and held up her hands in anticipation of the blow. I intercepted Kennedy's fist in midair and grabbed it, twisting her arm behind her back.

"Let go of me," she cried.

"Not until you chill out," I said.

As she struggled to free herself, we bumped into Victor, who was standing next to us. He stepped back and brushed off his clothes, cursing under his breath in Bulgarian.

My brain, which had been whirring a mile a minute to keep up with the fast-paced drama, suddenly quieted. I was still wrestling with Kennedy, but time seemed to slow down. "Wait a second," I blurted. "Zaria doesn't speak Bulgarian."

The whole room looked at me. I released my hold on Kennedy, whose rage had been replaced by confusion. "Huh?" she said, looking at me like I'd just donned a tinfoil hat.

"*Zaria doesn't speak Bulgarian*," I repeated.

"So what?" Zaria said, shrugging her pointy shoulders. "I have a degree in Classical Languages, and I'm fluent in French."

"Behind the screen, during the party," I said. "That wasn't French or any classical language. I recognized it. It was Bulgarian. Victor spoke to you in Bulgarian, and you responded. You said mm-hmm, like you understood what he was saying. But it wasn't you, was it? It was him pretending that a coatrack with a turban on it was you."

"Are you feeling okay?" Lola asked, concern creasing her forehead. "Did Kennedy hit you in the head?"

Ignoring her, I addressed Sonya and Pam. "He knew I wouldn't understand him, so he wouldn't have to pretend to carry on a full conversation. That would've been harder to fake. But in Bulgarian, he could get away with little murmurs in reply. Victor spoke Bulgarian because he was ad-libbing, trying to fill time."

"What are you doing? What happened to your poker face?" Sonya said, shaking her head rapidly.

I clapped my hand over my mouth. *Whoops.* Amidst all the confusion and drama, the realization had come to me so unexpectedly, my brain's usual filter hadn't engaged. And I'd thought kissing Capone showed what happened when a mix of alcohol and drugs lowered inhibitions. My latest big-mouth blunder could be its own anti-drug public service campaign.

The implication of what I'd said hit home with Jarka, and she spoke up. "Why would you do this, Victor? Pretend to speak to Zaria when she is not there? Where would she go? Unless . . ." She shook her head, her eyes growing wide with horror. "No! Is not true!"

"Jarka," Victor said, reaching across the couch toward her. "You must let me explain."

"You'll say nothing if you know what's good for you," Zaria seethed. "Idiot."

"Me, the idiot?" Victor wheeled back toward Zaria. "If I recall, you were the one who couldn't keep from stuffing a chocolate cookie into your mouth when you're supposed to be allergic to dairy." His ice-blue eyes simmered with fury. "I told you we should have left here hours ago."

"You'd have gotten us lost in the woods! You're useless when it comes to anything practical," Zaria said.

"If you'd handled Clemmons properly, none of this would've happened," Victor said.

"Don't say another word," Zaria hissed.

"Why should I be silent?" He asked the question to all of us, and then pointed a finger at Zaria. "This whole scheme was her idea."

"Oh, Victor," Jarka whispered.

He turned pleading eyes toward her. "She's the one who thought it would be more plausible if we posed as a couple. I never stopped loving you. There was supposed to be no real harm. Taking money from uncultured people who were easily fooled." He turned back to Zaria, his voice like sharpened steel. "Yet, *you've* made error after error, and it's led us here."

"You wanted the money just as much as I did. Probably more," Zaria snapped.

"Copying books is one thing," he said. "Murder is another."

"Fake books . . ." Pam breathed. "Of course."

I took a step back. "That's why Clemmons didn't handle them carefully. He knew they were forgeries."

"She's the one who panicked and killed Clemmons," Victor continued, not hearing us, speaking only to Jarka, trying desperately to justify himself. "I only wanted her to talk to him."

"As if you didn't know what would happen when I went upstairs. Clemmons wasn't going to see reason. He thought he was judge, jury, and executioner," Zaria said.

"Ain't that the truth," B.L. muttered.

"Well, I never touched Clemmons, nor Isabel," Victor said.

While they'd been talking, Capone withdrew his weapon from its holster. He kept it pointed to the floor, his eyes laser focused on Zaria and Victor. "You two need to come with me." With his free arm, he gestured at the rest of the group to clear the room. "Go. Get downstairs."

We began to move toward the door, but Victor and Zaria blocked our way. They were intent on each other now, seemingly oblivious to everyone else in the room. The rest of us looked at one another. Considering they'd just confessed to two murders, it wasn't clear how we could politely duck past them.

"This is *your* fault," Victor was saying to Zaria. "You dug the hole deeper and deeper. If you'd stayed calm instead of throwing the cane into the chute . . . If you'd simply taken the time to clean it off and place it at the top of the stairs . . ."

"Me? You're supposed to be acting as if you're my fiancé and you can't keep away from that weird waitress you used to date!" Zaria leveled her finger at Jarka.

"Keep her out of this. You'll never understand the passion Jarka and I have. I'm tired of pretending to be your fiancé when I can scarcely stand the sight of you!"

"The feeling's mutual!" Zaria yelled, removing a knife from her coat. I recognized it immediately as Sonya's missing paring knife, and I knew for a fact that it was kept razor sharp. "If I have to hear one more time about your 'art' or your 'passion' or how your great-grandpa was the archduke of some godforsaken corner of nowhere . . ." She took a menacing step toward him.

"Victor!" Jarka gasped. She grabbed a candlestick from one of the window bays and tossed it to her former lover. He caught it and swung the heavy silver base at his assailant. Zaria dodged the blow, which landed on the back of the couch.

Zaria thrust the knife toward Victor, but she, too, missed. The rest of the group surged backward, trying to get out of their way, but we were trapped in the narrow space between the massive couch and the windows. For a few frantic moments, we pitched backward and forward as they dodged and parried, skirting the edges of the round room like the hands of a clock gone berserk.

"Put down the weapons," Capone commanded.

The pair, wild-eyed, didn't comply.

I stood directly behind Victor. As he took another wild swing with the candlestick, I threw my arms out to shield everyone behind me. "Over the couch! Go!" I yelled.

Daniel hoisted Melody over first, and then helped the others to clamber across the massive piece of furniture to the relative safety of the opposite side of the room. Jarka was the last of the group to go. Daniel, positioned in the middle of the couch's circumference, held out his arms ready to lift her. Looking back over her shoulder, though, she hesitated.

"Victor, you must stop this. Please."

Victor looked up at the sound of her voice, as if suddenly awakened from a dream. Although his grip on the candlestick didn't relax, his eyes softened.

"Did you steal my father's paintings? His Jules Pascin paintings? We thought it so strange they should be forgeries. Experts assess them when he has bought them so many years ago. So strange that those experts should be wrong, we thought. But *you*. You could copy such things, replace them on his walls without him suspicioning you. You have such talent like this. Why you have thrown in the trash this talent doing these terrible crimes?"

Victor looked deflated as the accusation hit home. His shoulders slumped. "*Sŭzhalyavam*, my love. Forgive me."

"I cannot forgive such betrayal," she said quietly.

"If there is no hope for us," he said, "there is no hope for me."

The room was quiet, all eyes on Jarka and Victor. I heard Sonya whisper, "Holy melodrama, Batman."

Jarka took in a long, shaky breath. "Ever how could I trust such man as you? My love for you is dead. Now I am certain."

"Then I am dead, too," Victor said. He threw down the candlestick at Zaria's feet. His eyes darted back over his shoulder. He'd found himself right next to the doorway that led to the widow's walk—the widow's walk that jutted above the house, above the trees, above the bluff. Four stories off the ground. The sun had risen over the tree line, and the orangey-pink glare of it washed over him with dizzying brightness. *Don't*, my mind begged him. *Please don't*.

Capone, too, saw the direction of Victor's gaze and sprang toward him, trying to grab hold of the desperate man. But he was too late. Pivoting quickly out of Capone's reach, Victor was through the door and over the railing, sending himself into the blinding brilliance of the morning sun. Into oblivion.

A broken cry rose from Jarka's throat. She rushed out to the widow's walk, right behind Victor and Capone. Jarka and Capone leaned over the railing, peering downward after the fallen man. I could only imagine the horror that met their eyes. Jarka staggered backward, leaning on Capone for support.

I heard running steps and realized that Zaria had taken advantage of the disarray to flee back into the house. I was the only person left on the same side of the room as her, and without a second thought, I took off in pursuit. Victor had escaped justice in his own gruesome way. No chance I'd let her off the hook, too.

The stairwell was gloomy, especially after the sunrise vista afforded by the observation tower. In the servants' hallway, I stood for a moment, blinking in the thin gray light.

My ears pricked at a noise on the staircase, and I hurtled off in that direction. I paused on the landing, casting my eyes up and down the second-floor hallway. The door to the library, along with all the bedroom doors, remained closed. I saw no movement in the shadowy hall and heard nothing but the faint whispers and creaks emitted by an old house. Had Zaria ducked into one of the rooms? There were stairs at each end of the hall. Had she already slipped away? The emergency responders hadn't reached the house yet. Would she have time to make a break for it? Might she still get away scot-free?

My heart pounding from exertion and anxiety, I crept along the hallway. The floorboards groaned with each step I took. For the first time, I realized I'd rushed headlong after Zaria, totally unarmed. If it came to down to a *mano a mano* fight, I had the advantage over the much slighter-figured woman. But what if she snuck up on me? With her graceful, dancer-like movements, she could glide where I tromped. Did she still have Sonya's knife? She'd murdered two unsuspecting victims in the preceding twenty-four hours. I'd be foolish to underestimate her.

I'd nearly reached the opposite end of the hallway when I heard the swift clatter of footsteps on the stairway I'd just come down. I rushed back in that direction and encountered Capone barreling down the stairs.

"Thank god you're okay," he said, grabbing me by the shoulders, as if to reassure himself that I was intact. "Which way did she go?"

"I don't know," I said. "I lost her here."

He looked up and down the hallway. "We can't split up. You're unarmed."

"But if we pick the wrong direction, she'll make it to the woods or to the dock. She could already be outside. She could get away."

Before we could make a plan for pursing Zaria, though, a colossal shriek rang out, followed by a series of teeth-rattling thuds. We took off in the direction the sound came from—the main staircase, the one that led from outside the library down to the drawing room. The same staircase that Edgar Clemmons still lay at the bottom of.

Capone was the faster runner, and he hit the steps a few seconds before I did. Just as he was about to round the wood panels at the place where the staircase opened up to the room below, I had a sudden realization. We'd heard the unmistakable sound of someone falling down the stairs. How could a person as graceful as Zaria, presumably moving carefully to avoid detection, have fallen so clumsily down the stairs?

"Stop!" I screamed.

Capone clutched the banister, arresting his forward momentum so abruptly his shoulder slammed into the wall. I caught up to him a moment later. I looked from side to side. I'd been right. I pointed to the alcove that abutted the next step down. There, behind a large potted plant, was Butterball. The cat's muscles were tight, as he waited to confront whatever threat might come up or down the stairs. He arched his back in protest at our appearance, readying his paw for a swipe, but then, realizing we were familiar friends, he relaxed.

Capone nodded at the cat, one hand warily clutching his service weapon, the other keeping tight hold of my arm. As we rounded the corner of the last wooden panel, I heard a low moan. A second later, a macabre scene came into view, illuminated by the pink morning sunlight that streamed in through the room's floor-to-ceiling windows.

At the base of the stairs, Edgar Clemmons lay exactly where we'd left him, still covered with his tablecloth shroud. On top of his body, writhing in pain, lay an injured Zaria Singhal. Her right leg stuck out from the high slit in her dress at an angle I'd only witnessed once before, on a garage-sale Barbie doll that'd seen better days.

I took a few tentative steps toward Butterball. "Are you okay, sweet boy?" I asked the cat, bending toward him. I scooped him into my arms. He meowed and nuzzled against me.

Capone gave him a scratch on the head. "Looks like somebody inherited his mommy's talent for street fighting."

The three of us walked slowly toward Zaria. As we got closer, her agony-filled eyes confronted us, narrowing in anger. "That cat," she wheezed. She pressed her eyes closed and groaned again. "That damn cat."

CHAPTER 32

It felt good to be back in my element, my restaurant kitchen, surrounded by my own pans, my own appliances, my own carefully curated ingredients. The familiar scents of garlic and baking bread embraced me like a warm hug. Most of all, it felt good to be alone. The previous morning, once Zaria, Victor, Isabel, and Edgar Clemmons were carted off and the police took the initial statements of those of us who'd survived the night, I sent the rest of my crew home, while I stayed behind at Bluff Point to pack up the catering van. By the time I finally got back to Geneva Bay, it was late afternoon. I took a roasting hot shower and then crashed hard, dead to the world, until early morning. Luckily, the restaurant was closed on Mondays, so despite our epic misadventure, we hadn't missed out on any business.

The soap-opera-level outlandishness of our night at Bluff Point was already receding into the background as I pushed a pizza pan into the hot oven and shut the door. Thirty minutes until it was transformed into a molten circle of deliciousness. Soon, Auntie Biz, along with Capone and his mother, would turn up for dinner. Capone was still knee-deep in investigation paperwork, and at first he'd balked at his mother's idea that he pause his work for a nice dinner at my restaurant. She cajoled him into it, though—she told Capone that if our collective brush with death taught us anything, it was that life is short, and things like a nice dinner out with your mother shouldn't be put off any longer. I asked Auntie Biz along, knowing how much she adored Lola Capone's music. My way of extending an olive branch.

Outside, a car door closed. I wiped my hands on my apron and walked through the kitchen door into the empty dining room. I'd set the scene earlier, arranging a four-top table in front of the huge windows that overlooked the lake. The day was cold, but tranquil. Little waves rippled the lake like buttercream icing, and the vivid fall foliage that surrounded the water had dimmed to russets and browns. Instead of using the usual vases of cut flowers, I'd decorated the table with a small, rough-hewn crate filled with a seasonal cornucopia of mini gourds, pinecones, fall berries, and squat golden candles. A deep-dish apple pie stood among the seasonal bounty in all its flaky-crusted, gooey-fillinged glory. Sonya did most of Delilah & Son's baking, but the pie was one of my specialties, and it fit right in among the decorations—it was that pretty.

A whoosh of cold air blew in from the entryway as my aunt came inside. I hurried over to take her jacket. Melody had dropped her off a little early, but I was glad.

Biz looked around and tipped her chin approvingly at my tablescape. "Not half-bad."

I smiled at her. Following long-standing O'Leary custom, neither of us had fully admitted that we were sorry for the fight we had on the phone. We'd been unusually considerate to each other, though, bordering on downright kind.

"I have something to add to it," Biz continued. She

held up a pie carrier and extracted a stunning creation nearly identical to my own. But hers, it pained me to admit, looked just a *wee* bit prettier.

"Your aunt Sandra's recipe?" I asked, as Biz placed her baked offering next to mine on the table.

She gave a crisp nod of her white curls and leaned down to examine my pie.

In all of recorded history, no O'Leary woman had ever bought an "I'm sorry" card. The words "It was all my fault" had rarely passed our lips. But many a fruit pie had been baked and offered in penance. Aunt Sandra's apple pie was the ultimate act of contrition.

"Did you use three kinds of apples?" Biz asked.

"Granny Smith, McIntosh, and Braeburn," I confirmed.

"And lard for the crust?"

"Crisco," I admitted. "Sujeet and Big Dave need at least a day's notice to fill a lard order."

"Well, it doesn't look half-bad considering," she said. "I bet it'll taste just fine."

"I made it for you," I said. "I hope you like it."

She and I inspected each other's pies for a long moment, our eyes glistening with unspoken tenderness. Any outside observer could be forgiven for being oblivious to the profound emotional exchange that was taking place as two bullheaded women oohed and aahed over the pies.

"What else are you serving?" Biz asked, clearing her throat.

"As a starter, garlic knots and cold shrimp with a classic cocktail sauce and a melted, anchovy-infused butter dip."

"Anchovy butter will be a nice complement to the shrimp, and give some umami to the garlic rolls, too."

I nodded. I was in the mood to gild lilies, and none of tonight's guests had any dietary restrictions. I filled Biz in on the rest of the menu. Italian sausage and spicy pepperoni deep-dish pie—an extravaganza of meat, cheese, gluten. No calories spared. Nary a vegetable in sight. I hoped to purge the memory of the night by cooking food that was the exact opposite of free-from.

"I still need a salad, though," I said, tapping my fingers on my lips. "Otherwise, it's too meat heavy, even for me."

"What about a vegetable medley instead? We could do grilled eggplant, peppers, and onions," she suggested.

"Perfect. Let's drizzle the veggies in an arugula and walnut pesto."

Biz nodded. "And top them with toasted walnuts."

Biz and I had spent a few minutes in the kitchen putting that plan into effect when we heard the sound of voices in the dining room. We came out to find Capone hanging up his and his mother's coats.

I was a little nervous about Lola Capone laying eyes on my restaurant's décor for the first time. Long before I knew Detective Capone, I'd commissioned the artwork that hung from the high ceilings—whimsical, contemporary paintings of famous Chicagoans. There were images of luminaries like Michael Jordan and Oprah, but also a fair number of the city's less savory scions, including a painting that depicted a certain infamous scar-faced Capone forebearer as a diaper-wearing baby.

Lola took in the ambience, her gaze fixing on the Capone-as-baby portrait. She squinted, her mouth twisting into a frown.

I held my breath. Was she offended? I'd had the impression Capone's father had only been a fly-by-night romance. And surely she couldn't hold any affection for

Public Enemy Number One, a gangster who'd died before she was even born?

"Looks a little like Calvin looked when he was a toddler," she said. "Same eyebrows . . ." She turned to her son. "Same Pampers."

We all burst out laughing, and my fears evaporated.

Turning to me, Lola said, "So nice of you to cook for us on your day off. Especially after everything you've been through."

"I'm glad you suggested it," I replied, eyeing Capone. He and I still hadn't had a chance to speak alone, and I had no idea where things stood with us. Was he annoyed at the million different times my big mouth had caused trouble at Bluff Point? Did he regret our kiss?

"It's a shame Butterball couldn't join us," Lola continued. "He's the man of the hour, from what Calvin tells me. Caught the culprit all by himself."

"Don't let Butterball hear you say that." I laughed. "He'll get a big head."

"It'd match the rest of him," Biz mumbled.

Feeling magnanimous, I chose to ignore the comment. Instead, I sighed. "All kidding aside, I wish I was a better pet parent. We're lucky that it was Zaria he swiped at, but it could've been someone who *hadn't* just murdered two people. I know I spoil him too much."

"I think he knew what he was doing," Capone said. "Maybe the Geneva Bay PD needs a feline unit to match our K9 unit."

"I think so, too. He's a good cat," Lola said. "And I can tell you're a good mother to him. You love him, and you try to do right by him. That's the best any of us can do."

My eyes fell on Capone, who placed an affectionate arm around his mother.

I crossed the room to the bar and opened a bottle of Syrah I'd been saving for a special occasion. This definitely counted. The group joined me at the bar, where Capone leaned his elbows on the long wooden counter with a sigh.

"Long day?" I asked.

"Long few days," he answered, rubbing his hands over his face. "I was at the hospital all morning, interviewing the Count."

"I still can't believe that man survived a four-story drop," Lola said.

"The pergola broke his fall, but he's worse for the wear," Capone explained, taking the proffered glass of wine. "A lot worse. Broken ribs, a broken collarbone, and two broken legs. The doctor said he'll walk again, but with a limp. Pretty ironic that now *he'll* need a cane. Zaria's also got a broken leg, plus a fractured tailbone."

"Have her send the hospital bill to Butterball," I said, smiling.

"Have you slept at all?" Biz asked Capone. "You look worn out."

"He hasn't," Lola answered. "But he hasn't eaten, either, and right now, that's the priority."

"It does smell amazing in here," Capone said.

I doled out the rest of the wineglasses and got everyone settled in to enjoy the lake view.

"I'll bring out the appetizers," I said.

"I'll help," Auntie Biz offered, following me through the swinging door into the kitchen.

Dish by dish, we brought the food to the table. The pizza came out looking like a literal slice of heaven. Once I had the dishes arranged, Capone lit the candles. The four of us dug in as he brought us up to speed on the events of the day.

The pizza was every bit as indulgent as I'd hoped. I swallowed a spicy, cheesy bite and took a sip of my wine. "So Victor gave a statement?"

"Oh, yeah. Count Leka Simeon Victor Hohenstaufen-Chandon was ready to sing a three-act opera."

I raised my eyebrows, impressed that he'd nailed down the Count's convoluted moniker.

Noting my surprise, he explained, "You wouldn't believe how many forms I've typed that name onto today. And how many times I wished his parents had named him Joe Smith."

"I guess he's thinking if he throws his accomplice under the bus, he'll avoid the worst of what's coming," Biz said.

"Will he?" Lola asked her son.

"That's up to the DA, but I doubt it. Victor had too much of a hand in it all. Zaria didn't force him to get into the forgery business. He was already doing it when they met."

"So I hear," Biz said. "Melody told me this morning that Jarka's been in touch with her father, who made some calls. Apparently, some black-market Jules Pascin paintings were seized by Interpol this morning."

"As usual, you're more in the know than I am." Capone laughed. "I've got a friend at the FBI who said that several European countries are lining up to extradite Victor once we're done with him. *If* we're ever done with him."

"What do you mean?" I asked.

"There'd be plenty of charges filed here to keep him occupied for a long, long time, but I suspect the Feds will take over the prosecution. Zaria Singhal had an extensive client list, and not just in the U.S. I doubt it's a coincidence that once Victor came into her life, she suddenly started to be able to acquire some very rare, very expensive books, allegedly taking advantage of Victor's family connections with the great private libraries of Europe."

"I understand copying a painting, but how do you forge a book?" Lola asked.

"That's where Victor's skill as an artist and access to genuine rare books through his family connections came in. To mimic the font, age the paper, get the cover to look and feel and even *smell* just right"—Capone whistled—"it takes a skilled artist. Apparently, when they're done well, these types of forgeries are nearly impossible to detect."

"So they'll get him on the forgeries, but what about the murders? That seems like it should be the priority," I pointed out.

"We'll see," Capone replied.

Lola shook her head. "I don't buy for a minute that Victor wasn't in on the plans from the beginning. He must've known that Clemmons would end up dead after his meeting with Zaria, or at least that it was highly likely. If she was just going to have a friendly chat with him, why would they have gone to such great lengths to make sure they had an alibi?"

I put down my napkin, nodding. "Victor as much as admitted that he acted as the lookout while she killed Clemmons."

"And again while she drugged the gin and 'went to talk with' Isabel, or so he told me today," Capone said, taking a meditative sip of his wine. "The way the law works, a person can be charged with homicide if someone dies in the course of them committing a felony. Even if it's a totally different felony. He wasn't an innocent bystander."

"That's a fact," Lola said. "The important thing is they're in custody."

"And that we came out alive," I added. "So we can be here today with people we care about."

My eyes spontaneously locked on Capone's.

Picking up on the look that passed between the two of us, Lola turned to Biz. "Elizabeth, honey, would you mind giving me a tour of the kitchen before dessert? I'd love an in-depth look." She took my aunt by the elbow and led the way out of the dining room, leaving me and Capone alone.

CHAPTER 33

We finished off the bottle of Syrah I'd opened earlier, so when Lola and Biz headed to the kitchen, I walked to the bar to pop another cork. Capone trailed after me, sliding onto one of the stools. I came around the bar and took a seat next to him, bottle in hand.

"I still don't understand how it all went down," I said. "What put Clemmons on to them? If they'd been able to fool collectors, dealers, and appraisers, how did he manage to see through the scheme?"

"Rettberg was working on that very question most of the night while we were at Bluff Point. By the time I got back to the station, she'd tied up a lot of loose ends."

"Such as?" I asked.

"She pulled the records from the call Clemmons made on Sonya's phone the day he and Sonya were talking about old movies. He called an old coworker from the Newberry Library."

I raised my eyebrows.

"When you all did the pre-party walk-through a few days before the party," he continued, "Pam showed Clemmons her new books. He thought they were in unusually good condition. Still, he didn't think much of it at the time. Apparently, talking to Sonya a few days later jogged his memory. A first edition of *The Maltese Falcon* came up for auction during his time at the New-berry, so he was familiar with what it should look like. His old colleague now works for an auction house and made some inquiries there. No one was aware of any first editions coming up for auction recently, but someone mentioned that Zaria Singhal sold one last year. What's the likelihood that two pristine first editions of the same book would come into her possession in that timeframe?"

I tilted my head to one side. "Remember, I'm a bar-barian, but I'm streetwise enough to say 'fat chance.'"

"Right. Clemmons seems to have figured out how the scheme worked. Victor and Zaria would get ahold of a real copy of a rare book, create a small number of fakes, sell them to far-flung collectors, and double or triple their money. If the collectors wanted the book authenticated, they could swap in the real one, which they'd hang on to. Then they'd switch the books back after the fact. Victor must've learned his lesson when he forged the paintings from Jarka's father's collection. He hadn't swapped the originals back before the insurance appraiser examined them. He'd sold them. He was lucky he wasn't caught that time, and he apparently learned to be more careful."

"Books, paintings, being sinister as a moonlit gar-goyle—Count Victor is a man of many talents," I ob-served.

He smiled. "There's less scrutiny in the rare book world than in the art world, or so my friend at the Bureau tells me. Less infrastructure to detect fraud."

"The funny thing is, Victor was the first person I sus-pected. Do you remember in the pantry? I was sure it was him." I pointed to my forehead. "Evil eyebrows."

Capone chuckled. "People said that about my great-grandfather, too. Maybe you're on to something." He raised his wineglass overhead to the canvas that depicted his famous forebearer.

I joined in the toast. "To evil eyebrows." I looked out the window and sighed. "I'm not used to the bad guy being the bad guy."

"Well, usually the bad guy *is* the bad guy. Your crime-fighting experience has been atypical."

"How did Zaria and Victor find out Clemmons was on to them?" I asked. "Zaria mentioned that they'd changed their plans at the last minute to come to the library gala. They must've realized they needed to shut him up ASAP."

"Unfortunately, Clemmons played his cards a little too close to his vest. His colleague at the auction house didn't realize anything fishy was going on, because Clemmons didn't explain himself, or let on that the guy should keep quiet about their conversation," Capone explained. "Clemmons's questions to him were all very cryptic."

I had to cover my mouth to avoid spitting my wine all over Capone. I swallowed and straightened my face, trying to exhibit appropriate respect for the dead man. "You don't say?"

"By unfortunate coincidence, the auction house was in the midst of a deal with Zaria, and this guy, the former coworker, innocently mentioned Clemmons's call to her and told her Clemmons was inquiring about the books. That was the day before the party. I talked to him earlier. He feels awful, as you can imagine."

"It wasn't his fault," I said. Maybe I was more inclined to forgive considering the trouble my own loose lips had caused.

"No, it wasn't. But it did put Zaria's wheels in motion. She called Pam and Isabel about the free-from pizza to gauge whether they were on to her. She figured if

Clemmons had told anyone, it would be them. When that conversation went smoothly, Zaria and Victor decided to get to Bluff Point early, intending to steal the books before the party. They figured that without the evidence, Clemmons had no proof of his suspicions."

"Let me guess," I said. "Clemmons was already in the library, so they couldn't steal the books. And I'm guessing he gave them a chance to turn themselves in? To come clean to Pam?"

Capone's eyes darted toward the kitchen door, but his mother and Biz were nowhere in sight. I imagined Lola was trying to give us *alone* time. Little did she know that Capone and I usually spent our alone time hashing through the details of criminal investigations.

"Seems to be his MO," Capone said quietly.

"Well, with an MO like that, it's a miracle Clemmons survived as long as he did," I said.

"It's a good lesson to leave the crime solving to the professionals." He took a long drink from his wineglass and raised a cheeky eyebrow over the rim. "Anyway, I'm guessing that's when Zaria came up with the idea of staging an accident during the party, if she hadn't already been planning it, that is."

"What about Jarka? Did Victor know she'd be there?"

He shook his head. "No. Jarka's father hired a private investigator when she left, but they hadn't been able to find her." He drained the last of his wine and I topped up his glass. "Victor was shocked to see her. He described her as the love of his life, and I think we all saw how deep his devotion ran. When you and Rabbit intervened in Victor's reunion with Jarka, he realized that you were the kind of person who'd stick close by in a situation where you thought someone was being threatened. Or, as Victor put it, 'I realized she couldn't mind her own business.'"

I crossed my arms. "I'm tempted to head down to the hospital and see if there are any bones he *didn't* break in the fall."

Capone smiled innocently. "I'm just telling you what the man said. Your, let's call it, *propensity for intervention* made you the perfect alibi witness. They could summon you whenever they were ready to thank you for the free-from pizza."

I pressed my palm to my forehead. "I feel so stupid for not realizing how strange it was for her to thank me *before* the meal. In all my years in the restaurant business, I can't think of another time that's happened."

"It was busy and chaotic—the perfect time to catch you off guard. They arranged to meet Clemmons upstairs, telling him that Pam would come, too, so they could confess to her about the forged books and he could witness it."

"That explains the change in Clemmons's demeanor between the first time I saw him and when he gave me the books. He was much more guarded the second time. Savvy enough, I guess, to make sure the books were away from the library in case they were planning to pull a fast one."

"But still idealistic enough to think they'd actually confess," he observed. "They also had a lucky break with Butterball being there. They couldn't have asked for a better explanation of how Clemmons fell. And the power going out worked in their favor, too. Made it easier for them to sneak around."

"Geez. With that many lucky breaks, it's a miracle they *did* get caught in the end." I said. "What about the pills?"

"Once Zaria overheard you saying that Sonya might be privy to a clue that would unmask the killer, she took the pills from my mother's purse to use to poison Sonya."

I took in a sharp breath. So Sonya had dodged not one, but two murder plots.

"Zaria realized, though, that it'd be difficult to get a lethal dose of Xanax into *just* Sonya's food or drink, so she decided to go with Victor's plan."

"Which was?"

"Drug everyone and destroy the books," he said.

"What about Isabel? She figured it out, I guess?"

"Yeah. When they went to the library to get the books, Isabel was there, having a closer look. When Zaria came in, she saw that Isabel was handling the books roughly, flipping through the pages. She immediately realized that Isabel must know the books were worthless. Isabel was too careful a librarian to handle rare books like that. Zaria grabbed the books from her and threw them into the fire. Isabel reached in to pull them out and they struggled."

"Why would Isabel try to save the books if she knew they were worthless? I guess she wanted to preserve evidence?" I asked.

He smiled sadly. "It was more than that. Victor said her last words were, 'I'll be damned if I'm going to stand here and watch a book burn.' To Isabel, all books had value."

"She was something," I said. We fell quiet for a moment, lost in our memories of the dynamo of a librarian. "And that's when Zaria strangled her?"

"Yes, while her back was turned."

A mixture of anger and disgust boiled up inside me. "Why use the boa? She must've brought it with her. That means it was premeditated."

"Victor swears it wasn't. He said they planned to

create confusion. Zaria noticed that Pam and Melody both had boas. She stole Pam's earlier and then took Melody's when she came upstairs to attack Sonya. She planned to plant feathers in the library and near the stairs to throw suspicion on Pam and Melody for Clemmons's murder, but after the confrontation with Isabel, she ended up using one as a weapon and burning the other one in the fire. A bit of the old *Murder on the Orient Express* routine."

I furrowed my brow in confusion.

"I forgot. In that book, they stage the evidence to implicate multiple people . . ." He shook his head. "Oh, never mind. Get a library card, okay? For Isabel."

I nodded. "I think I just might," I said. "*The Maltese Falcon* sounded like a good book. Although I don't know where I'll find the time to read it."

"They rent DVDs, too, so you have no excuse."

"Speaking of which, did Victor explain why they went after Sonya after all? You said he'd convinced Zaria not to," I said.

"After Zaria killed Isabel, they realized Sonya might be the next one to figure it out. For all they knew, Clemmons left other clues for her or told her other things that could lead back to them. They were hoping that if they could brazen it out, they could flee the country before we had enough evidence to arrest them. At that point, they were in so deep, what was one more body?"

"God, that was so scary. I really thought she was dead."

We were silent for a long moment. Capone reached for my hand and gave it a squeeze.

I flashed a half smile. "If we were going to have to go through all that, I'm glad you were there."

"Me, too."

We lapsed into silence again, his warm hand still holding mine. What a strange series of events. How different it all could've been. *If Victor had been content being with Jarka the hardworking doctor. If Clemmons had just reported his suspicions to the authorities like a normal human being. If Butterball hadn't been inadvertently shipped to Bluff Point. If the storm hadn't arrived with such unexpected force.* The sound of approaching voices from the kitchen roused me out of my contemplation.

Capone leaned forward on his stool, his face close to mine. When he spoke, his warm breath tickled the skin on my neck. "Hey, how about you and I watch *The Maltese Falcon* together sometime? Maybe I could take you out to dinner first? For real."

"You mean without my aunt and your mother coming along?" I asked, letting the corner of my mouth curve ever so slightly.

"Just us." He placed a hand on my thigh.

The warmth of his touch zinged through my entire body. I traced the rim of my wineglass with my index finger and looked up at him through my eyelashes. "At a restaurant that *isn't* mine?"

"Any. Place. You. Want." He gently touched my lower lip as he spoke each word.

"And *without* anyone getting killed?"

He drew back and held out his hands. "Based on experience, *that* might be asking too much."

I hopped off my stool, planted a kiss on his lips, and threw my arms around his neck. "Well, guess I can't have *everything*."

***

RECIPES

ITALIAN BEEF CROSTINI

This is Sonya, bringing you a crowd-pleasing shortcut recipe for our Italian beef crostini appetizers, using heat-and-eat beef. This is just between you and me, okay? Pinky swear? Delilah doesn't need to know that we're cutting corners by not making the beef from scratch . . .

Chicagoans know that an Italian beef sandwich is a heaping mess of beef, sliced razor-thin and piled on a crusty-yet-soft roll, topped with zesty *giardiniera*. From there, you have a choice to make. Do you dab on a little of the au jus (a brothy, meaty sauce otherwise known as gravy), or have your sandwich served "wet," i.e., doused with a firehose of gravy?

Delilah had a moment of genius when she adapted a notoriously messy Chicago classic into a finger food, suitable for event catering. While not exactly dainty, these crostini capture the yum factor of an Italian beef sandwich without the change-your-shirt-three-times, take-a-face-bath-in-meat-juice messiness of the original.

At Delilah & Son, we make our own Italian beef and *giardiniera* in house. But any recipe that starts with "cook 13 pounds of beef sirloin" and generates appetizer portions for sixty to seventy people is going to have home cooks running for the hills. If you're making these apps at home, you want something quick, easy, and scalable, so you can focus on the main event. Here goes.

Preparation Time: 10 minutes
Cook Time: 15 minutes
Yield: 20–30 crostini portions, enough for 10–15 people as an appetizer

Ingredients:

- 1 long, skinny French baguette, cut into ½-inch rounds
- 3–4 tablespoons garlic-infused olive oil (or regular olive oil)
- 1 lb. Italian beef,* heated in its own gravy
- 1 jar mild *giardiniera* (For catering orders, mild is safer, but if you know your crowd likes spice, feel free to go with hot!)
- 10 slices of provolone or low-moisture mozzarella cheese

Directions:

Preheat the oven to 450° F. Using a pastry brush, paint both sides of each baguette slice with oil. Arrange the oiled pieces in a single layer on a large baking tray, and place the tray in the oven.

Bake slices for 4–5 minutes. Flip 'em. Bake for another 4–5 minutes or until golden.

Remove the bread from the oven and layer each slice with drained Italian beef and *giardiniera*. Top with a cheese slice. Depending on how big your slices are, you may need to cut the cheese. (*Hahahaha!* Sorry, sometimes I'm five years old.)

Turn broiler on low.

Broil 2 minutes, or until the cheese is melted. Serve immediately.

* Obviously, the closer you get to the motherland (Chicago), the more authentic the flavor of your Italian beef, and the more choices you'll have in the purveyor. In most instances, the beef and gravy are sold together as a kit. Since you'll only need the gravy for reheating, you'll have a fair amount left over. This makes a great soup base or braising liquid or, what the heck, just take a face bath in it.

  You can order the real deal from Portillo's at www.tastesofchicago.com, but expect to pay a pretty penny for shipping. Buona Beef is tasty and sold in many Midwestern grocery stores. Viennabeef.com is a cheaper option and Sam's Club sells 5-pound catering tubs of beef in gravy.

DELILAH'S FREE-FROM DEEP-DISH PIZZA

Real talk: I've never made a gluten-free pizza crust that's as good as the genuine, wheat-based article or tasted vegan cheese with the melting creaminess of mozzarella. To paraphrase Sonya, I'm a chef, not a magician. But for many, many people, gluten and dairy are a no go, so it's important to me to create a recipe that's a tasty and satisfying substitute for the original. Assuming you or your guests have only one set of preferences, allergies, or intolerances to deal with, you can pick and choose which elements to replace with the following recipes.

GLUTEN-FREE PIZZA CRUST

Preparation Time: about 1¾ hours, including
*   rising time*
Cook Time: 30–40 minutes
Yield: one 9-inch pizza, feeds 2–3 people

A few tips if you're new to GF baking. First, *check all labels.* Sometimes gluten hides in weird places, like yeast or baking powder. Tip number two: Some people are highly sensitive to even small amounts of gluten, so you'll want to use squeaky-clean equipment (knives, bowls, cutting boards, et cetera) to prevent cross-contamination. Before you begin, calibrate your expectations: this will not behave like normal gluten-y pizza crust. Despite the challenges, this recipe delivers a tasty crispy-on-the-outside, fluffy-on-the-inside texture that can be hard to find in GF crusts.

Ingredients:
- 1½ cups (234 g) King Arthur Gluten-Free All-Purpose Flour*
- 2 tablespoons almond flour or almond meal
- 1 teaspoon baking powder
- 1 teaspoon salt
- 1 teaspoon xanthan gum
- 1 tablespoon granulated sugar
- 1 cup warm water (approx. 110° F)
- 4 tablespoons olive oil, divided
- 1½ teaspoons instant yeast

*Everyone seems to have their preferred GF flour blend, which makes recipe results highly variable. For the sake of reproducibility, I'm going to specify that you use King Arthur Gluten Free All-Purpose Flour and weigh it on a kitchen scale. If you use a different commercial flour mix, check if it already contains xanthan gum. If it does, leave out the teaspoon of xanthan gum. I can't guarantee results with other flours, though! If you don't have a kitchen scale, spoon the flour gently into your measuring cup; don't pack it down.

Make the Dough:

Place the all-purpose flour, almond flour/meal, baking powder, salt, and xanthan gum into the bowl of a stand mixer. Mix with a beater attachment on medium-low until thoroughly blended.

Place the sugar, warm water, 2 tablespoons of the olive oil (reserve the other half), yeast, and about ½ cup of the dry mixture into a small bowl. Stir to combine; a few lumps are okay. Set aside for 30 minutes or so, until the mixture is bubbly and smells yeasty.

Add this mixture to the dry ingredients and beat on medium-high speed for 4 minutes. Again, use the beater attachment, not the dough hook. The mixture will be thick and sticky. This will not look like ordinary pizza dough and will not hold its shape. Do not try to mix or knead this dough by hand. It's too sticky.

Cover the bowl, and let the dough rise for another 30 minutes.

Bake Your Pie:

Preheat oven to 425° F.

Drizzle the remaining 2 tablespoons of the olive oil onto the center of a nonstick 9-inch round cake pan. I know it seems like overkill to use that amount of oil in such a small pan, but trust me on this. Using a silicone spatula, scrape the dough from the bowl onto the puddle of oil.

With wet fingers, start at the center of the dough and work outward, pressing it to fill the pan and go up the sides. Let the dough rest, uncovered, for 15 minutes. Smooth out the shape.

Bake the crust for 8–10 minutes, until it's just beginning to firm up; the surface will look dry. Remove from the oven and add your toppings. If anything unexpected has happened with the shape, this is your last opportunity to press it back into submission.

Top and Finish:

Ingredients:

- 1.5–2 cups vegan or regular mozzarella
- vegan or regular pepperoni
- cooked vegetables of choice
- marinara sauce or No-Mato Sauce (page 301)
- olive oil, for brushing the crust
- vegan or regular Parmesan

For deep dish, you add cheese, *then* toppings, *then* sauce. It's more important than ever to ensure that your toppings are as moisture-free as possible. I like to use a thick layer of mozzarella (vegan or real), then a layer of large pepperoni (vegan or regular), then veggies, *then* sauce. You'll want to use quite a bit of cheese on this. I typically use 1.5–2 cups. I usually paint a little more olive oil on the exposed edges of the crust to help with browning. Add a generous sprinkle of Parmesan (vegan or regular) to the top of the pizza.

Return the pizza to the oven to finish baking, about 15–20 minutes. The crust should be brown at the edges.

Remove from the oven and allow to cool for a few minutes. Transfer to a cutting board to cut into slices. Serve warm, and eat immediately.

Note: The texture of this dough is slightly springy, akin to the personal-pan pizzas you used to win at Pizza Hut for doing the BOOK IT! reading program. Although I'm a barbarian now, I used to read in elementary school, when pizza was the incentive. Maybe I'll talk to the Friends of the Library about doing an adult BOOK IT! program at Delilah & Son . . .

NO-MATO SAUCE

This recipe is perfect for the person who is dodging nightshade vegetables for whatever reason, but it's also a less-acidic tomato alternative for reflux sufferers and a great way to use up a late fall garden glut of pumpkins, beets, and squash. This recipe makes a big batch, and it freezes well. You can use this anywhere you'd use marinara sauce. It's delicious in a veggie lasagna, ground-beef casserole, or your favorite pasta bake.

Yield: Lots! Enough for 4 pizzas.
Total time: about 1 hour

Ingredients:

- 2 tablespoons extra-virgin olive oil
- 1 large onion, diced
- 5 cloves garlic, crushed
- 1 cup diced carrot (approx. 2 medium carrots)
- ½ cup diced celery
- 1½ cups butternut squash, cubed*
- 1 cup cooked beets (roasted or canned), cubed
- 2 teaspoons sea salt
- 1 teaspoon dried thyme
- 1 teaspoon dried oregano
- 1 teaspoon dried basil (or 1 tablespoon fresh)
- ¼ cup good-quality red wine vinegar
- ½ cup canned or cooked, pureed pumpkin
- 2 cups water
- 1 tablespoon maple syrup
- Salt and pepper, to taste

*Buying frozen, pre-cubed squash saves you from
   having to do a lot of knife gymnastics.

Directions:

Heat the olive oil in a large stockpot over medium heat.
When the oil is hot, add the onion, garlic, carrot, celery,
and butternut squash and sauté 4–5 minutes, stirring
frequently.

Once the onions begin to become translucent, add in
the beets, salt, and dried herbs and sauté 1–2 minutes.

Next, add in the vinegar, pumpkin, and fresh (if using) basil and cook, allowing most of the vinegar to
evaporate.

Finally, add in the water and maple syrup. Bring to a low boil and reduce heat.

Simmer on low for 30 minutes or until the vegetables are soft. Stir occasionally and add a splash of water if the vegetables become too dry.

Remove from heat and allow everything to cool a little.

Blend ingredients into a smooth sauce using an immersion blender or carefully transfer to a blender in batches and blend until smooth. Season with salt and black pepper as necessary once blended. Remember, red pepper flakes, paprika, and chili powder (along with any other chili pepper–derived spices!) are nightshades.

I CAN'T BELIEVE IT'S NOT PARMESAN!

Sounds weird. Is tasty.
- ¾ cup raw cashews
- 3 tablespoons nutritional yeast*
- ¾ teaspoon sea salt
- ¼ teaspoon garlic powder

*If you're not familiar with "nooch," it may sound exotic, but most large grocery stores carry it.

Directions:

Add all ingredients to a food processor and pulse until it reaches the consistency of grated Parmesan cheese. That's it! Store it in the fridge, and it'll last up to a month.

DANIEL'S HANKY PANKY

Although the Friends of the Library fundraiser didn't turn out to be too friendly, that's no reason not to enjoy this strongly flavored cocktail from Prohibition times. *Gracias a Dios* that I was not born in those sad times when the pleasure of alcohol was forbidden. If you make this, be aware—as I told Delilah, this drink is bold. It doesn't hide behind sugar syrups or fruity flavors. It is the drink of a strong person—spicy and a little bitter, like Delilah's aunt Biz.

Ingredients:

- 1½ ounces gin
- 1½ ounces sweet vermouth
- 2 dashes Fernet-Branca, or any other bitters that you like
- Orange twist*

Directions:

Add the gin, sweet vermouth, and Fernet-Branca into a mixing glass with ice and stir until well chilled.

Strain into a chilled cocktail glass. Garnish with an orange twist.

> * Lean in close and let me tell you how to make
>   a perfect citrus peel twist. First, hold a whole
>   fruit in the palm of your hand with a firm
>   grip. Flex your biceps a little as you do this to
>   show them off. Use a canelle or paring knife,
>   cutting into the citrus peel just deep enough
>   to pick up the colored peel and a thin layer of

the white pith. Roll the fruit around in your hand with a smooth, even motion, like you are stroking the curves of a beautiful woman. Stop peeling when you have the desired length or when the peel naturally ends. Roll the peel into a tight spiral, give it a tender squeeze— you must coax it, never force it, as if you were wooing this same woman. To keep your twists tighter and more pliable, drop them into icy water immediately. Never do this to a beautiful woman, unless of course she asks you to. In which case, *felicidades*, because you're in for an exciting night.

TIRAMISU COOKIE BARS

Sonya again. We invented these bar cookies for catering gigs, to pack the flavors of tiramisu into a sturdy dessert that travels well, serves easily, and requires minimal on-site prep. They'd also be a great option to bring to a dinner party or potluck.

Preparation Time: 1 hour, including 30 minutes chilling time
Cook Time: 20 minutes
Yield: 20 cookie bars

For the Cookie Base:
- ½ cup unsalted butter, softened
- ½ cup granulated sugar

- 1 small egg, beaten
- 1½ tablespoons vanilla extract
- 1¼ cups all-purpose flour
- ½ teaspoon baking powder
- ¼ teaspoon salt

For the Tiramisu Topping:

- ¼ cup extra-strong brewed coffee or espresso
- ¼ cup Kahlúa
- 8 ounces cream cheese, softened to room temperature
- 1 cup mascarpone, softened
- 1 teaspoon pure vanilla extract
- ½ cup confectioners' sugar
- 1 small bar semisweet or bittersweet chocolate

Prepare the Base:

Beat together the butter, sugar, and egg with a mixer until creamy, then beat in the vanilla extract.

In a separate bowl, whisk together the flour, baking powder, and salt, then add into the butter mixture and beat on low until evenly combined with no dry pockets. Chill the dough for at least 30 minutes.

Using a rolling pin, roll the dough into a rectangle approximately the size of a 9×13-inch cake pan. With your fingers, press it in a flat layer to completely cover the bottom of the ungreased pan. Lightly cover with plastic wrap and place in the refrigerator for at least 15 minutes. In baking as in life, chilling is important!

Preheat the oven to 400° F.

Bake the cookie base for 15 minutes or until golden brown. The edges may be slightly more brown but shouldn't be too dark. Let it cool completely in the pan before topping.

Make the Topping:

Stir together the coffee or espresso and Kahlúa. Pause here and take a good swig or two of the Kahlúa straight from the bottle. This is optional, but cooks *should* test the quality of their ingredients. Just sayin'. Spoon 2 tablespoons of the mixture into the bowl of a stand mixer or a large mixing bowl. Add the cream cheese, mascarpone, and vanilla extract and beat until smooth and creamy. Sift in the confectioners' sugar and beat until fluffy.

Use a pastry brush to brush the remaining coffee/Kahlúa mixture evenly over the cookie base. Take another swig of Kahlúa from the bottle (optional, but recommended).

Spread the mascarpone mixture evenly over the cooled cookie base. Grate the chocolate bar with a fine grater over the cream topping. Cut into approximately 20 cookies and serve.

THE O'LEARY WOMEN'S DEEP-DISH APPLE PIE

This is Elizabeth O'Leary, but my friends call me Biz. Since you and I are not friends, you may call me Miss O'Leary.

This is my aunt Sandra's recipe. She only made one pie per year, and we kids all fought over the who got the last piece. Sandra didn't share recipes. Or rather, she'd give you what she *said* was the recipe, but she'd change a quantity here or leave out an ingredient there to make sure yours could never come out as good as hers. Believe it or not, when she died in 1974 she asked to be buried with her recipe book. I obliged . . . after I mimeographed the whole book on the ditto machine at the high school where I used to teach.

This is a good pie to make if you ever you want to apologize to someone. Because anyone can buy a card, but making a pie shows effort. Besides, who wants some two-bit dime store card when they could have a pie?

Preparation Time: 3 hours, including making and chilling the crust
Cook Time: about 50 minutes
Yield: 8–10 slices

Piecrust:

- 2½ cups unsifted all-purpose flour
- 1 teaspoon sugar
- 1 teaspoon salt
- ½ cup vegetable shortening or lard, very cold, cut into small pieces
- ½ cup butter, very cold, cut into small pieces
- ½ cup very cold water
- 1 teaspoon cold white vinegar

Mix the flour, sugar, and salt in a large bowl using a fork.

Add shortening or lard and butter and mix with a pastry blender or two forks until it crumbles. You should leave a few slightly larger chunks of fat to help with flakiness, but nothing larger than pea size.

In a small bowl, mix together the water and vinegar. Add the water mixture a little at a time to the flour and fat mixture and combine with a fork. Once the mixture starts to hold together, stop adding the liquid. If you use too much water, the pie dough will require more flour and it'll be tough. If too little water is added, you'll see that the dough is too crumbly when you try to roll it out and handle it.

Using a well-floured rolling pin and a well-floured work surface, shape dough into two even disks about 1 inch thick with smooth edges. This step makes the dough much easier to roll out and helps prevent cracking. Cover the dough disks and chill them in the fridge for at least 1 hour.

Filling:

- ¾ cup sugar (you can go as low as ½ cup if you have sweeter apples)
- ¼ cup all-purpose flour
- ½ teaspoon ground nutmeg
- ¾ teaspoon ground cinnamon
- A pinch of salt
- 7 cups of thinly sliced and peeled tart apples (about 10 medium apples)*
- Juice of half a lemon (optional)
- 2 tablespoons margarine or butter, cubed
- Pastry for 9-inch Two-Crust Pie (previous page)
- 1 egg beaten with a splash of milk, for egg wash

Directions:

Preheat your oven to 425° F. Mix the sugar, flour, nutmeg, cinnamon, and salt. Stir in the sliced apples. If you want a tarter flavor, add lemon juice. Let the mix rest while you roll out the dough.

Let one of your pastry disks stand at room temperature until slightly softened, about 5 minutes. Sprinkle it with flour; roll it into a circle a little bigger than your pie plate. Deep-dish pie plates are about ½ inch deeper than ordinary pie plates, so you will need to roll out a larger circle. Carefully fit dough into the deep-dish glass pie plate, leaving a 1½-inch overhang around the edges.

Spoon the apple mixture into your pastry-lined pie plate. If the apples have given off a lot of juice, spooning them into the crust prevents the pie from being too soggy. Dot the apples with cubed margarine or butter.

Take out the other dough disk and let it soften for a few minutes. Roll out that dough disk for the top. Before you place it on top of the apple filling, cut slits in the dough disk to vent the steam. If you have extra dough, you can cut out pretty shapes with a cookie cutter to decorate your pie.† Cover the apples with the top crust. Seal and flute the edges, trimming off any extra dough.

Lightly brush the top of the piecrust with the egg wash. Place a strip of foil around the edges of the crust to prevent it from overbrowning.

Place the pie onto a large baking sheet lined with parchment paper and bake for 20 minutes. Remove the foil. Return the pie to the oven, turn the temperature down to 375°, and bake for an additional 20–30 minutes.

After 45–50 minutes total, your crust should be brown and juice should bubble through the slits in the crust.

Transfer the pie to a wire rack, and cool at least 1 hour prior to serving.

*Be sure you cut the apples in slices and not
    chunks so you can fit more apples in the pie.
†Lattice tops are generally not recommended
    for apple pie. The apples benefit from being
    steamed inside a solid crust.

Last Notes: Sandra always insisted that the best apple pie was made from three different kinds of apples with different levels of tartness and sweetness. The recipe says 10 apples, but that's using apples from the 1950s and '60s. You'll have to use your common sense about the number of apples and fill the crust until it's slightly mounded but not overflowing, because nowadays apples are pumped full of GMOs or whatever they do to make them genetic freaks. I saw a Granny Smith at the Stinebrink's Piggly Wiggly the other week that was the size of a church-league softball. When they're selling an apple that can feed a family of four, you know the world's gone nuts.